"INTO TOMORROW"

by Anita Richmond Bunkley

Living together on the Texas Gulf Coast, Audra and her widowed sister, Bertice, find the ghosts of their past coming between them as Audra thinks of returning to the husband who once betrayed her. . . .

"HOMECOMING"

by Sandra Kitt

When film star Renee Saxon makes a whirlwind visit to her New Jersey hometown, she faces not only Gena, the sister she left behind, but the daughter she left for Gena to raise . . . and Gena must confront Renee's handsome manager, the man she secretly loves.

"GUESS WHAT'S COOKING"

by Eva Rutland

Marrying into money will get Darlene and her teenaged sister, Tonya, out of their Brooklyn flat and into a Long Island home. Tonya, however, has plans of her own: an audacious scheme to match her sister with a man who may not make her rich, but who can make her happy.

SISTERS

SISTERS

by

Anita Richmond Bunkley,

Eva Rutland,

and Sandra Kitt

A SIGNET BOOK

SIGNET
Published by the Penguin Group
Penguin Books USA Inc., 375 Hudson Street,
New York, New York 10014, U.S.A.
Penguin Books Ltd, 27 Wrights Lane,
London W8 5TZ, England
Penguin Books Australia Ltd, Ringwood,
Victoria, Australia
Penguin Books Canada Ltd, 10 Alcorn Avenue,
Toronto, Ontario, Canada M4V 3B2
Penguin Books (N.Z.) Ltd, 182–190 Wairau Road,
Auckland 10, New Zealand

Penguin Books Ltd, Registered Offices:
Harmondsworth, Middlesex, England

First published by Signet, an imprint of Dutton Signet,
a division of Penguin Books USA Inc.

First Printing, December, 1996
10 9 8 7 6 5 4 3 2 1

Printed in the United States of America

PUBLISHER'S NOTE
These are works of fiction. Names, characters, places, and incidents either are the product of the author's imagination or are used fictitiously, and any resemblance to actual persons, living or dead, events, or locales is entirely coincidental.

CONTENTS

INTO TOMORROW
by Anita Richmond Bunkley

Chapter One

Audra glanced nervously at her watch, then peered down the winding asphalt road, expecting to see Tami's red BMW swing into sight at any moment. She was amazed that Micere and Anika had agreed to let Tami drive, and was not surprised that they were running late. She could not ignore the glimmer of hope that perhaps her friends had canceled their plans and were not coming after all.

Looking anxiously back at the house, Audra prayed that her sister, Bertice, would at least be polite—act civilly toward her guests—despite the fact that she had called them an intrusion on her privacy.

The house, a weathered two-story lodge fronted by a line of palm trees tilting precariously toward the north, had once rocked with laughter and music when upscale African-Americans from Houston, Dallas, and San Antonio had flocked to the seaside resort for weekends of soul food, fishing, and boisterous beer parties. But that was years ago, before the accident. Now all road signs pointing to Marina Manor had been removed, all the empty rooms had been boarded up, and Bertice contented herself with living alone in the isolated resort on the shady Texas cove, convinced that her deserted, lonely refuge suited her just fine.

Today the relentless Gulf coast winds blew gently off the bay—excellent weather for the crush of holiday vacationers out in their sailboats, motorboats, jet skis, and big cabin cruisers that crowded the glittering water. Memorial Day weekend was the start of the summer season, and Audra was not surprised to see the myriad colorful dots zipping across the blue-green water spread out behind the lodge.

Pulling off her sandals, Audra walked down to the beach and headed toward the abandoned pier that jutted from the shore out over the water. Warm waves lapped at her ankles as she waded into the shallow water. Gripping the boards with both hands, she hoisted herself up onto the rotting walkway, padded to the end of it, and sat down. Stretching her legs out, she tugged her jeans up to her knees to catch a little sun. With her palms flat against the splintered wood, Audra turned her soft brown face to the sky and focused on a scattering of wispy clouds that were drifting over the water as she thought about the weekend before her.

As much as Audra missed partying and shopping and chatting with her sorority sisters, she was nervous about seeing them again after eight months of living in isolation at the coast. How could she ever convince them that her self-imposed exile had healed her wounds or erased the shock of Neal Foster's betrayal? And how in the world was she going to make it through the next two days without breaking down? Watching a top-heavy cabin cruiser sail off into the horizon, Audra began to regret her impulsive invitation.

Looking down at her hands, Audra frowned. Her nails, on which she used to spend as much as fifty dollars a month to keep perfectly manicured, were now split and cracked, devoid of polish. Her work as a court reporter in Houston had dictated that Audra's dress and grooming be impeccable. But since fleeing her suburban home to live the carefree life of a seaside dweller, entering a styling salon or sitting in front of a manicurist's table had suddenly become a very low priority.

Sighing, Audra pushed her hair back under the Houston Astros baseball cap that she had pulled on to hide her grown-out perm. *What the hell?* she thought gloomily. *Tami, Micere, and Anika are my sorority sisters, not really company. It doesn't matter to them how I look.*

When the purr of Tami's BMW sounded at the end of the road, Audra turned around in surprise. They *had* come, she thought, pushing her reservations aside. Standing to watch them get out of the car, she was unable to keep from smiling at the assortment of baskets, coolers, and bags of groceries they pulled from the backseat and the trunk.

"Hey, girl," Tami cried out, tossing her Dooney & Bourke bag to the grass. She raced toward the rotting pier.

"Tami!" Audra cried out, and jumping down, she moved to hug her best friend tightly. "I was getting worried about you guys." She was telling the truth because Tami, who worked as a regional representative for Jemila Cosmetics, spent twelve hours a day zipping around Houston, dodging in and out of retail outlets, amassing as many speeding tickets as product orders.

Tami flipped a rope-of-a-curl out of her eyes, swept one hand over the mass of twisted hair that was held back from her round face by a bright red scarf, and pushed her sunglasses atop her head. "We would have been on time if Anika hadn't insisted on stopping at every antique shop we passed. Since she's expanded her shop, she's insatiable. That girl bought more junk than Ma and Pa Kettle ever had."

Laughter bubbled up, and Audra enjoyed the sense of relief her first real laugh in months brought with it. She and Tami hooked arms, heading back to the car.

"Well, stranger," Anika said, putting down a dusty picture frame to embrace Audra. "God, it's good to see you." She stepped back and ran her eyes up and down in an exaggerated fashion. With her ringed fingers propped at her tiny waist, she admonished, "Audra, I know you turned thirty last week, but dag, girlfriend, you look like somebody's grandma. We gotta get you together. That cap has got to go."

"Ease up, Anika," Micere shouted across the top of the car, waving at Audra as she started around. "We're hanging loose this weekend, remember? Leave Audra alone." Micere wrinkled her stubby freckled nose at Anika, shaking her head vigorously, her layered shag swinging as she spoke. "I can't wait to get in the water, and I'm gonna wrap my head like Aunt Jemima for the next two days, so y'all better not say a word."

"Micere," Audra burst out, kissing her sorority sister lightly on the cheek. "I'm so glad you came. Really."

"She almost didn't make it," Tami said. "One of her *children* can away."

"Which one? Kassie? Don't tell me Kassie ran away." Audra's jaw dropped open in horror. She knew Micere, a divorced mother of two, was having difficulty with her ten-year-old daughter, but Audra never suspected it might come to this.

"Oh, no," Micere quickly replied, playfully slapping at Tami. "She's talking about Billy Bradford, the most difficult case I have. He's been on probation less than two weeks and has already broken it twice."

Audra sighed in relief, awed by Micere's ability to keep up with the seventy-some juvenile probationers under her supervision. "I don't think he's gonna make it," Audra said.

"Me neither. He's probably already across the border."

Laughing, the four gathered up suitcases, boxes, and bags, chatting as they crossed the shady lawn.

"And where is my godchild hiding?" Tami asked.

"I let Jason go play with the Wilson boys down the road for a few hours. Five-year-old twins. Their mother swears the boys are a lot less trouble when Jason comes for a visit. Don't worry, he'll be home after lunch."

"Marina Manor," Anika read the brass plaque, darkened by salty sea air, that was nailed above the door. "This place is wonderful. I see why your sister never sold it."

"Where is Bertice, by the way?" Micere asked.

"She's got a summer cold. Can you believe it? She's lying down, but you'll see her at lunch, I'm sure."

"A summer cold? That's a bummer," Tami said.

"Yeah, well, she does too much. This place is really a lot to manage alone," Audra replied, leading her guests onto the wide cool porch that was screened in all around. "Bertice no longer takes in guests, paying guests that is," she added playfully, "so the place has deteriorated quite a bit since . . . the accident." Audra fell quiet, surprised at the tremor that slipped over her at the mention of the boating accident that had taken the lives of her brother-in-law and her four-year-old niece three years ago.

She swallowed and pushed open the front door.

"I'm going to help Bertice do some renovations over the summer."

"You?" Tami said wide-eyed. "I was your roommate in college, remember? Tell me . . . when did you learn the difference between a pair of pliers and a wrench?"

"Give me a break," Audra said, grinning. "Bertice and I are going to take a few of those do-it-yourself classes at Builders Supply and try to do most of the work ourselves. Might be fun."

Anika nudged Micere in the ribs, jerking her head to one side. Micere got the clue. "This summer? Audra, I thought you were coming back to Houston next week. I talked to Judge Rawlins. He's expecting you to work in his court. A big case is going to trial, and he wants you. What happened? Why have you changed your mind?"

Audra didn't answer right away, leading her friends into the cavernous front hallway that was dominated by a huge stone fireplace. She stopped and set down Tami's suitcase. "I don't think I'm ready to get back into the hassle of working full-time, wearing suits and heels everyday, making that god-awful drive into town. I don't miss the Southwest Freeway at all."

Tami stared in surprise at Audra. "Who says you've got to move back to your house in Missouri City? It's a beauty and I know how much you loved it, but if I were you I'd sell it. Maybe lease it. Forget life in the suburbs . . . take a small apartment closer in."

"Well, maybe. But I don't want to think about that now. Besides, Jason wants to stay here over the summer . . ." Audra said.

"Jason?" Anika asked, one professionally arched eyebrow lifted. "Since when did you start letting your four-year-old son make decisions about your future?"

"He likes it here, and it's a good place for him to spend his summer," Audra said stiffly.

"Not very convincing, girlfriend," Tami started. "I thought Jason was supposed to spend the summer with Neal . . . in Houston. Wasn't that the agreement you two worked out?" Tami thumped her heavy cooler to the floor.

"Yes," Audra hedged. "But Neal doesn't deserve to see his son."

"Be careful, Audra. I'll bet Neal's attorney would see things differently."

"I'm sure Neal knows better than to challenge me on this."

"Just wait until you get to court," Micere cautioned. "Once your son's future is in the hands of the judge, everything changes. Neal may have been quiet about visitation so far, but believe me, he can make you look like a monster for depriving him of time with Jason."

"I . . . I don't want any trouble, but . . ." Audra stammered, suddenly feeling a little fearful. When she had left Houston she had warned Neal to stay out of her life, away from his son. To her relief he had heeded her warning, but now it might come back to haunt her.

Tami put her arm around Audra. "I don't want to get in your business, but it sounds like you're avoiding a face-to-face with Neal and using Jason as a buffer. Your son ought to spend some time with his father."

Audra let Tami hug her, tears of embarrassment gathering in her eyes. She forced a smile. "Not get in my business? Tami, who are you trying to fool?" She tugged her cap lower onto her forehead. "You know you can't wait to get on my case. Admit it . . . you think I was wrong to move away from Houston and keep Jason from his father. Don't you?"

"It's not my place to say if you were wrong or right," Tami said, looking wounded. "But you ought to think about returning to civilization, Audra. Pull yourself together. This is not you. And you know it."

Audra looked from Tami, to Micere, then to Anika, who lowered her eyes and pursed her lips, agreement evident on her face.

"We'll talk about it later, okay?" Audra said, picking up Tami's suitcase, heading toward the stairs. As she slowly mounted the wide stone staircase, her thoughts whirled. *These are the best friends I have in the world,* Audra thought, *and I value their advice. But I won't let them pressure me into making a decision I may not be ready to live with.*

Chapter Two

Bertice removed the half-empty bowl of crabmeat salad from the picnic table and started back into the house.

"Lunch was delicious, Bertice," Audra said, wishing her sister had made an attempt to join in the conversation. Unable to pull Bertice into the social setting, Audra had given up, chatting and laughing with her friends while Bertice kept busy running back and forth between the sunny patio and the kitchen, waiting on everyone in stony silence.

"Right," Anika said. "I feel guilty letting you do so much. We could have helped you fix lunch."

"No problem," Bertice said coolly, pursing her lips, drawing her pinched features into a severe mask. Her heavy brows, which she had long ago stopped shaping with tweezers, divided her sallow face in an unflattering thick line. Her wavy hair, of a texture that could be worn naturally in soft gentle curls, hung in a shapeless mass on either side of her face, stopping in a blunt cut just below her prominent cheekbones.

It was obvious that Bertice took no interest in her appearance and had completely abandoned all efforts to even make herself presentable. "You and your young friends are on vacation. Relax, enjoy yourselves."

Audra frowned. Bertice was only five years older than she, but dressed and acted as if she were about to enter menopause. Since her surprise appearance on the patio to serve lunch, Bertice had barely acknowledged her visitors' presence, speaking very little, feigning a sore throat. But Audra knew it was a ploy to remain withdrawn and that as soon as the table was cleared, she'd retreat again to her gloomy, musty bedroom.

"Please sit down. You haven't even eaten," Audra said.

"I'm not hungry," Bertice replied, her dark-ringed eyes flitting nervously over the faces of Audra's guests. Her thin hands tightened together at her stomach.

"Maybe if you ate, you'd feel better," Tami volunteered. "My momma always said feed a cold, starve a fever." She gave up a short chuckle, then resumed eating her crabmeat salad.

Anika tilted her champagne glass and drained it, towel-drying her short soft natural with the other hand. "It's so nice of you to have us here, Bertice. Marina Manor is lovely. But don't consider us guests, we've been like sisters to Audra since college." She slathered a handful of conditioner into her wet hair.

"Yeah," Micere broke in, lowering the straps on her bathing suit to even out her tan. "And we're not ashamed to tell you, we miss Audra terribly and want her back in Houston." She lifted a finger, shaking at Audra. "Pronto. This vacation is over, sister."

"Right," Tami said. "Time to get back to the real world."

Bertice slammed the bowl down on the table, a stunned expression on her face. "And what makes you think this is not the real world?" she asked icily. "Why should Audra return to Houston? To accommodate that no good bastard Neal Foster? He doesn't deserve to see her or his son."

Micere rolled her eyes toward the sky and grimaced, pulling her Ray-Bans over her eyes. "Exc*uuuu*se me!" She clamped her mouth shut and tilted her face to the sun.

Audra had shot to her feet. "Bertice! What a rude thing to say!" She walked around the table and stopped in front of her sister. "I can't believe you said that. Micere was merely expressing her concern for me."

Bertice sniffed. "Concern? You don't need concern, Audra. What you need is to keep yourself as far away as possible from the man who betrayed you and broke your heart. If you go back to Houston, you know what will happen."

Unable to resist joining in, Tami prompted, "What?"

Bertice spun around to glare at Tami. "What?

Audra will fall for Neal Foster's lame-ass excuses and wind up forgiving him. That's what."

Tami glanced at Audra, then spoke. "I don't see that as so bad. If they can patch things up, why not?"

In the silence that followed, Audra slowly set her champagne glass down on the picnic table as if she were gaining time to pull her thoughts together. "If you guys don't mind," she began, "I think I can speak for myself. I *may* return to Houston . . . when I'm ready. And if I do, it will only be for Jason's sake. I can assure you the last thing on my mind is going back to Neal. Our divorce will be final August first, and after our day in court, I hope I never see him again."

Bertice gave Tami a triumphant glare, snatched up the leftover crab salad, and stomped back into the house.

"Whew!" Anika said, sitting up to spread a glob of suntan lotion over her parchment-colored legs.

"Yeah, Anika," Micere started in, trying to lighten the mood. "Brown it up a little, girl. You're too damn pale."

Anika playfully tossed the plastic tube of suntan lotion at Micere, then asked, "Audra, what's eating your sister?"

Audra sank back into her seat, pulled the chilled bottle of Korbel out of the cooler, and refilled her glass. "Remember when I told you that her husband and daughter were killed in a boating accident?"

"Wasn't that years ago?" Anika asked. "She ought to be over it . . . and what's it got to do with you?"

"What exactly happened?" Micere broke in. "I never did hear the whole story."

Audra nodded. "Walter and Bertice used to be a happy couple, real party animals, throwing big festive bashes here all the time. But on their daughter Sara's fourth birthday, which was to be a real fancy affair, Walter wanted to take Sara for a boat ride. Bertice told him not to because it was very windy, but when she left to go into Corpus to pick up Sara's cake, he and Sara went out in the boat anyway. It capsized. Both Walter and Sara drowned . . . their bodies were found washed up on the beach. It was a nightmare for her . . . our entire family."

"Gee, I see why she's emotionally scarred," Micere said, "but she ought to get over it. I take it she hasn't been able to do that?"

"No, and I'm not sure she ever will," Audra said. "Bertice's bitterness at Walter for defying her orders is as intense today as the day of the accident. I worry about her, believe me, but she refuses to consider therapy and will not even discuss the issue."

Micere sniffed loudly. "Sounds like she's convinced herself that men cannot be trusted."

"Hey," Tami broke in. "I'm sorry, but that's her problem." With a sideways glance at Audra, she added, "I hope you haven't bought in on her attitude."

Audra looked away, rubbing her thumb over her fingernails. "Of course not," she finally answered.

"Good, 'cause Bertice seems to have lost her ability to trust anyone."

"That's close to the truth," Audra admitted, "but I sympathize with her. She's never gotten over her loss."

"I can understand that, but maybe you ought to listen to us and not let Bertice influence you so much," Micere said.

"She hasn't influenced me," Audra said testily. "She stuck by me when my world fell apart. I cratered completely when I came down here. I don't know what would have happened if she hadn't helped me, and Jason, get over the pain Neal caused. Bertice is all right. She's just lived alone too long." Audra sank back in the chaise lounge, glaring at her friends as if daring them to say another negative word about her sister.

"Hey, guys, let it go," Anika said. "Let's enjoy what's left of the afternoon." She closed her eyes. "If I fall asleep, please, somebody have a heart and wake me. Don't let me lie here and roast."

"Sure," Micere said, rising from the table. "I'm going inside to finish reading that slow-ass sci-fi novel I started. How that book got on *Essence*'s best-seller list I'll never know." At the door she paused. "I'll set the oven timer for you, Anika. Okay?"

Anika sat up, scowled at Micere, then lifted her chin to the sun.

Audra looked apologetically at Tami, who tried to ease the tension by asking, "How are the shell pickings on your beach?"

"Pretty good," Audra said, pulling on her sunglasses, knowing it was best to get off the topic of her future. "Let's head over toward the Wilsons' pier on the other side of the next dune. We can pick up Jason on the way back."

The hard-packed sand was cool and comforting under Audra's bare feet. "Have you seen Neal?" She was comfortable enough with Tami to bring up the subject.

Tami nodded, eyes cast to the dark brown sand. "Uh-huh. Several times. I was in his office last week for a checkup. He found a crack in a filling, so I guess I'll have to go back."

"So, you still go to Neal?"

"Sure. He's the best," Tami said, bending to pick up a conical brown and white flecked shell.

Audra's heart thudded in her chest and she held her breath, trying to keep a tremor from her voice. "How is he doing?"

"He's a wreck," Tami quickly replied. "Seems to be at loose ends. Edgy."

"What about Delores?"

"I didn't get much out of him, but after he'd skirted around the issue, he finally got his message across. He's not seeing Delores. Whatever was going on must have died shortly after you found out about it. I thought you might have heard."

Audra felt smugly elated to hear that the "other woman" was out of Neal's life. "Heard? How? No one tells me anything but you . . . and why did you hold back this tidbit?"

"I thought Neal may have already talked to you."

Audra stopped walking, surprised. "Not hardly," she tossed back tightly.

"Well, I guess I have to fess up, Audra. That's one . . . but only one . . . of the reasons I wanted to see you this weekend. You know that I've known Neal Foster longer than any of your friends. Remember, I was the one who introduced you two."

Audra shrugged in agreement, but said nothing.

Tami went on. "Neal is truly a changed man. He wants you back. When I was at his office, he told me he was going to call you. Everyone talks about how different he is. We never see him in the clubs, on the social circuit anymore. He used to be the first to arrive and the last to leave. The life of the party, you know that." Tami kicked at the sand. "He told me that he's miserable. He wants to reconcile. Very much."

"Hell. He surely doesn't think sending a message by you will erase all the pain he caused me."

"He didn't send a message. I'm just telling you. I am convinced he truly regrets what he did. He's serious about making things up to you."

"He hasn't called."

"Would you talk to him if he did?"

"No," Audra said adamantly, shaking her head.

"No way. Everything I have to say to him, he will hear in court."

"Well, then. What do you expect?" Tami tossed the shell out into the water, then waded farther into the rippling waves. Standing with her back to Audra, she shaded her face with one hand and watched a water-skier zip past. The waist-high waves rolled toward her, creating an undulating ripple of froth. She stood her ground, then screamed and skittered back as a huge wall of water caught her in the face. Laughing, she headed back to shore.

Audra's curiosity kicked in as she considered Tami's revelation. "What do you know about Neal and Delores's breakup?" she asked, suddenly anxious for every bit of information Tami had, and she wanted it in full detail.

During the night, Audra lay listening to the sloshing sound of water lapping at the beach, unable to stop the relentless tug-of-war that pulled her thoughts from what she wanted to what she feared. After a marathon gabfest about the ups and downs of mutual friends, Audra had settled her guests into the cleanest suite of rooms in the east wing, then hurried down the musty hallway to her sparsely furnished bedroom on the other side of the manor. Now, as the hour hand on her porcelain clock swept toward three, she tossed off her thin cotton sheet and went barefoot to the open screened window.

The sight before her was comfortably familiar, a

sandy landscape she and Bertice and their two sisters, Kathleen and Teresa, had romped on and fought on while growing up. Audra grinned as she spotted the tall pine tree near the pier, where her only brother, Douglas, had caught her kissing a boy she had met on the beach. Of course he had run to tell her parents, who immediately confined her to this very room for the remainder of the weekend.

When Bertice married Walter, they had honeymooned at Marina Manor, eventually scraping up enough money to buy the place five years later, as soon as it went on the market. The family reunions and good times had continued—until tragedy struck. Then everyone stayed away—except Bertice, who stoically refused to abandon the site of her heart-shattering loss.

Tami may be right, Audra thought, unable to recall ever feeling so lonely and unhappy at Marina Manor. *Maybe I don't belong here after all.*

Moths and mosquitoes fitted past the rusted screen, and a gentle salty breeze lifted the filmy curtains from the buckling, water-stained sill. With one hand under her chin Audra stared out over the moonlit water, mentally creating an image of Neal Foster's face in the black ebb and flow of the undulating waves.

She ran a hand over the swell of her breasts, her thin cotton nightgown, unable to smother the warmth of her throbbing flesh. She ached for her husband's familiar, gentle touch, and felt her nipples grow hard as memories of their passionate relationship came back.

In this very room they had often made love after coming in from a late afternoon swim. She smiled to remember how the gritty sand, still clinging to their sun-warmed skin, would chafe and sting as their bodies meshed during the precious moments they were able to snatch while the rest of the family romped on the beach.

For eight months she had struggled to keep all thoughts of Neal repressed beneath her still simmering rage at his selfish infidelity. But after talking with Tami, the frightening possibility of a reconciliation had forced itself into her mind.

So he wanted her back. He was sorry. But could she trust him? Audra wondered. Or better yet, could she forgive him for the cavalier way he had treated the sanctity of their marriage? Shuddering, Audra didn't see how she would ever be able to forgive Neal or wipe from her mind the sight of him groping and kissing a half-naked woman on the sofa in her beige-toned living room. Why there? she often wondered. He could have taken Delores to a hotel. To her place. It was almost as if he had wanted to be caught.

Tears warmed the back of her lids. It was difficult for Audra to forget the dead-calm expression on Neal's rugged face when she had entered the room or his stuttering attempt to explain away his diversion while Audra had been away. The horror of it all—to Audra at least—was not the act itself, but the fact that Neal had not seemed to understand, or be able to admit, the seriousness of his infidelity. During the past eight months of separation, Audra had had plenty of time to think about what she ought to do, and forgiving Neal Foster had never been an option. Until tonight.

Her mind went back to the early years when they had endured a commuter engagement. Neal had been studying dentistry at the University of Texas in San Antonio, and she had been in Houston working as a court reporter. Had he been unfaithful to her then? she wondered. And when he introduced her to Delores Belton at his graduation celebration two years later, had her fiancé and the raven-haired dentist already been in bed together?

Audra groaned. Had she been so much in love with Neal that she had blinded herself to the embarrassing fact that he was the ultimate playboy? And to think that during their six-year marriage Audra had welcomed Delores into her home on several occasions.

Rubbing her temples, Audra went to sit on the edge of her bed. She picked up a blue ceramic-framed photo of Jason and studied it. She saw, smiling up at her, Neal's rich tan coloring, the same curious eyes that seemed to glimmer and dance with a mischievous life of their own, and the innocence she knew in her heart she would go to any lengths to protect. How could she force her son to grow up without a father? Neal loved Jason as much as she did, and according to Tami, he'd broken into tears while describing his anguish at being separated from his son.

Audra slid back under the cool sheet and turned onto her side. Lying in the dark, her heart pounded rapidly and her mouth went dry. Neal Foster might be repentant and want his family back, but she'd be damned if she'd allow him to make a fool of her again.

Chapter Three

Sunday began in an early-morning whirl of activity as Audra and her girlfriends, with Jason in tow, jammed themselves into Tami's red convertible and started off to Sea World, home of Shamu, the killer whale. The place was crowded with holiday visitors: Senior citizens, teenagers, parents with small children, and groups of tourists with cameras around their necks all streaming through the tall iron gates to pack the outdoor stadium.

Audra felt a twinge of jealousy when a young couple with a son about Jason's age squeezed past and sat down next to her. Immediately Jason and their little boy began chattering. She scooted over and changed seats with Jason so the two boys could point and laugh together at the antics of the water clowns, who were somersaulting on skis to warm up the crowd.

Jason clapped his tiny hands, squealing in delight when Shamu shot out of the water in a streak of black and white. Audra was struck by her first pang of guilt for lying to her friends about Jason's wanting to stay at Marina Manor for the summer. She looked around the stadium at other fathers enjoying the show with their sons. Jason ought to have the opportunity to share experiences like this with Neal, she admitted. Certainly, her son enjoyed himself with her, but she worried that her evasive, noncommittal answers to Jason's probing questions about his father were wearing a trifle thin.

Feeling ashamed of her selfish behavior, Audra reached over and took Jason's hand. Holding it tightly, he thought of Tami's warning. Depriving Neal of access to his son might bode poorly for her at the upcoming divorce hearing. She'd like to rectify the situation, but initiating visits would mean facing Neal, talking to him, involving him in her life again, shattering her calm, insulated existence. Her anger at Neal for creating this complicated situation with their son flared, and she swallowed the lump forming in her throat.

Looking down at Jason, she caressed him with a loving gaze, though a kernel of resolve hardened inside. *All right, Neal Foster,* she decided. *I'm not about to give you any ammunition to use against me in court.* She'd call Neal at his office Monday morning, as soon as Tami, Anika, and Micere left, and inform him that she was willing to bring Jason into Houston for a visit on Saturday, but only for the day.

From Sea World they headed to Corpus Christi Beach, where the U.S.S. *Lexington* was berthed, and after touring the vintage wartime carrier that was longer than three football fields, they stepped back into history again with a visit to the replica fleet of Christopher Columbus's seafaring ships, the *Niña,* the *Pinta,* and the *Santa María.*

At noon, exhausted and parched, they stopped playing tourist long enough to eat boiled shrimp and drink iced tea at the Bayfront Café, before heading for the white sandy beaches at the remotest tip of Padre Island.

Once Jason was engrossed in constructing turrets on his sand castle and Tami and Anika were strolling far along the shore, Audra summoned the courage to ask Micere for advice.

"Judge Rawlins wants me back in his courtroom?" she prompted, easing into the subject of her future. If she decided to allow Neal access to his son, eventually she'd have to move back to Houston because she definitely planned to be nearby. Tami may not have seen Neal on the social circuit lately, but Audra doubted he was living a celibate life. Who knew what Neal's lifestyle was like now that he was technically single?

"Yep," Micere replied, taking a sip of her Coke. "The judge stopped me in the hallway on Friday. Asked if I'd heard from you. When I told him I was coming down, he said to tell you he wants you in his courtroom for the Salinas trial that starts in a few weeks."

Audra bit her lip. She loved her work and missed

her coworkers, but dreaded facing the aftermath of her breakup with Neal—a subject that had caused a buzz of gossip that had swirled through the employee lunchroom like dust at the center of a tornado.

Sensing Audra's hesitation, Micere said, "You *can* go back to your job and your home in Houston without involving Neal in your personal life, you know?"

"True," Audra replied, wondering how she could ever live again in the four-bedroom house that both she and Neal had abandoned. And was she strong enough to go into the restaurants and clubs where they had dined and danced knowing he had probably taken Delores there, too? Audra tugged her big straw hat lower to keep the sun off her face, scooped up a handful of sand, and let the warm grains slip through her fingers. "Tami told me that Neal and Delores are not together." She tilted her head, squinting. "I take it you know about his desire to patch things up?"

Micere nodded, eyes riveted on Audra's sun-shaded face. "Think about it, Audra." She reached over and put her hand on Audra's arm. "Neal Foster is too good a catch for you to let get away. I admit, he messed up . . . big time. You have every right to be pissed off. But, damn, girl, he's sorry."

"So Tami said, but it sounds like a bad case of the guilties if you ask me," Audra grumbled under her breath.

"Probably. I know he cheated on you," Micere

said, "but he still loves you. Always has. And he was devastated when you moved out."

"I had to leave. That scene with Delores was a sight I'll never be able to forget." Audra tried to keep her voice low enough not to be heard by Jason, while struggling to keep the tears burning her eyes from spilling over. "I wonder how long he was carrying on with that woman before I found out."

"It couldn't have been much of a relationship, if that's even the right word to use. Call it an interlude. A brief liaison . . ."

"A big mistake," Audra cut in.

"Okay. Whatever," Micere sternly agreed. "Besides, it's all over."

"How can I be sure?"

"Because Delores Belton is hanging on the arm of some bigwig politician from Washington, D.C. I heard she's moving up there. Probably already gone."

"Fast work."

"Oh, it just means that she and Neal were never serious. I think they had one of those flirtations that got out of hand."

"Damn straight. *Way* out of hand."

"Oh, Audra, don't make yourself crazy imagining things. You and Neal have been in love since you were both sophomores at Prairie View. You were absolutely inseparable on campus. Remember? I used to be so damn jealous of you two. Perfect. That's what you were. The perfect couple. You had so much going for yourselves. Don't let it all slip away, Audra. Neal just let himself get off track. Think about it."

"Yeah. He had to wait until I went to Phoenix for the court reporters' convention to bring the bitch into my house."

"Maybe Delores seduced him," Micere said.

"I really don't know . . . or care who initiated it," Audra shot back. "But he was my *husband*." Now tears flowed down her sunburned cheeks. "He ruined our marriage, my life."

"Maybe the marriage, but not your life. Get over it, Audra. Neal *is* sorry . . . and he's Jason's father. Remember?" Micere lifted her can of Coke to her lips, pulling down her sunglasses to peep over them at Audra. "And don't even think about telling me you no longer love the guy."

Bertice waited until Tami's BMW disappeared down the road, then pulled the shade back over her bedroom window and frowned.

With the book she had been reading still in her hand, Bertice left her bedroom and headed downstairs. At the foot of the stone staircase she stopped, waiting until Audra and Jason came inside.

"Well, you're up," Audra remarked, a look of surprise on her face. "Feeling better?" She handed Jason his box of crayons and patted him on the head. "Your cocoa is on the table, and just one doughnut," she told him, pointing him toward the kitchen.

"Much better. The girls got off okay?" Bertice asked in an uninterested tone.

"Yes," Audra said. "It was really great to see them again." She smiled and started toward the bright den off the hallway. "I think I'm going to indulge myself with a morning of watching talk shows."

Bertice followed Audra into the rustic room that was filled with oversize oak furniture upholstered in red and green Indian prints. After settling herself into the lodge-style sofa, she said, "Don't turn on the TV just yet."

Audra raised one shoulder in a halfhearted shrug. "Sure."

Shifting to face Audra, Bertice sighed aloud, then slumped back as if she were exhausted. "Now that your company has left, let's enjoy the peace and quiet. Maybe things can get back to normal."

"Hey, what's normal? Not much changes around here."

"I meant we can finally start planning our renovation project. I'm so glad you want to say here and help." Bertice set her book on the coffee table and pierced Audra with expectant eyes. "Moving to Marina Manor was the best decision you ever made, Audra." She nervously clasped her hands together. "After filing for divorce that is."

Audra twitched uncomfortably. "I don't want to talk about it."

The skin on Bertice's forehead wrinkled into furrows, and she sat up straight, prepared to have her say. "Audra, playing Scarlett O'Hara is not going to work. You'd better face what's happening now. Don't think I didn't pick up on the enormous pressure your friends put on you all weekend. They want you to leave me. Leave Marina Manor. Don't they?"

Audra pushed her Astros cap to the back of her head. "That's not fair, Bertice. You were a lifesaver during a very low time in my life, and I don't know what I would have done without your help. My time here with you has been healing, but maybe I'd better start thinking about Jason instead of myself. Tami, Anika, and Micere all agree. He deserves access to his father."

"Humph," Bertice mumbled, blinking as if she didn't want to hear what Audra had to say. "They certainly are generous with advice about how you ought to live your life."

"That's what sorority sisters are good at. We help each other through the tough times—celebrate the good ones, too," Audra replied.

"I just hope they haven't convinced you to make any rash decisions you'll regret later."

"They haven't, but I am seriously considering returning to Houston."

"What a foolish idea," Bertice said curtly, shaking her head in disgust.

"Why?" Audra snapped. "I have a job and a lovely empty home waiting for me. Why am I being foolish? Neal has been sending money regularly, and I've managed to save most of it. I can get back on my feet and be a single mother. Lots of women do it. It may be difficult at first, but I have to think beyond my own selfish needs."

"Oh, Jesus," Bertice groaned sarcastically. "Sure, Audra, go ahead and listen to them. Not one of them has a husband . . . or even a decent relationship. What do they know? And I can't believe you've got the nerve to think you've been selfish. What about Neal Foster? He is the most selfish man alive. He filled his own needs at the expense of his marriage. And you think you can live in the same city with him and not be hurt again?" Bertice scooted to the edge of the couch, her bony knees poking out of her denim shorts like two gnarled knobs of wood. She balled her hands into fists. "If you go back, you'll be sorry. He'll hurt you again."

"Not if I don't give him the chance."

Bertice's face darkened, as if Audra had insulted her. Jumping up, she put her hands on her hips. "How can you even think about leaving me after all those promises you made about staying here forever, helping me bring the place back to its former beauty so we could open it to the public again? Why'd you say those things if you didn't mean them?" Bertice gulped air into her lungs as her body quivered in agitation. She glared at Audra.

Rising, moving nose-to-nose with Bertice, Audra replied. "I said those things because I meant them at the time, but now I see that I was only groping for a way to stay isolated, to keep from involving myself in the day-to-day struggle that living as a single mother would be."

"That's right," Bertice said rapidly, eyes gleaming. "Stay here with me and you will never have to struggle. Jason would have a wonderful childhood growing up here at the coast."

Audra pulled back to assess Bertice. "I wish I understood you better," she started. "You never came to Houston to visit me in happier times. The only time I saw you was when the whole family came here for holidays. And after the accident, you shut yourself off from everyone. I can't do that. I thought I could when I was at a low point, but I can't stay here and I can't keep Jason isolated, either."

"Why are you so anxious to please Neal Foster? He has no right to see my nephew. He gave up his rights when he trashed your marriage."

"Stop it, Bertice," Audra cautioned. "Neal had an affair, that's true. But he was a good father. What he did has no bearing on his love for Jason."

"Sounds like you've made up your mind to go back to him."

"No, I haven't. The only thing I am sure of is that keeping Jason away from Neal is wrong, and I plan to rectify that."

The corners of Bertice's mouth turned down in a smirk. "I don't think Jason needs to be in the company of the man who destroyed his family. He's almost five—old enough to remember the pain Neal caused his mother. That child watched you cry yourself sick. For weeks. I'm telling you, Audra, if you start taking Jason to visit Neal, you'll be making the biggest mistake of your life!"

Audra lifted her chin and calmly assessed her sister. In a firm voice she said, "It's not *my* life I'm concerned about, Bertice. It's Jason's happiness I'm thinking about."

Chapter Four

Grinning so broadly he could feel the skin on his cheeks pull back from his teeth, Neal Foster hung up the phone. He closed his eyes in thankful prayer that Audra had come to her senses. Well almost, he reminded himself, not daring to expect more than what she'd offered. Bringing Jason for a visit was a start, but it was still a long way from anything remotely resembling an overture for a reconciliation.

Neal thought back over their brief conversation, cursing himself for not trying to keep her on the line longer, and wishing he'd been able to convince her to stay in Houston overnight. He would gladly foot the bill at any hotel in town if it meant the chance to have another day with his son. But her voice had been practical and firm, mesmerizing him with its familiar huskiness that had seduced him the first time he had heard it ten years ago. Remembering the sound of it now initiated a flush of desire that pushed his blood racing through his veins. Somehow, he *had* to get her back in his life.

She had come right to the point, openly admitting her mistake in keeping Jason away so long, barely giving him enough time to tell her his address and the time he wanted her to drop Jason off before the phone had clicked off in his hand. She wasn't going to be easy to talk to, he knew, wishing he could stall the rapidly approaching court date.

Maybe it was just as well I didn't ask her to stay longer, he decided. If she'd turned him down, his elation at seeing Jason would have been overshadowed by her rejection. As it stood, the mere fact that she was coming to Houston was encouraging, and he wasn't about to let his opportunity to show her how much he had changed slip by.

Audra is still very angry, he thought, and he didn't blame her in the least. He'd made an ass of himself, a sham of their marriage. Though his attorney had urged him to press for visitation rights long ago, Neal had declined, too disgusted and disappointed with himself to face her or Jason at the time. But eight months had passed. He'd learned his lesson, and now all he wanted was the chance to prove it.

Neal opened his drawer and took out a heavy brass frame that held his favorite photo—the two of them standing on the Riverwalk in San Antonio—the last vacation they had taken before Jason was born. As Neal devoured the picture with his eyes, he could not help remembering the filmy white peignoir Audra had worn that weekend, or the way she had made love to him with a yellow rose behind her ear.

A thin smile replaced his wide grin, and his hand began to sweat as he gripped the photo tighter. A magical two days of incredible passion, that's what it had been. And they had laughed in joy, not at all surprised, five weeks later when Audra's doctor had confirmed that she was pregnant. His love for Audra washed through him at the memory. Slowly, he replaced the photo in the drawer, locked it, and stared glumly at the insurance forms on his desk, grasping at the hope that someday he would hold her, kiss her, make love to her again. Pressing his eyes shut, he cursed himself for taking Audra's love for granted.

The intercom buzzed on his desk.

"Yes, Sherry?" he asked his nurse.

"Mrs. Tucker is here. The root canal, remember?"

He wanted to say, "How could I forget," reminding himself that he'd have to be very gentle with the seventy-five-year-old woman, who carried on like a frightened baby whenever he gave her a routine dental examination.

"Get her prepped, please. I'll be right out."

"And after her, you've got one more appointment. Tami Rogers, at six."

"Fine," Neal replied. He pushed the button, then got up from his polished cherry desk, clearing his thoughts of the foolish possibility that Audra might give him a second chance. Yet, as he flipped through Mrs. Tucker's X rays, he knew he was going to try. *I may not deserve a shot at getting Audra back,* he morosely conceded, *but if I can get her alone for just one hour, I know she'll listen to what I have to say.*

The drilling and scraping and suctioning went on for over an hour. Carol, the receptionist, left at five-thirty, leaving Sherry alone to assist Neal. When Tami arrived for her appointment, she found no one at the front desk, and the cleaning service was busy vacuuming and dusting the reception area. Tami could hear the buzzing of a drill in one of the cubicles, so she walked to the back and stuck her head in to let Sherry know she was there.

"Hi, Tami," Sherry said.

Neal looked around. "Running a little late. Just have a seat in my office until we finish here. Won't be much longer."

Tami entered Neal's office and sat down in a chair fronting his desk. She noticed a pink slip of paper stuck to Neal's calendar. Carol must have put the message there before she left so Neal would be sure to see it. It was not difficult to read: "Call Iris Chargulis before you leave." Tami raised an eyebrow at the sight of Iris's name. Tami knew that name, how could she forget it? Iris was the woman Neal had been dating on campus before Tami introduced him to Audra. Why was Iris suddenly popping up in Neal's life? Tami grit her teeth as she waited.

Soon Mrs. Tucker emerged from the cubicle, and Tami could hear Neal talking to her. "You just rest this evening, Mrs. Tucker. Take the pain medication only if you really need it."

"Thank you, Dr. Foster," the old lady mumbled, hurrying out of the office.

After she left, Sherry escorted Tami into the next cubicle and began to set up the instrument tray. When Neal came in to get started, they made small talk, avoiding the mention of Audra's name. He administered the dreaded novocaine. As the painkiller began to take hold, Tami was suddenly relieved that her tongue was getting numb because she had been on the verge of asking Neal outright just what was going on with him and Iris Chargulis, even though she knew it was none of her business.

The steady warm spray of water over her scalp almost put Audra to sleep. As the shampoo girl massaged her head, she relaxed, letting the accumulation of tension that had gathered over the last two weeks ebb from her stiff shoulders. The weight of worry she'd been carrying around was finally about to be lifted, and there was no way to turn back now. She'd given Neal her word, and she planned to be at his apartment in the Galleria area at exactly ten o'clock on Saturday. And after dropping Jason off, she was going to meet Tami at Marshall Fields and go on a marathon shopping trip. Getting her hair cut and styled was only a start. If she was going to be spending a lot of time in Houston, she'd better pull her image together.

Still shaken by the awful argument she'd had with Bertice, Audra bit her lip, regretting the icy barrier that now kept them tiptoeing around each other, taking caution about what they said and how they said it. Not used to being at odds, Audra sometimes wished she and Bertice were the type of sisters who fought loudly and openly, getting the cutting criticisms out of the way so they could move past whatever their differences were. But they didn't fight like that and Audra hated the way Bertice now tuned her out, avoiding conversation unless it was absolutely necessary.

The uneasy situation at the house hurt Audra, but what could she do? Her decision was final, and she'd be damned if she'd disappoint Jason. He was so excited about going to see his father, he'd already packed every toy and book he owned into his purple Barney bag despite Audra's continual reminders that they were going to Houston only for the day. Yet he kept packing, telling her that he wanted to take all his toys with him just in case they decided to stay. Her heart had nearly broken to hear his innocent expression of hope that his parents might get back together.

After the relaxing shampoo, the manicurist pulled up her table and attacked Audra's nails while the stylist blew her hair dry and began snipping away to the sound of Whitney Houston singing on the radio.

Thirty minutes later, wet nails held out to dry, Audra gingerly took the hand mirror to examine her new look.

Well, she thought, *this is truly a new me!* Her hair,

which she had worn for years in a gently waved shoulder-length pageboy, was now short on the sides, long on the top, feathered in a pixie cut around her heart-shaped face. Audra ran her palm along the sides of her head. "Really short, huh?"

"Low maintenance. That's what you said," the stylist said, rather coolly.

"Oh, no," Audra laughed. "I'm not upset. In fact, I love it! This is just what I need." She paid her bill and left the salon, wondering if Neal would like her new look.

When she entered the house through the back door, Bertice was at the kitchen table talking on the phone.

"Mother," she whispered to Audra, one hand over the mouthpiece.

Audra shook her head back and forth, indicating that she didn't want to talk.

After Bertice hung up, Audra explained. "I'd rather call Mother on Sunday, after the visit. I don't want her to get the wrong idea."

A shadow of perplexity flickered over Bertice's face. "Wrong idea? What's that supposed to mean?"

Audra plopped down in the chair across from Bertice and let out an exasperated sigh. "If I tell her I'm going into Houston, she's going to get it in her mind that Neal and I might get back together. You know how she is. I don't want her to get her hopes up, because this trip is solely for Jason's sake."

Bertice chuckled under her breath. "It's not likely that Mother will get the wrong idea."

"What has she said to you?" Audra felt a chill run over her arms. She recognized that knowing chuckle, the sly look on Bertice's sallow face. Something was going on. As children, Bertice had always been the ring leader, the plotter, the one who got Audra and her sisters into big trouble, then blithely went on her way. "What did you two talk about?" she asked.

"I said, it's not likely that Mother will get the wrong idea. She's not sitting at home rooting for you to get back with Neal."

"I don't believe you. Mother and Neal always got along very well. When we broke up, she told me that she hoped we'd work things out."

"Get real, Audra. That was just polite, comforting talk. She didn't want to tell you the truth."

"Which is?"

"There has never been a separation, let alone a divorce in our family. Manning women choose men who are faithful. Don't you remember Mother telling us that?"

"That was years . . . a generation ago."

"It still holds true. Mother thinks Neal is a monster, an absolute failure. She hates him for what he did to you and wishes you'd use a go-between when you drop Jason off for his visits. You know, let Tami take Jason to see his father."

"You told her about the visit!" Audra was shocked.

"Yeah, and she agrees with me. You're making a big mistake."

"Damnit, Bertice, I wish you'd stay out of my affairs." Audra pushed back her chair and stomped out of the room. In the hallway at the foot of the stairs, she yelled back into the kitchen. "Why don't you get a life for yourself and stay the hell out of mine?"

Chapter Five

The television set in the kitchen was tuned to the channel that ran Saturday-morning cartoons. Neal Foster grinned at the heroic antics of the Power Rangers while absently pulling items from his shopping bags. Next to the gigantic jar of peanut butter, he piled two bags of chocolate chip cookies, four boxes of Cracker Jacks, three different flavors of Kool-Aid, and a dozen jelly doughnuts. Scattered over the butcher-block table were coloring books, packets of crayons, and a new Creepy Crawlers kit.

I wonder which one of the rangers Jason likes best, Neal thought, making up his mind to buy one of the young action figures for his son. He picked up the phone book to find the address of the nearest Toys "R" Us store, then stopped—hand in midair. What if Jason didn't like the teen heroes at all? Or any of the stuff he'd bought? Neal's enthusiasm wavered, and he worried that perhaps he was expecting too much.

After shopping, we'll go to the zoo, then eat dinner at Pizza Junction, Neal planned, struck by the realization that he knew little about what Jason liked to eat, play with, or talk about. Glancing at the clock, Neal began to feel uneasy. Ten o'clock was fast approaching. Soon Jason and Audra would be standing at his door and somehow he had to reestablish a rapport with his son while facing Audra for the first time since she slammed out of his life in the middle of the night, leaving him stunned in the hallway of their French colonial home.

God, how could he face her, knowing how much he'd hurt her? And how was he ever going to broach the subject of asking for her understanding, let alone her forgiveness?

He lowered the volume on the TV and went into his living room, crossing the white plush carpet to the sliding glass door that opened onto his patio/ balcony. He'd have to be diligent about keeping the door securely locked whenever Jason visited, Neal thought as he pushed the heavy glass aside and went to stand at the stainless steel railing circling the sunny plant-filled area. As he took in the panoramic view of the busy Galleria area, he grew more anxious. What if Jason had forgotten him? What if he started crying when Audra left? A flicker of panic curled in his stomach at the idea that his son might think him a stranger.

Audra checked her rearview mirror, then swung into the exit lane that fed from the Loop onto Westheimer. As she inched down the clogged thoroughfare, weaving in and out of traffic, her grip on the steering wheel tightened. The closer she got to Neal's apartment, the more tightly her insides coiled in apprehension, but she was not going to give him the satisfaction of canceling. The last time Neal saw her, she had been crying hysterically. Now she was determined to return with her emotions in check to let him know she was doing just fine.

Jason pressed his nose to the window, murmuring in excited recognition as they passed places he remembered—places they had gone to as a family. Yet, his chatter went unanswered because Audra kept her eyes on the road, too unsure of her voice to say anything.

Picking up the directions she'd scribbled on a scrap of paper, she watched for the landmarks Neal had given her. At the corner of Sage and Westheimer she turned right, pointing her silver Camry north until she passed through the busy shopping area and saw the Exxon station and turned left. Her breath caught in her throat at the sight of the quietly elegant neighborhood, where Neal's pink granite apartment building rose up from a tropical forest of flowering shrubs and spiked palm trees.

"Is this it?" Jason asked, scooting back down in his seat.

"Yes, baby," Audra said, surveying the Jaguars, Mercedes-Benzes, and Porches parked in the adjoining spaces. "This is where your daddy lives."

After parking in the visitors' area, she spoke to the

security guard, who pressed a button and directed them to a bank of gleaming brass elevators behind glass doors. The elevator whisked them skyward in near silence until the doors slid open on the twentieth floor.

Audra stepped out, head held high, tugging Jason along as if leading him to battle. She glanced over, glad to see him smiling. A good sign, she thought, relieved that her less than positive feelings about Neal, which she knew Jason had overheard her express, seemed not to have affected his adoration for his father.

The walk to Neal's apartment seemed a long one. Outside his door Audra fluffed up her bangs, loving the carefree way her new haircut made her feel, then tugged at the sides of her white cotton jeans. Maybe she had gained a few pounds eating Bertice's cooking, but she knew she still looked good—good enough to make Neal regret cheating on her with Delores Belton.

She pressed the buzzer, waiting as she heard Neal's familiar step on the tiled entry inside the apartment. Suddenly, the door opened, and there he was, looking more attractive and seductive than she remembered. And there she stood, feeling as awkward and tongue-tied as a teenager, thankful she'd taken Tami's advice and sprung for the new hairdo and manicure before facing him again.

Swallowing dryly, not daring to look Neal in the eye, Audra ran her eyes down the buttons of his banded-collar shirt to his creased, stonewashed jeans, unable to keep from smiling at the sight of his silver belt buckle—the one he had bought on their vacation in San Antonio.

"Jason!" Neal scooped his son up in his arms and buried his face against the child's neck. Jason wrapped his arms around Neal and hugged him fiercely, then leaned back to peer into his father's face. Neal kissed Jason firmly on the cheek, then clutched him to his chest as if he feared he might evaporate. "Thank you, Audra," Neal said in a throaty voice. He stepped back to let her enter. "Really. Thanks for bringing Jason over."

Shaken by the emotional reunion, Audra smiled softly and nodded. A tightness gathered in her chest at the sight of tears on Neal's tan face.

Brushing them away with his thumb, he said, "Please come in. Sit down for a minute. You don't have to run off, do you?"

"No," Audra said, anxious to see the rest of the elegantly appointed apartment. "Nice place, Neal."

"Thanks. It's home," he said rather flatly.

Audra followed Neal into the living room and perched stiffly on the edge of his white leather sofa. Neal sank down onto an oversize ottoman across from her, Jason still firmly in his arms.

"Let me look at you, buddy," he started, easing Jason to the floor. "Boy, you've grown."

"Yeah," Jason piped up. "About two inches!"

Neal laughed. "All of two inches? How do you know that?"

"Aunt Bertice measured me," Jason said matter-of-factly, squirming away from Neal to explore the bright sunny apartment.

Audra kept a close eye on Jason, a little nervous about the high-rise patio door. "Is the door locked?" she asked, meeting Neal's eyes for the first time, feeling the familiar slow burn of the magnetic current that had always flared between them.

"Oh, yes. Don't worry. It stays locked. He won't be out there unless I am with him." He pulled her toward him with his gaze, then broke the spell when he turned to speak to Jason. "Go through that door over there and look on the kitchen table. You might find something you like."

Jason grinned and scurried off. Audra raised an eyebrow. "Cracker Jacks, I suppose?"

Neal nodded. "He still likes them, doesn't he?"

"More than ever," Audra said, glad Neal was making an effort to keep their strain from showing.

"Good," Neal said, "because I realized this morning that a lot can change in eight months. We'll have to get used to each other again."

"Oh, don't worry. It won't take long. Jason has been primed for this visit all week." She twisted her fingers together. "He's really missed you, Neal. A lot."

"And I've missed him." Neal got up and went to sit beside Audra.

She stiffened, inching closer to the end of the sofa.

"I've missed you, too, Audra," Neal confessed, sitting at an angle, his back to the arm of the sofa. "I hope we'll have time to talk while you're here. There is so much I'd like to say to you."

Audra met his gaze, her icy resolve to keep Neal Foster out of her life melting like snowflakes in June as she faced him. "I don't think there's much to talk about, Neal. I'll be heading back to Corpus this evening." She pulled her shoulders back as if attempting to create a solid front to shield herself from Neal's disturbing gaze. *Oh, God,* she thought. *Bertice was right. This is a terrible mistake. I am not ready to be this close to Neal or deal with his unnerving charm.*

"Do you have to?" Neal asked. "Couldn't you stay over? I'd pay for a hotel."

"No, Neal. I could stay with Tami. That's not a problem. I promised Bertice I'd be back tonight, and I think it's best not to change our plans now."

"All right," Neal said, quickly backing off. "I was just hoping that . . ." The telephone rang, interrupting his sentence. "Damn. I hope it's not my service. I told them Dr. Caroway would take my emergency calls." He got up and went into the foyer and answered the phone.

Audra stood, easing toward the patio door to stand with her back to Neal, trying to block out the one-sided conversation.

"Iris! Yes. I got your message."

Audra pulled her lips between her teeth, pretending to survey the view, her ears tuned to Neal's voice.

"Well, my son is with me . . . yes . . . he's visiting today. I'll be busy all afternoon."

Now Audra licked her lips, trying to slow the rapid thudding of her heart against her ribs. She held her breath, determined not to overreact to something that did not concern her in the least.

"I'm sorry you canceled, too," he said.

Audra could feel the strain in his voice as he tried to camouflage his emotions.

"Later? Sure, Iris. That'd be great. Okay. Seven o'clock? Fine. I'll see you then."

The sound of his hanging up the phone cut into Audra's stomach. She could feel him approaching behind her, yet gave a startled jump when he reached around her and pulled on the heavy sliding door.

"Would you like to step outside? Great view."

"No," Audra said flatly, feeling his offer was an attempt to soften the impact of his telephone conversation. How could he make a date in front of her, after just confessing how much he had missed her? And he had wanted to talk! About what? she fumed inwardly. If he had anything to say, it would have to wait until they had their day in court. She headed across the living room back toward the sofa and picked up her beige leather purse. "I have to meet Tami at the Galleria in ten minutes. I'd better go. This is your time with Jason. I don't want to interfere."

Neal came closer, reaching one hand out toward

her, then seeing the defiant look in her eyes, he let his hand drop to his side. "I understand," Neal said curtly. "I'm sure you have things to do."

Turning away, Audra went into the kitchen to find Jason, who was stuffing his mouth with Cracker Jacks, mesmerized by the Power Rangers on TV.

"I have to go now," Audra said, not sure if she was happy or sad that her statement brought no words of protest from Jason. In fact, he barely took his eyes off the screen as Audra pecked him on the cheek.

"Bye," he said cheerfully.

"I'll be back to get you at six."

"Okay, Mommie," he said, chewing as he spoke.

Neal held the door open as Audra approached.

"Thanks again," Neal said. "I'll have him back here by six."

I'm sure you will, Audra thought, *if you've got a date at seven.* "Fine," she told him, brushing past Neal to hurry down the hallway.

The walk back to the car seemed interminable, and when she finally settled in her seat and locked the doors, she pulled on her seat belt, then buried her head in her hands. The tears that spilled from her eyes and soaked her palms confused Audra. Was she crying because Neal had proved Bertice right? Or was she shedding tears of disappointment because it appeared as if Neal had someone new in his life? How stupid of her to think he had changed, or that seeing him would not rekindle the feelings she had struggled for months to ignore.

Chapter Six

"You sound like someone who cares," Tami told Audra as they strolled through the cosmetics department of Marshall Fields.

Audra cocked her head to the side. "I don't think so," she flippantly replied. "Who Neal spends his time with is not my business."

"Iris Chargulis! That snooty psych major who told everybody she'd get Neal back if she ever got the chance."

"That was aeons ago, Tami. It's not important now. If Neal wants to see her, it's his business."

"If you say so, girlfriend," Tami tossed back, mocking Audra's disinterest. She stopped and sprayed a sample of Liz Taylor's White Diamonds on her wrist. "Wow. I can see how Liz catches so many good-looking men if this is what she uses." Tami pointed the bubble-shaped container at Audra.

Holding up one hand in protest, Audra backed off. "No, thanks. That's the last thing I need."

"Maybe not," Tami said, replacing the glittery bottle on the mirrored counter. "But if Iris is moving in on Neal, you may need Liz's help if you want to get him back." She giggled, bending over to smell a box of rose-scented soap. "I remember the time you spent one hundred and fifty dollars on bath oil and candles to seduce Neal on that Caribbean cruise you two took to celebrate your first anniversary."

"Please, Tami," Audra threw back, not ready to trip down memory lane and dredge up painful reminders of the good times she and Neal had shared. "Please be serious. I told you I can't go back with Neal. How could I after what he did?"

With a low groan, Tami offered her opinion. "Try. I told you . . . the man still loves you and is heartbroken that you filed for divorce. Didn't he say he wanted to talk?"

"Yes, but a conversation with me must not have been high on his list of priorities. He was pretty darn quick to set a date with Iris."

"Right. He could have put her off if he really had something to say." Tami measured Audra's remark. "Maybe he got cold feet."

"Face it, Tami. Neal Foster has not changed. He'll always accept an invitation to go anywhere . . . do anything . . . if a pretty woman asks him. Don't you get it?"

"I don't remember Iris as being that pretty."

Audra shifted her shopping bag from one hand to the other. "Give me a break, Tami. Do you think for one minute that Dr. Neal Foster would be seen in public with any woman who wasn't?"

During the rest of their afternoon outing, Audra avoided further discussion of Neal or her future, pumping Tami for the latest on Micere's mystery boyfriend. No one had seen him, but Anika told Tami that Micere had gone out to dinner with her new acquaintance three times last week and was planning to go to Dallas with him next weekend.

"Good for her," Audra said. "If anyone deserves a second chance, it's Micere."

Tami's brown eyes flew open, and she tossed a twisted curl from her cheek. "Oh? That's just great, Audra. Put yourself down, why don't you?"

"I'm not."

"Okay. But I'm telling you. Don't be so stubborn that you live to regret not giving yourself a second chance, too."

After a late lunch at Café Annie's, Tami drove Audra back to the parking garage in the Galleria to get her car.

"You drive carefully and call me when you get back, you hear?"

Audra hugged Tami. "I promise . . . on both counts. See you next time."

"Oh," Tami stopped, one hand on her gearshift. "So there is going to be a next time?"

"Well, yes," Audra admitted. "There's no reason for me not to let Neal see Jason. His personal life has nothing to do with that."

Tami shook her head. "Okay, Audra. If you say so." Waving, she drove off into the crush of traffic and disappeared around the corner.

Audra turned the key and started her car. As she drove toward the street leading to Neal's apartment building, she foolishly let scenes of the Caribbean cruise enter her mind. God, she really did miss him. And love him more than she dared admit to Tami. So why hadn't he pursued an opportunity to talk with her? He was the one to confess to Tami his desire for a second chance, then do nothing about it. What was going on with him and Iris? Audra wondered, struggling to remember just what the woman looked like.

Bertice set her coffee cup down very carefully and stared at Audra over the breakfast table. "Why did you do that?" she sighed, letting her shoulders droop. "You need to talk to your attorney."

"Don't overreact," Audra said, glancing out the window at Jason, who was playing in his sandbox in the backyard. She paused, as if deciding exactly how to phrase her explanation. "The visit went very well. Jason cried when he had to go. It was so sad. How can I refuse letting him visit again?"

"But every two weeks? The next visit will be close to the July fourth weekend. You promised to take Jason to the fireworks display at Sea World."

"We'll work it out," Audra tossed back, determined to remain calm in spite of the obvious obstacles Bertice threw in her way. "I'll take Jason for a one-day visit, and Neal said he'd make time whenever I could get him there."

"You'd better be careful," Bertice cautioned, her thin face quivering with anxiety. "Visitation arrangements ought to be handled by the judge . . . as part of the divorce. You'd be better off staying out of it."

"Ah, Bertice. It's not that easy. Jason is just a little boy. He doesn't understand these grown-up problems. If he wants to see Neal, I'm not going to make a fuss about it."

"You are such a pushover, Audra. Don't you see what Neal is doing?"

"No, what?"

"Using Jason to get to you. The more you bring Jason to see him, the more opportunity he has to work on you. If you forgive him and take him back, he won't have to pay child support and maintenance on that big house. Making up would be a whole lot less expensive than getting a divorce."

Audra tossed her napkin to her plate, tired of Bertice and everyone else's speculation about her future. "That is the craziest thing I've ever heard you say." Now she deliberately raised her voice, tired of pussyfooting around the subject that was causing so much strain. If they were going to disagree, Audra was going to let Bertice know exactly how she felt. "Neal makes a very good living. Money is not the issue. I told him he could sell the house for all I cared. He's the one hanging on to it. Neal will pay whatever the judge tells him to, and I can assure you he doesn't want me back. He's probably already got someone new in his life." Her voice cracked, and her fingers flew to her lips, as if she were trying to put back the shocking revelation she had let slip out. Horrified, Audra watched wide-eyed as a sly smile eased over Bertice's face.

After drawing a long, thoughtful breath, Bertice spoke. "So. He's already moved on, huh? Hurt you again, didn't he? You see . . . he's found someone new . . . and after all that garbage he told Tami about wanting you back. I told you not to go to Houston. But listen to me? Oh, no. Well, now you understand, Audra. Neal Foster can't be trusted. *You can't trust any man.* If you do, you are going to be stepped on, crushed by their selfish, arrogant ways."

"Stop it! Stop talking like that," Audra shouted. She jumped up and banged out the back door, fleeing to the beach, where she waded into the water without taking off her tennis shoes. Standing with the waves lapping at her knees, she wrapped her arms about her stomach and squeezed her eyes shut. Tears of regret and shame slipped over her cheeks as she realized Bertice was right.

"I expected Neal to ask me to come back to him," Audra admitted in a whisper swept from her throat into the roaring water. "I never thought he'd play games with my feelings again. But I was wrong, and as long as I keep trusting him, I'll never be able to start over."

* * *

It had been easier for Audra to admit to her foolish hope that she and Neal might find a way to reconcile than to admit her romantic imaginings to Bertice. In fact, Audra had said nothing about her disappointment, choosing to let the matter drift away as the summer days slipped past.

For a week she moped along the beach, letting her new hairdo go untended, her nails unpolished, wearing her usual baseball cap and jeans. She refused all calls from Anika and Micere, swearing Tami to secrecy about her current state, and submerged herself in the stack of books she had checked out of the library in Corpus. Though Jason kept asking about his next visit to his father, Audra put off making the arrangements.

A week before the July fourth weekend, she and Bertice were sitting in the den watching a rerun of *Family Matters* on TV. When the show ended, Bertice shocked her with an unexpected announcement.

"I've decided to hold a family get-together here at Marina Manor over the July fourth holiday weekend."

Taken aback by Bertice's uncharacteristically upbeat attitude, Audra's lips parted in surprise. "Why? Jason and I might be going to Houston about that time."

"So? You said you were only going for the day. Why don't you take Jason to see Neal on Friday—the second. We'll have the reunion on the fourth. It won't be a problem at all."

Audra could not believe her ears. Bertice was actually sounding enthusiastic—not only about Jason's upcoming trip to see Neal but about having the family intrude on her carefully guarded privacy. After living like a hermit for so many years, Audra was suspicious of this abrupt change of heart.

"The fifth of July will be Mother and Dad's fortieth wedding anniversary, remember?" Bertice said.

"Yeah," Audra replied, mentally reminding herself to get them a card.

"Well, why not have a party? A big blowout barbecue like the old days—when all of us were younger and . . ." she paused, frowning, "happier. It'll be fun. We need to liven things up a bit around here." Bertice propped one foot on the old oak coffee table, and pulled a pad and pencil from the end table drawer. She balanced the notepad on her leg. "Teresa, Kathleen, Douglas, and their families surely will come." She scribbled their names. "That's twelve right there. Aunt Martha and Uncle Joe would drive over from Alvin, and I'll bet cousins Theodore and Patty would probably fly in from Baton Rouge. What do you think?"

Audra could not suppress a smile. Looking around the gloomy room, she shook her head. "It's been so long since we've gotten together here at Marina Manor." She shivered at the sight of the dust covering the high mantel, the spiderwebs clinging to the beams overhead. "It will take a lot of work to get ready."

"I'll spring for a professional cleaning service if I have to in order to whip this place into shape," Bertice said in the gayest voice Audra had heard her use in years.

Laughing, Audra asked, "Is this you? What's going on? I never thought I'd hear you say you'd spend money for something you could do yourself."

Bertice's face took on a serious expression. "I've been doing a lot of thinking since we had that awful argument. I didn't mean to upset you, Audra, you've already been through enough, and you are right. I shouldn't have interfered. But Kathleen and Teresa are concerned about the possibility that you might go back to Neal and be hurt again. Now that you've made up your mind not to, maybe getting together like this will help you settle into your new life here."

"You discussed my situation with Kathleen? Teresa?"

"Yes," Bertice said in an authoritative manner. "And Douglas, too. They all want the best for you and are happy you've decided to live at Marina Manor with me."

Audra got up and paced in front of the dark empty fireplace. It was so damn hard to keep from screaming, but she managed. In a very controlled voice, she told Bertice, "I know you mean well, but I prefer to be the one to tell my family about any decisions I make about my life."

"I'm sorry," Bertice said. "You're right, and I promise never to discuss you with them again." She tipped back her cup of coffee and took a sip. "Now, what kind of barbecue should we have? Brisket or chicken?"

Shaking her head in amazement, Audra said, "Why not both?" Then she settled on the sofa next to Bertice to help plan the family gathering.

This may be just what I need, Audra thought, glad to finally have something to occupy her mind besides the image of Neal Foster in Iris Chargulis's arms.

Chapter Seven

The dismal gray clouds hanging on the horizon matched Audra's disheartened spirits. When a special weather bulletin interrupted the music she had been absently listening to, she stepped on the gas, hoping to get to Houston before the threatening clouds let loose.

"A tropical depression north of Havana is being watched very closely," the weather reporter said. "At the present time surface winds are thirty-five miles per hour and all signs indicate that the storm has little chance of affecting the Texas Gulf Coast during the upcoming July fourth weekend."

Damn, Audra thought, *just when Bertice emerges from her shell and decides to pull the family together, we have to deal with the possibility that a hurricane is brewing in the Gulf.*

With only four days until the Fourth of July, she had promised Bertice she would be back that evening in order to help with party preparations and grocery shopping in the morning. The plans for the family reunion were going full steam ahead, but Audra had lost her enthusiasm, not looking forward to her parents' interference or her sisters' advice on the decisions she had made about her future. A flurry of phone calls had gone back and forth, and now Audra gripped the wheel, staring glumly into the nearly deserted road, the reality of the approaching encounter with Neal weighing like a stone in her stomach.

Nothing seemed right anymore. Why did she feel so off-kilter? Regretting her impulsive decision to wear her jogging suit and faithful Astros cap, Audra thought about turning her car around to head back to the haven Marina Manor had become. She dreaded seeing Neal at all, let alone facing him when she looked as depressed as she felt. Though Tami would have been a willing go-between, Audra had opted not to call on her friend. She was not in the mood for a "sister" pep talk, and besides, she had to start dealing with Neal on strictly nonemotional terms whenever Jason was involved. She'd drop him off without going in, then head to the Cineplex and take in a movie or maybe go over to the Museum of Fine Arts to see the new John Biggers exhibit.

By the time Audra parked her car at Neal's apartment building, a fine misty rain had begun to fall. Hurricane season was in full swing, and Audra knew the thick gray sheen overhead meant the type of weather that Houstonians dreaded was on its way—heavy rains and flash floods that could wipe out side streets in a matter of seconds. Worrying about making the long drive back to Marina Manor, Audra pulled her umbrella and Jason's overnight bag from the backseat. Though she had not mentioned her idea to Bertice, Audra knew—if Jason asked—she was going to let him stay overnight and she'd come back for him on Friday.

After unbuckling Jason's seat belt, Audra held him closely under her red-striped umbrella and scurried into the building. Nodding to the security guard, who smiled in recognition, she led Jason into the mirrored elevator. When the doors slid open on the twentieth floor, Audra knew that the giddy anticipation she had felt a few weeks ago was now a steely sense of relief. No false hopes clouded her mission now. She would deliver Jason safely into his father's care, then get on with her plans for the day.

When Neal appeared at the door, cream-colored shirt open at the neck, a wide smile on his face, her resolve melted under his gaze. Her mouth grew dry, and she balled her hands into fists at her sides, silently cursing the effect he still had on her. Audra cleared her throat, declining his offer to come in. "I've got plans," she stated, handing Jason his bag as he slipped past Neal to disappear into the kitchen to see what goodies might be there for him. The door slammed shut behind Jason.

Neal laughed and shook his head.

Audra could not help smiling. "Guess he's right at home, huh?"

Neal nodded.

Audra took in a deep breath. "Neal, the weather's pretty awful. I think I'll head over to the museum before it gets too bad."

"The Biggers exhibit?" he asked.

She nodded, afraid to trust her voice, remembering the Biggers painting they had bought at Black Heritage Gallery on their first wedding anniversary. As far as she knew, it was still hanging in the bedroom at the house in Missouri City.

Neal still hadn't made a move to close the front door. He eyed her thoughtfully, rubbing his hands on the sides of his brown slacks. "Audra?"

"Yes?" she said, wondering why he seemed so uncharacteristically agitated. Neal rarely let anything get to him. Audra had begun to believe that most doctors had similar personalities in order to stay calm while facing emergencies.

"Please come in," Neal said, his request sounding more like a plea than an invitation. "Just for a few minutes. Please. There's someone here I want you to meet."

Audra felt as if an airplane had just dive bombed inside her stomach as the seriousness of Neal's words filtered into her brain. Dreading what she was about to hear, she stepped inside the door.

"You have company?" Audra managed in a cool voice, determined not to give Neal the satisfaction of knowing he had shaken her with his news.

Without answering, he walked in front of her into the living room. Audra followed on weakened legs, feeling as if she had just gotten off a roller coaster, coming face-to-face with a vaguely familiar and definitely attractive woman sitting on Neal's white leather ottoman. Audra held her breath, waiting for Neal to make the introductions.

"You remember Iris Chargulis, don't you?" Neal began, approaching his guest—a gorgeous honey-toned, thirty-something woman who was completely encased in beige. Her linen pants were crisply creased, her silk shirt softly tied in a bow at her neck, and her pedicured feet were clad in pale brown leather sandals that Audra recognized as Charles Jourdans.

Feeling shabby in her baseball cap and comfy, nylon jogging suit, Audra cringed inwardly. "Yes. Of course," she managed, stepping closer to extend her hand.

Neal turned around and faced Audra. "*Dr.* Iris Chargulis," he stressed.

Audra gave Iris's perfumed fingers a limp shake. "Oh? how nice," she commented in as calm a voice as she could muster. "It's good to see you."

"Yes. It's been years," Iris replied in a voice that Audra was certain must be the kind you heard if you called those 1-900 sex lines.

When Neal put his hand gently on Audra's arm, she jumped, looking at him in surprise "Dr. Chargulis is my therapist, Audra," he said softly. "I hope you don't mind but I wanted to tell you about this in her presence."

"Oh? Your therapist?" Audra asked in amazement.

"Yes. Iris recently moved her practice here from Denver. I went to see her shortly after we . . . after you left. I was deeply depressed, Audra. I didn't know what to do. I'd lost my wife, my son, my home. Everything that I thought mattered. Why? I kept asking myself. Why did I treat our marriage so shabbily?"

Audra lowered her eyes, recognizing the same questions that had been rumbling through her head, now coming from his lips. *Yes,* she thought, *why?*

Neal went on. "I knew I had to change my attitude toward commitment—really change whatever was in me that made me approach our marriage so lightly. I was confused. In a lot of pain. I put myself in Iris's hands, and I've been attending counseling sessions with her once a week for the past six months."

Iris nodded at Audra. "And he's made a lot of progress."

Audra stared at the doctor, humiliated that the woman knew so much about her personal affairs, yet grateful that she was helping Neal discover and explore the roots of his behavior. Maybe there was hope after all.

Neal took Audra's hand in his, holding it firmly as if he feared she might run away. "Iris has helped me better understand why I hurt you, Audra." He pulled her down next to him on the sofa. "I only ask one thing."

"What?" Audra whispered, her lips barely moving.

"I want you to hear me out. I couldn't do this alone—I tried to when you brought Jason the last time, but I chickened out. With Iris's help I want to tell you how sorry I am."

During the next forty-five minutes, Audra heard, for the first time, the real story behind why and how Neal's father, Harry Foster, had died. It was not exactly news to her, she had heard bits and pieces of the tragic incident in which Neal's father had been gunned down in a random drive-by shooting. Neal had been fourteen years old at the time and very close to his father.

The loss had paralyzed the family, and they soon fell on very hard times. Then Neal's mother pulled herself together, determined to get her children away from the circumstances that she thought had killed their father. After completing her degree in computer science at Texas Southern, she got a good job and managed to move the family from their shabby apartment into a modest middle-income neighborhood. From there, Neal went on to dental school and his sister, Margarite, became a lab technician at the Veterans Hospital. That was all Neal had told her, but what Audra was hearing now about Harry Foster was an entirely different story.

"On a cold February night inside a bar in the heart of Third Ward," Neal began, "my father . . . a handsome, flashy charmer who prided himself on bedding as many attractive ladies as he could . . . was bragging about some woman named Olivia. He called her his latest conquest and described in rather detailed terms the good time they'd had the night before. Well, when Dad stepped outside at two in the morning, he was shot to death in front of several of his drinking buddies. They refused to talk to the police, assuming that the killer was Olivia's outraged husband, justifiably seeking revenge."

"How do you know this?" Audra asked softly, stunned at the picture he was painting.

"I always knew most of it. I overheard my mother on the phone. I was old enough to put it together, but then I blocked it out of my mind and created a more acceptable version."

"Have you talked to your mother? Lately?" Audra liked Nellie Foster and had great admiration for her mother-in-law, although she was shocked to hear she had had to put up with a philandering husband, too.

"Yes," Neal said. "During my therapy, we have talked quite a bit. She has confirmed what I have been trying to deny for so many years: My father was adulterous and thought he had every right to be. She has also been brutally honest about the way my father's behavior influenced me when I was young. She was shocked, and very sorry, but not surprised to hear that I had done to you what my father did to her. She hated to see the behavior come full circle and was devastated to learn that you had walked out on me."

Audra sat quietly as Neal finished telling her how much influence Harry Foster had had on him. When

Neal spoke of how he had idolized his philandering father, Audra's heart broke for him.

Iris held up a hand to give Neal space to stop talking and pull himself together. "Audra, Neal has been reliving some very painful times from his childhood. Through intensive therapy he has come to understand that the example Harry Foster set for him unconsciously became his own foundation for relationships, especially marriage. In other words, Neal truly believed that having extramarital affairs was expected of a man . . . a *true* man . . . and the thing he had to worry about was not getting caught. Rather like a game of intrigue that would keep him in a constant state of excitement. Unfortunately, Neal grew up listening to his father joke and laugh about his sexual exploits."

Audra nodded, thinking, *So this was the atmosphere in which Neal formed his opinions about relationships, women, and marriage.*

Neal faced Audra fully and clasped her hands in his. "With Iris's help I have searched the painful roots of my feelings and expectations about you . . . our marriage. I know now why I threw my marriage away for a casual affair with a woman I didn't care about. My father had always bragged to me about his escapades, encouraging me to enjoy the ladies, but get married and have a family. Oddly, that was important to him. He always said, 'Keep 'em guessing. That way you'll never look weak.' "

By the time Neal finished telling Audra how

clearly he now saw the error of his ways and how much his therapy sessions had helped him, she was in tears.

"So, Audra," Iris began, "Neal has finally been able to reject the picture his father had instilled in his mind of men as fun-loving, carefree spirits who can do as they please as long as they don't get caught. Young boys imitate their fathers. It's just too bad that some fathers don't have very good habits and attitudes to imitate."

"Right," Neal said. "You know, during the time that I now know my father was running around, I never saw my mother cry, though I'm sure she did. I never heard my parents argue. On the surface, everything appeared normal, but now I see it was all a sham. My father was never faithful, and my mother never challenged him. Somehow I got the screwed-up idea that it was all right for Dad to do as he pleased, because he loved my mother, was proud that she was the mother of his children, and as far as I could see, he never openly treated her badly."

"Except to sneak around behind her back and betray his marriage vows," Audra stiffly clarified.

"I know," Neal admitted, "but I mean he never got loud, physical."

"There are plenty of other ways to hurt someone besides physical abuse, you know."

Neal nodded. "Do I ever."

Audra sank back onto the sofa, arms folded across her chest, absorbing Neal's revelation. From the corner of her eye, she watched him wipe a tear from his cheek with his thumb. He looked wounded—like a little boy who has been forced to tattle on his best friend. When he drew in a deep ragged breath, her heart fluttered, and she suddenly wanted to reach out, pull him into her arms, and tell him how glad she was that he had come to terms with his past. Loving Neal again was all Audra wanted, but she waited, emotions in check, determined not to forgive him too quickly and end up disappointed once more.

Chapter Eight

Pale pink impatiens that had somehow survived the winter without Audra's tender care struggled to hold their blooming heads upright in the steady slant of rain. Audra smiled, glad to see the front of her home looking as if someone lived there. She slammed her car door and dashed across the soggy lawn, passing the blooming flower beds that looked as if they had been recently weeded and mulched.

I guess Neal has someone looking after the place, she thought as she nervously stuck her key in the lock, halfway assuming it wouldn't work. But it did and when the door swung open, the sense of longing that swept over Audra stopped her at the entryway.

It was such a lovely home—the two-story French colonial she had always dreamed of living in, with an island kitchen and decking all around the back. She eased the beveled glass door shut, then took off her hat and ran her fingers through her hair, thankful that her new haircut sprang back to life after being crushed under her cap. As she fluffed up her bangs, she crossed the black and white marble entryway and stepped down into the sunken living room. The custom-made drapes she had spent so much time choosing still hung at the windows, not faded by the sun. As she walked through the room, she was surprised at how well kept the place looked, considering the fact that no one had lived there for at least eight months.

Instead of going to the museum, she had wound up driving around, thinking of what she had just learned about Neal. Her heart went out to him, and she now understood how his childhood experiences had influenced his adult relationships. He seemed anxious to be the kind of husband and father Audra wanted, but Dr. Chargulis, who had been pleasantly supportive, urged them to proceed slowly if they planned to give their marriage a second chance.

Audra's joy at the mature, responsible way Neal had discussed his problem had initiated thoughts of a reconciliation, subconsciously spurring her back to their house—the house where she and Neal had shared not only some heartbreaking moments, but some very wonderful ones, too. As soon as she turned onto her old street, a sense of belonging had filled her, invoking a feeling of hope.

A rush of memories crowded her heart as she glanced into the near empty rooms, some still holding the few pieces of furniture neither she nor Neal had opted to claim. She had feared the place might have been vandalized, but the neighborhood security was tight, and along with the alarm system they had installed, the house remained virtually the same as the day she had walked out.

She wandered into the kitchen, checking the cabinets for traces of any mice who might have taken up residence. Finding none, she slowly climbed the curved staircase to the master bedroom at the end of the hall. Inside, she found the king-size bed she had once shared with Neal, a quilt thrown over the mattress, an old copy of *Jet* magazine on the floor. She stooped and picked it up; the date was October 4, 1994. Two weeks before she had left Neal.

"We'll get back together," Audra said aloud as she roamed about the spacious bedroom. She stopped to gaze up at the John Biggers painting, both pleased and annoyed to see it still hanging in the abandoned house. "I love Neal, and he knows it. There's got to be a way for us to work things out."

She took off her damp shoes, loving the feel of the plush gray carpet beneath her feet. At the window seat overlooking the deck below, she sank down, placing her chin on her arms. Staring out over the backyard, she weighed the options before her: Forgive Neal and move back into the house to try to reconstruct her family as it had been. Come back to Houston but move into an apartment and take the reconciliation slowly. Or stay at Marina Manor and protect herself from ever being hurt or betrayed again.

Rain pounded the cedar deck below, and Audra

watched clear rivulets of water drain over the rocky ledges of her cactus garden, knowing she had to leave Marina Manor. Living with Bertice was not an option, but telling her that she was moving out was going to be a painful ordeal. As much as Audra loved her sister, she had her own life to live and it had been on hold far too long.

If only I could turn back the clock and erase the complicated situation facing me now, she thought. Dropping the divorce proceedings would be easy enough, a phone call to her attorney would take care of that, but breaking the news to her family was going to take some careful planning.

The sound of footsteps on the outside walkway startled Audra, but she relaxed, assuming it must be her good friend and neighbor June Trevir, to whom she had waved when she turned onto the street. June's boy, Tommy, was the same age as Jason and the two mothers had become very close, running back and forth for play dates, sharing birthday parties and other outings.

Primed for the chime of her doorbell, Audra waited, but when Neal's voice called out her name, she jumped up and spun around. She could hear the front door close, then his footsteps on the stairs. He emerged from the darkened hallway and stood in the doorway, his brown slacks and cream-colored shirt splattered with drops of rain.

"Oh, my God! You startled me." With one hand

to her chest she stared at Neal. What on earth was he doing there? Had he followed her?

"Sorry. I didn't mean to scare you," Neal said, wiping beads of water from his cheeks.

"Where is Jason? Why are you here?" Audra asked.

Neal smiled. "I guess entertaining a four-year-old on a rainy day requires some imagination. After Play-Doh and fingerpaints Jason asked if he could visit Tommy Trevir. I telephoned June. She was delighted that Jason was back in town and wanted to take the boys for pizza. After I dropped Jason off, I drove past the house . . . I saw your car."

"Oh" was all Audra could manage. She felt anticipation building—for what she didn't know. But being alone in the house—in their old bedroom—created a dizzying awareness of Neal's physical presence and stirred up the attraction she knew had never gone away. In a stilted voice she said, "Fine. That was nice of June. Jason has missed his friends."

"Right. I hoped it would be okay with you."

Audra waved her hand in a dismissive manner, more in an attempt to gain time to gather her wits than to put Neal off. "When Jason is with you, you're in charge. I trust you to make the right decisions, Neal. You wouldn't do anything that might harm our son."

Neal stepped from the hallway into the room, his dark eyes leveled on Audra. She inched back toward the window seat, burning under his stare, feeling as if he could see right through her clothes to the fire he'd ignited inside her.

"Thanks," he said in little more than a rough whisper. "It means a lot to hear you say that . . . you trust me." His words rang with sincerity.

Touched by his confession, Audra felt the tug of desire that was so familiar begin to coil inside and prayed she'd be able to keep her emotions under control. But the longer Neal raked her with his sensuous gaze, the more weakened her resolve became.

"Your trust means a hell of a lot," Neal reiterated, leaning against the frame of the open door, his tall lean body seeming to dominate the dusky room.

As the rain intensified and the clouds grew thicker, the room had gradually eased into semidarkness. Audra glanced around for a lamp to turn on, her heart skipping a beat when she realized there was none. "The house is in good shape," she said, trying to find a common, nonemotional topic to keep the conversation going.

"I contracted with a cleaning service and a gardener to keep it from going to pot."

Audra eased down onto the padded window seat, tugging a small cushion from beneath her hips. She toyed nervously with the fringe on it as she spoke. "Good idea. It was quite an investment."

Now Neal crossed the room and sat beside her. "*Was?* Don't speak in the past tense. This *is* a good investment, and it's still our home."

"I'm sure the judge will order it sold," Audra replied coolly, though her heart was burning at the thought of strangers moving into the house she and Neal had so lovingly and carefully designed.

"Never," Neal said adamantly. "I'll never sell this house." He put both of his hands on Audra's arms. Quivering, she let him run them up to her shoulders and draw her nearer as he spoke. "I'm hoping we will live here again, Audra. Me, you, and Jason, a family once more."

Though craving his touch, Audra pulled gently away. "Neal, please don't. It has not been easy to move past what happened. We've both been through a lot. I'm glad you've been able to get to the source of your problems, but we can't move too quickly. I don't want to create more pain for either of us . . . or Jason."

"I know," he said dejectedly, arms settling at his sides. "I'm willing to wait. I'll hold onto this house and wait as long as you want me to."

A low murmur of a chuckle escaped Audra's lips. "Don't you think that's putting quite a bit of pressure on me to make some sort of a decision?"

The room was silent except for the splatter of rain against the house. Audra tucked her legs beneath her, trembling inside, suddenly wishing Neal would reach up and massage her shoulders as he had done many times while sitting in the window seat.

"I don't mean to put pressure on you," Neal said, his voice deep and contrite. "But I can't help it if I want you . . . and Jason back in my life." He placed one hand flat against his leg and rubbed his palm along the length of his thigh.

With lowered eyes Audra watched the rhythmic movement of his strong hand—the left hand—surprised to see he was wearing his wedding band. Had he had it on earlier? If so, how had she missed seeing it? She pressed her legs together, trying to still the warming glow she felt spreading from her stomach to the moist, pulsing core of her womanhood. Swallowing dryly, she told him, "I know you don't mean to pressure me, but I feel as if you expect more from me than maybe I can give you right now."

Neal edged closer until his knee touched hers, then searched her face as if asking for permission to go on. When Audra didn't move, he said, "We've lost eight months, and I don't want any more time to slip past us. I can prove to you that I've learned my lesson, and I need the chance to show you and Jason that I can be the perfect father, the perfect husband."

Shaking her head, Audra relaxed, letting her knee rest against his, absorbing the current of desire that traveled between them. She touched the side of his cheek and whispered, "Nobody's perfect, Neal. Nobody."

"If you give me a chance, I'll be as damn near to perfect as any man could be." His voice broke, and he glanced away. Then, lifting imploring eyes to Audra, he said, "We could be happy again. You know we could. Let's start over. All I need is for you to say when."

She hesitated, twisting her fingers together, then pierced him with a look that pulled all of her love for him to the surface. Her answer was a soft reassuring kiss on his cheek that left her shaken, but still in control. "Neal, I don't hate you. I am not holding any grudges, and my anger at what happened has been tempered by the talk we had with Dr. Chargulis. I'm proud of you for getting professional help. It was the best . . . the only thing to do. But start over? I don't know if I'm ready . . ."

Her sentence was lost to the urgent press of Neal's fingertips to her lips. "Don't say anything more," he asked.

Audra narrowed her eyes in puzzlement.

Neal faintly trailed his fingers from her lips, over her cheek, along her neck to the warm spot at the base of her throat. Then he kissed her fully on the mouth. Drawing back, he murmured, "We'll both know when we're ready. Let's not set any timetable we can't keep." He relaxed, easing his body toward the opposite end of the seat. "If you want me to, I'll leave."

Audra said nothing, but she tilted her chin upward as if inviting Neal to kiss her again.

A glow illuminated his face in the semidarkness, and Audra's mind spun when he gave her a dazzling smile. He bent toward her. She let him slip his arms around her waist. When he angled her into a half-sitting position, she settled onto his muscled arm and accepted his mouth with hers. The probing search of his tongue against hers unleashed a burst of passion that Audra found seductively familiar. His unspoken knowledge of what she wanted, craved, and needed, made his tender overture feel naturally correct.

Audra felt as if a magnet was pulling her back to the source of the love she had treasured. Driven by the flame of her long-suppressed desire, she responded to Neal's embrace by slipping down onto her back. With her head on a small velvet pillow, she broke off the kiss and gazed at Neal, seduced by the tingling sensation caused by looking at him.

"I can't lie, Neal. I want us to find a way back. I've been miserable without you." Tears brimmed at her lashes. "Miserable," she said, nearly choking on the word.

"It's been hell for me, too," Neal whispered, tracing one finger down the front of her jogging suit. "I love you. I always have."

Closing her eyes, Audra drew in a wisp of breath. "I love you, too, Neal. I never stopped loving you, but I was very angry. Too angry to think beyond my disappointment."

"You had every right to hate me, but it's all behind us now, isn't it?"

Grinning, Audra put one hand behind his neck, pulling his lips closer to hers. "I think it could be," she said in a smoldering voice. "If you show me how sorry you are."

Challenge flared in Neal's brown eyes, and he

broke into a boyish grin. "You really want me to show you?"

Beaming like an impish seductress, Audra nodded vigorously, her bangs swinging over her tawny brow.

Without saying a word Neal began to unzip Audra's jacket, showering her face and neck with kisses as he pulled off her soft nylon top. When the garment rustled to the floor, Audra was struck by undulating currents of desire that fired her ache for Neal.

Slipping his hot hands beneath her white cotton T-shirt, Neal delighted Audra with a roaming caress of her torso. She moaned under her breath when he unfastened her satin bra and fondled her taut nipples between his thumb and forefinger as he eased the bit of lace from her body. Her skin begged for his touch, her body longed for his embrace, and Audra knew he was going to meet her challenge.

With his head pressed to her breasts, Neal let Audra unbutton his shirt and yank it back from his shoulders. Before it fell completely away, he captured a hardened nipple through her soft T-shirt and pressed it between his lips. She groaned aloud, let go of his shirt, and put her hands beneath his chin, forcing him to look up at her.

"Neal. Neal. I missed you so much" was all she could say before he impatiently stripped her torso bare, then cast his shirt to the carpet. When his smooth warm chest descended onto her throbbing breasts, she shuddered and closed her eyes, thrilling to the familiar press of Neal's body against hers.

Arching her back, Audra pressed closer, as if trying to meld her flesh to his in a guarantee they'd never be parted again. The past eight months had been a long, lonely time, and she willingly surrendered to Neal's embrace.

Shifting to accommodate him on the small window seat, Audra steadied herself with one hand on the floor. Neal burst out laughing at the cramped spot they had chosen for their reunion, shattering the urgency of the moment.

Abruptly, he sat up and leaned back, shaking his head. Then he grabbed Audra's hand, pulling her upright beside him. "We can do better than this," he laughed, guiding her to the bed.

Audra scrambled to the center of the bed, its familiar bounce making her feel as if she'd truly come back home. Sitting on her knees, she was conscious of her bare breasts inviting Neal to touch them. He advanced toward her. She teasingly scooted back. But he lunged forward again, this time bending low to capture her in a viselike grip. Feeling Neal grow hard and firm against her thigh brought a ragged breath to Audra's lips. She tugged at his slacks, eager to free him, anxious to feel the soft firm maleness of him touching her innermost core.

His manhood emerged stiffened, and Audra stroked it lightly before slipping onto her back. She snuggled beneath Neal, letting him kiss each breast tenderly, then suckle them hard until she was swept away by the aching pull that tore through her in a blinding white flash. Caressing him, she bent her head over his, rocking gently back and forth as she cradled him in her arms.

For Audra the experience was unbearably familiar, comforting in one way, but tenderly painful in another. Neal had been her first true love—the only man to ever bring her to fulfillment. He knew exactly how to stoke her passion and how to prolong it until she cried out for him to stop. Now, aroused to an excruciatingly delicious point, Audra shivered when Neal ran his tongue over the curve of her abdomen. She drew herself even closer to him, her body taut in anticipation.

Neal stripped off her sweat pants in a fluid, controlled gesture, then shed his slacks and settled between her legs. A gathering tightness coiled in Audra's chest, threatening to cut off her breath. When Neal's fingers trailed like feathers up her calves to the soft mound of hair at the top of her thighs, she quivered, waiting for him to touch the place she knew he was edging toward.

His fingers grazed the sensitive source of her satisfaction. Audra let out a small moan of pleasure and opened herself to Neal, simultaneously crushing her mouth against his as he entered on the wave of her surrender. Audra spread her hands over Neal's smooth back, and urged him deeper inside her. Kissing his shoulder as her body pulsed beneath his, Audra experienced an explosive collage of emotions that soared through her, transporting her beyond any reservations she may have had about loving Neal Foster again.

Gently, urgently, Neal made passionate love to Audra, whose heart beat in tandem with the rhythmic hammering of her lover's. Spiraling away from the advice and caution of others, Neal and Audra were swept together to the pinnacle of their union and catapulted into the sweet unknown of their future.

Chapter Nine

Lightning exploded like fireworks outside the window, and a crash of thunder jolted Audra awake, then rumbled through the house like an angry echo. Sitting up, Audra pulled the sheet to her neck and groped for the alarm clock.

Blinking at the luminous green face, she saw that it was four-fifteen. As she set the clock back on the nightstand, she rubbed the back of her neck. It was still stiff and cramped, just as it had been when she had pulled into the garage three hours ago. The drive back to Marina Manor had been a nightmare, taking twice as long as usual, with rain pelting the car, forcing her to pull over three times.

While waiting for a break in the downpour, she had listened to the radio, alarmed to hear that the depression in the Gulf of Mexico had been upgraded to a tropical storm. With sustained winds of fifty-five miles per hour, the storm was heading due west, gathering strength by the hour.

It's a good thing I left Jason with Neal, Audra

thought, knowing her son would have been terrified by the lightning and thunder that had bombarded her during her journey.

Audra slid back under the sheets as another flash of lightning tore through the sky, but instead of trembling, she smiled, determined to push the storm to the back of her mind and savor her memories of making love to Neal.

During the long drive back to Marina Manor, she had relived each moment of their exquisite encounter, satisfied with her decision to move back to Houston. It was all set. On Monday, she'd call her attorney and halt the divorce proceedings. Then she'd give Judge Rawlins a call, and hopefully, arrange to be back at work in his courtroom as soon as his next case went to trial. By July fifteenth, she wanted to be settled in her house in Missouri City, though Neal would stay in his apartment until they felt more comfortable with the reconciliation. As Audra squirmed under her sheets, she hoped Neal did not plan to stay out of her bed very long.

"You did what?" Bertice said, reaching to turn the radio down, interrupting a prediction that the tropical storm would probably be upgraded to a hurricane by late afternoon. The forecaster explained in an optimistic voice that landfall would most likely be somewhere between Gulfport and New Orleans, sparing the residents of Corpus Christi.

"I left Jason in Houston with Neal," Audra said, casually pouring herself a cup of coffee.

"I wish you hadn't done that," Bertice stated, lowering her voice. "What if this storm makes landfall closer to Houston? Jason could be stranded . . . for days."

"Well, they'll make out," Audra replied, wishing Bertice could be more optimistic. "Neal isn't a monster, you know? He used to get Jason ready for nursery school everyday when I was working. Neal can manage. Jason will be fine."

"Humph," Bertice grumbled. "What about the reunion? You've got to go back to Houston to pick Jason up."

Audra looked at Bertice in astonishment. "If this weather doesn't clear, there won't be a reunion."

Bertice visibly stiffened. "That would suit you just fine, wouldn't it?" she said.

Audra felt a slow burn edge onto her cheeks. "Why do you say that? I told you I think getting the family together is a good idea. As a matter of fact, Neal is going to bring Jason back tomorrow." She walked to the table and sat down across from Bertice. "I hope you don't mind, but Jason invited Neal to stay here for the holiday fireworks, and I couldn't say no. So Neal will be here for the reunion . . . if there is one."

Bertice scowled, shaking her head. "Why did you agree to that? Neal is no longer a part of this family.

He forfeited his rights when he threw away your marriage. Having him here will be a disaster."

Audra narrowed her eyes at Bertice, wanting to stay calm. She sipped her coffee and thought about her response, not ready to tell Bertice of her impending reconciliation. "I don't see this as a disaster at all. Having Neal here will make Jason happy, and if I can put my emotions aside and accept his presence for a day or two, then so can the rest of the family."

Bertice shrugged, folding her arms around her waist. "Don't count on it" was all she had to say.

Knowing it would be useless to try to convince Bertice that all was not ruined, Audra pushed their discussion past the subject of Neal Foster. "I do believe the weather is going to break, and we have a lot to do before Sunday. Watch . . . by the day after tomorrow, the skies will be clear, and the sun will dry everything out." When Bertice said nothing, Audra went on. "Even if it's still rainy, we can have our celebration inside."

A doubtful expression came over Bertice's face. "That's not what I had in mind when I planned this reunion."

"I know," Audra comforted, "but we'll have a good time. It's going to be fun." What she wanted to add, but couldn't, was that she hoped everybody would welcome Neal back into the family and support her decision to hold onto her marriage.

"I don't know how much fun it's going to be,"

Bertice said dryly, "but if Neal Foster really has the gall to show his face down here, it's going to be interesting at least."

"Why can't you try to be a little more tolerant about this?" Audra lashed out, not caring if she hurt Bertice's feelings. "This funky attitude of yours is disgusting, and I've had enough. Give it a rest. Neal *will* be here for the reunion, and you'd better not ruin it for Jason."

"Oh, please!" Bertice shot back. "Don't you dare try to lay a guilt trip on me. If anyone ruins anything, it will be you."

Holding her breath, Audra gave Bertice a look that reflected her mounting anger. "You can hate Neal Foster for the rest of your life and say as many nasty things about him as you please, but there's one thing you can't do, Bertice. You can't make him go away. He's your nephew's father, and like it or not, Neal will be connected to me, to you—to our family forever."

For the rest of the morning the two spoke very little as they continued the preparations for the party. Bertice baked two pies and a chocolate cake and put them in the freezer. Audra washed plates and polished tableware that had been in storage for years. Together they opened up long closed rooms, swept away cobwebs, and put fresh linen on all the beds. When they finished, Marina Manor sparkled with the inviting warmth it had been famous for during Audra's childhood.

While the sisters readied Marina Manor for its guests, the rain continued to fall, relentlessly pounding the water-soaked earth. Late in the afternoon, the sky grew even darker, casting everything in drab gray shadows. When Bertice went upstairs to take a long soaking bath, Audra went to stand at the wide bay windows at the back of the house, watching the water in the Gulf being whipped into a white-foamed frenzy.

So far, the forecasters had not totally doomed the upcoming holiday weekend, and as long as the airport remained open, Audra was determined to keep a positive attitude, while praying that Neal's presence would not set off a family uprising.

Bertice didn't emerge from her room for the rest of the afternoon, and Audra stayed in the den, listening to updates on the storm. By seven o'clock, the weather was still awful, though it seemed as if the storm was going to behave itself and turn eastward after all.

Audra ate dinner alone, then tried to read the paper, but by ten o'clock, she knew things had changed when a beeping weather alert flashed onto the television screen. The tropical storm, now officially a hurricane, had been given the name Alberta. A map appeared, and Audra cringed to see the swirling white dot on a dead-line course toward Galveston Island. Shivering, she worried; if landfall was going to be only two hundred and thirty miles up the coast, Corpus would experience a hell of a storm surge.

She listened intently as the weatherman urged residents of the Corpus Christi area to stay tuned for advisories, reminding them to fill their cars with gas and to stock up on emergency supplies like batteries for radios and flashlights, and plenty of drinking water. No major evacuation order was issued, but people living along the shoreline and in low-lying areas were encouraged to move inland toward higher ground.

Audra jumped up from the sofa and headed to the stairs, anxious to give Bertice the latest update, but changed her mind and grabbed the telephone instead, nervously dialing Neal's number. When she put the receiver to her ear, her breath caught in her chest. The line was already dead.

"Bertice," Audra yelled up the stairs. "Bertice! Come here!"

The door to Bertice's bedroom creaked open, and she appeared at the top of the staircase, her faded terry robe belted around her waist. "What's going on?" she asked, leaning over the banister as she held her unruly hair from her face.

"The storm is getting worse." Audra could see that Bertice had been sleeping, in spite of the thunder and lightning that had been bombarding the coast for hours. "Do you think we'd better try to get out?" Audra asked.

"What's the latest?" Bertice replied, hurrying down the stairs. She moved quickly across the hallway to the windows at the front of the house.

"We're under a hurricane watch," Audra told her. "The last weather report officially upgraded the storm to a hurricane. Landfall is predicted about two in the morning at Galveston." Audra picked up the phone again. "The line is dead! What should we do?"

With the take-charge attitude of a hurricane veteran, Bertice spoke in a clipped levelheaded manner. "You said we're under a hurricane watch, not a warning?" she clarified.

"That's right," Audra replied.

Bertice turned again to peer out into the darkness, one hand to the side of her face. "Sure is a mess," she said flatly. "I can tell by the level of the water in the ditches along the driveway . . . the main road to the freeway is already under."

"Under water? We're cut off?" Audra asked, panic beginning to rise. She'd lived in Houston all her life and had weathered many storms, including Hurricane Alicia in 1983, but she'd never ridden out a storm at the coast and had no desire to do so now. "Can we get out by boat? Will an emergency rescue team come this way?"

"I doubt it," Bertice replied. "They know I won't leave, even if they come. Marina Manor is so isolated. I've been through a lot of bad weather out here, and the emergency squad always tried to get me to leave, but I never do . . . and won't now, either."

"Damn," Audra cursed, angered by Bertice's selfish attitude. "You mean we're *really* stranded?"

"Looks that way unless you want to walk, and I wouldn't advise trying that. You'd be swept out to sea by the force of that water." Bertice crossed the flagstone walkway and went into the den. Plopping down on the sofa, she pressed the remote control until she came to a Bette Davis movie. "God, this is a good one, Audra. Have you ever seen it?" She settled down, propping up her feet, ready to lose herself in the film.

"What are you doing?" Audra pressed. "Shouldn't we be taping up the windows, moving furniture upstairs? Doing something?"

Bertice shook her head. "Relax. I've lived at the coast for ten years, and water has yet to get into this house. Marina Manor is very well built. I guarantee you we have nothing to worry about."

Audra sucked in her cheeks to keep from screaming, then turned on her heel and left Bertice watching Herbert Marshall struggle to get to his medication as hard-hearted Bette Davis stood by and watched.

At the kitchen sink Audra began filling plastic bottles with water. Sadly, she remembered that the car was on empty because she had not wanted to stop for gas last night, and their closest neighbor was half a mile away and had probably already moved inland. Audra turned off the water and opened a drawer, rummaging until she found some batteries and a large roll of masking tape. With shaking hands, she put the batteries into the radio, listening to the weather reports as she started taping up the bay windows that were vibrating under the continued assault of the wind and rain that gusted off the Gulf.

"Maybe Bertice doesn't care about what happens," Audra mumbled, "but I plan to see my husband and child again. I have too much to live for to sit around and let this thing wash me out to sea."

Chapter Ten

Like a caged lioness, Audra prowled the house—pacing from room to room, window to window, searching the black mist for signs of rescue activity, unwilling to believe that no one was coming to help them. Bertice lounged on the sofa watching TV, seemingly unperturbed by the howling storm that raged outside. Pummeled by torrents of rain, the roof groaned and creaked, sounding as if it might fly right off the house. The sturdy lodge trembled on its foundation, and Audra wondered if this might be the storm to break Marina Manor's forty-year record of holding its own against the capricious Gulf coast weather.

A crack of lightning split the sky, propelling a shower of sparks from a power box atop a pole at the edge of the property. Immediately, the house was plunged into darkness. Audra screamed, jumping back from the window as if she had been shocked by the electrical wires now dangling dangerously above the driveway. Rushing into the den, she watched Bertice calmly light the two oil lamps that had always sat, unused, atop the heavy pine mantel. According to their mother, the tall glass lamps had been carried in their great grandmother's lap all the way from Georgia when she came to settle in Texas in the late 1800s.

"So, those old things work, huh?" Audra said, pleasantly surprised at the amount of light the tall chimneys gave off. The yellow glow warmed the cavernous room, stilling Audra's fear that the storm was getting the upper hand.

"They sure do," Bertice said, "and there are two more like these in the attic. Come on. Help me get them down."

"Do you think we ought to go up there?" Audra asked, afraid they'd be swept away with the roof and hurled out to sea.

"Don't get panicky on me," Bertice admonished, picking up a burning globe to light the way. "This old place is like a fortress. It may creak and groan like a wounded bull, but, I assure you, it's not going to collapse."

At the end of the hallway that ran the length of the second floor, Bertice handed the lamp to Audra, then reached up and pulled down the overhead trap leading to the attic. The contraption unfolded with a thud. Bertice placed one foot on the first step just as a thunderous roar descended over the house, making the pictures on the walls rattle in their frames. She glanced over her shoulder at Audra, a puzzled look on her face.

"Better not go up there," Audra advised.

The roar grew louder, similar to the sound of a jet plane barreling toward the house.

"It's okay. Wait here," Bertice said, gripping the railing firmly with both hands, continuing her assent.

The noise expanded, enveloping the top of the house in a mournful wail that resembled a chorus of crying children. Audra put a hand of caution on Bertice's shoulder. "Come back. Let's go downstairs. There're some candles in the kitchen we can use."

Bertice stopped halfway up the rickety ladder, measuring Audra's advice. Glancing up, she assessed the dark opening into the attic as if expecting ghosts to emerge. She visibly shuddered as she took another step up. "This one is really coming in hard," she murmured, cocking her head to one side, listening to the screaming storm. "The last hurricane I rode out here in Marina Manor was back in . . ."

But before she could finish her sentence, the high double-paned windows at the opposite end of the hallway burst out of their frames, forcing a shower of water and shattered glass through the air.

"Watch out," Audra screamed, ducking to shield her face from the flying shards. Dropping to her knees she crouched with her face to the carpet.

"Oh, God! I've been cut." Bertice cried, scrambling down the ladder, kneeling on the floor next to Audra. She groped toward the banister, grabbing it to steady herself, cringing as another blast of seawater and rain whipped through the gaping hole in the wall and soaked them.

"Let's get out of here," Audra shouted over the roar of the frenzied waves surging in the Gulf. Jumping to her feet, she pulled Bertice upright. Together they fled downstairs, into the kitchen. Lightning flooded the room with a burst of white light, followed by another blast of shattering glass that whirled through the pitch-black lodge.

"The pantry," Bertice shouted. "It's the safest place in the house."

Quickly, they entered the huge windowless walk-in pantry that had a thick wooden door with an old-fashioned transom at the top. After kicking the door shut, Audra steadied the lamp on a wooden crate that had once been filled with apples, then collapsed on the floor. Bertice adjusted the small rectangle of a window atop the door until it was fully tilted to let air in.

"Let me see your arm," Audra said.

Holding her arm under the lamplight, Bertice scowled at the sight of blood running from a gash near her elbow.

"This looks as if it's going to need stitches," Audra said, "but for now let's try to stop the bleeding."

"There are some clean white towels over there," Bertice offered, pointing to the top ledge of a dark pine shelf. "You can tear them up if you have to." She cradled her elbow in her palm.

"Great," Audra said, grabbing the white cloth. She immediately began tearing them into strips. "This will have to do until we can get you to a doctor."

A glum expression on her face, Beatrice sat quietly while Audra bandaged her arm.

"Don't look so worried," Audra comforted. "It looks a lot worse than it is. You're not going to bleed to death, but you'll definitely have a scar."

"Oh, it's not my arm that's worrying me," Bertice sighed. "I was just thinking about the reunion. Guess it's off . . . for now, anyway." She rested her bandaged arm on her lap. "Mother and Dad were so excited about celebrating their anniversary here . . . with everyone together again."

"Yeah," Audra agreed, tearing extra strips of cloth. "Forty years of marriage ought to be celebrated." She stopped making bandages and rested her head against the wall. "Mom has been lucky to have someone like Dad to share her life with."

"Right," Bertice said. "Men like Dad . . . honest and faithful . . . don't seem to exist anymore."

Audra flinched, annoyed by Bertice's negative statement. An image of her and Neal and Jason together as a family flared into her mind. "That's not necessarily true," she replied, miffed that Bertice always seemed to have nothing good to say on the subject of men.

"All right," Bertice tossed back. "I admit there are probably a few exceptions walking around, but unfortunately, neither you nor I were lucky enough to find them."

Thankful that the shadows kept her face partially concealed, Audra scowled, taking a deep breath before plunging ahead with the news she had kept to herself all day. "I was going to wait until everyone got here, but since the reunion will most likely be canceled, I may as well tell you now . . . Neal and I have decided to reconcile."

Bertice shifted on the hard wooden floor until her face loomed pale yellow in the lamplight. She pierced Audra with an incredulous expression. "Why?" She scrambled closer. "Why in the world are you going to do something so stupid?"

"Going back to Neal is not stupid," Audra countered. "We have a child. Sometimes parents have to think beyond their own selfish needs."

"Using Jason as an excuse to go back to Neal is wrong!"

Gritting her teeth, Audra pressed on. "Jason is not the only reason I want to go back to Neal."

"What, then? What else would lead you to such a crazy decision?"

"There was a lot about Neal that I never knew . . . until recently. While I was in Houston, we were able to really talk. I learned some things about his past, his views on marriage and women that I never knew before."

"And?"

"And now I finally understand what motivated

him to act as he did, and he understands himself a lot better, too. We broke through all the resentment and anger that had built up since we separated and looked each other in the eye. Neal is sorry. He has changed. And I know he loves me, respects me. We can make it. Our marriage may never be as it was before, but maybe it's not supposed to be."

"Love? Respect? Are you insane?" Bertice hissed. "You've seen Neal Foster two times in the past eight months, and you're seriously talking about going back to the man who broke your heart? Trashed your marriage?" She sank back on her heels. "You need to stay right here at Marina Manor and forget about Neal Foster. Go back to him? Why? It won't work."

Audra bit her lip to keep from crying, desperate not to let Bertice's doomsday prediction get to her. "I am grateful to you for letting me and Jason live here when we had no place else to go. But I can't hide from life anymore . . . and I won't let you make me feel guilty because I've decided to save my marriage." Audra lowered her steely voice, cautiously edging away from Bertice. "Please let's not fight about it, okay?"

"Oh, no," Bertice threw back sarcastically. "Let's *not* fight. Let's forget about the past and act as if Neal Foster never even had an adulterous affair. My God, Audra, do you expect me to sit by and watch you ruin your life with that no-'count man who is as slick as a greased pig?"

Audra shot to her feet, pacing the tiny space . . .

two steps to one side, two to the other. Raising her chin, as if pulling her courage to the forefront, she accepted Bertice's challenge. "I am going back to Neal because I love him. I understand him, and I want my marriage back."

"Why? What lies did Neal come up with to make you talk like this? How much bull did he feed you this time?"

Audra suddenly lowered herself to the floor, sitting directly in front of Bertice. "He didn't tell me any lies," she said, her tone serious and low. "He introduced me to his therapist."

"His therapist?" Bertice said suspiciously.

"Yes," Audra said. "I was wrong when I assumed he was dating someone new. The woman I had mistakenly thought was his girlfriend turned out to be Iris Chargulis, a well-respected family therapist, and a very professional, warm woman who has helped Neal a great deal."

Audra plunged ahead, telling Bertice about Neal's childhood with a philandering, handsome father, and how he'd been wrongly influenced to believe that adulterous liaisons were expected of a man.

Bertice sat quietly, listening without interruption until Audra finished, then expressed her opinion. "Well," she started, "all that sounds interesting, but I'll bet he is having an affair with that woman. They've duped you, Audra. How long do you think Neal Foster can last without taking up with another woman?"

Audra raised her hand in horror, as if to slap Bertice's smug face. "That's an awful accusation. Unfounded and mean. What in the world makes you so goddamn suspicious? Just because Walter didn't do as you *ordered* him to, and Sara drowned, you condemn all men." Easing her hand down slowly, she glared at Bertice. "You are not being fair, and your attitude is very upsetting. I know you've been talking to Mother, Kathleen, everybody in the family, trying to convince them that Neal is a monster. What is it with you, Bertice? Huh? Tell me, where does this poison come from? Where?"

"You have no idea how horrible it was to lose my child. You can't understand the pain I have lived with since . . ."

"Oh, I do," Audra interrupted. "But it's time you moved past it. Stop wallowing in self-pity."

"That's cruel!" Bertice spit through clenched teeth. "Walter did as he pleased. His selfishness cost me my child . . . my marriage . . . my future. Why should you have a second chance? I didn't!"

Audra's breath caught in her throat. "What?" A ripple of fear threaded through her body. "What did you say?"

"I said why should you get a second chance? My husband and child are dead. I didn't get to reclaim my happiness. How can you sit here and act as if I could ever be happy?" A torrent of tears rushed down Bertice's cheeks, yet she made no effort to wipe them away.

Audra struggled to keep her voice from breaking. "You want me to be as lonely and miserable as you are, don't you?"

Bertice lowered her head, not answering.

"Answer me!" Audra screamed. "You want me to forever hold a grudge against Neal . . . just as you have against Walter. Don't you? Your twisted jealousy feeds your twisted opinion of men. Isn't that it, Bertice?"

Bertice raised a tear-streaked face to Audra. "No! That's not it!"

"Then, what in God's name is it?" Audra pressed, unwilling to let her sister avoid searching her soul for whatever it was that made her so distrustful and unhappy. It was time to clear the air.

"I loved Walter," Bertice began. "I trusted him, and what did I get for my trust? He took my baby out in the boat against my advice and killed her!"

"Stop it, Bertice. You know Walter did no such thing. It was an accident."

"An accident? Ha!" Bertice threw back her head in a curt laugh, shuddering as she positioned herself in a challenging way. "You don't know! You just don't know!"

"Know what?" Audra prompted, anxious for Bertice to purge herself of whatever was making her so miserable.

"You don't know what it was like, having to bury my husband and my child side by side . . . having to face a future without them."

"No, I don't," Audra admitted. "But why don't you tell me? Talk about it, Bertice. What more do you want me to know?"

Bertice's eyes flew open, and a frightened expression swept over her face. "I told you everything! Walter killed my baby!"

Audra pushed harder. "Killed? Why do you keep saying that? It was an accident. Wasn't it, Bertice?"

"Yes! Yes. It was an accident." Threading her fingers through her hair, Bertice pressed her hands to her temples. "It was an accident that *I* caused."

Audra's chest rose and fell as she gulped in air, suddenly feeling claustrophobic in the small, warm pantry. "You?"

"Yes! Me!" Bertice screamed, tilting her body toward Audra. Rising to her knees, she went on. "I caused the accident that destroyed my family."

Shocked, Audra reached out to place a comforting arm around her sobbing sister, then drew back, confused. What in the world was she talking about? "Why do you say that? What really happened, Bertice? Tell me the truth!"

The lamplight sputtered, then failed. Audra immediately fumbled with the knob until she turned up the wick and relit the lamp. Stalling for time, she wanted to give Bertice a chance to pull herself together.

Wiping her eyes, Bertice began to speak haltingly, her words coming out on a wave of pain. "It was the day of Sara's birthday party."

"I remember," Audra said, trying to help her sister along. "You told me you had arranged for a man from Corpus to come out to Marina Manor and put on a puppet show."

Wiping her face, Bertice nodded. "Yes, and I had to go into town to pick him up." She hesitated, a glimmer of panic in her eyes. "If only I hadn't insisted on going into town . . . Sara would still be alive." Bertice grabbed Audra's arm. "It was all my fault," she sobbed. "I made Sara go out in the boat. I wanted her out of the way while the puppet man set up his stage. It was going to be a surprise."

Alarmed by the way Bertice was shivering, Audra gripped her shoulder firmly. "Go on."

"Sara was crying. Screaming. She did not want to go out in the boat. Walter asked me to let her stay on shore, but I insisted they take a ride." Bertice shuddered, then rubbed the taut skin at the sides of her face.

A blast of thunder broke over the house. The sound of splitting timber followed, then the floor beneath them vibrated as a pine tree crashed through the roof. Drawing closer in the dark, the sisters clung to each other, waiting for the walls to cave in. Nothing happened, and the house grew oddly quiet once more.

"Go on," Audra urged.

Bertice continued her story. "Sara cried and carried on something awful. Those were the last sounds I heard from my baby as I put her into the boat."

Bertice's body shook convulsively with each sob. "When I returned with the puppet man, I was greeted by the Coast Guard. The boat had somehow capsized in the middle of the bay. Walter and Sara were dead."

"You can't blame yourself for what happened," Audra comforted, "but you've got to get over how it happened."

Bertice wrapped her arms about Audra, murmuring against her shoulder, "Mother, Dad, the whole family—I knew they'd never forgive me if they knew the truth."

Audra stroked Bertice's quivering back. "It is not their place to judge you. All they ever wanted to do was love you, help you through your tragedy. But you chose to isolate yourself with this awful secret, forcing everybody to tiptoe around the subject." She felt herself go limp with regret. "Maybe we are just as much to blame, Bertice. We shouldn't have let you stay here alone all this time."

"It's what I wanted," Bertice admitted.

"I know, but why didn't you tell me the truth? We used to be close. I wished you had trusted me. How could you think I'd blame you?"

"I don't know. I was confused, miserable. I'm so sorry," Bertice cried. "I know I've been selfish. I wanted you and Jason to stay at Marina Manor with me. It's been wonderful having a child around. Like having my family back."

"I'm sure it felt that way, but Bertice, just as I have

to take a chance on trusting Neal again, you have to take a chance on living your life. Maybe that will mean moving out of Marina Manor, away from the coast, going to a place where you will have to start over alone. Maybe not. That's a decision only you can make."

Bertice gave Audra a tight hug, then looked at her in a quizzical way. "I realize that now." She folded her hands together and sat thinking. "What do you think the chances are that I can really start over?"

"Excellent," Audra said, smiling. "About as good as the odds that the skies will clear tomorrow."

Bertice sniffed back her tears, then laughed. "Sounds good to me. From my experience, it's a good bet that the storm will be halfway across Oklahoma by daybreak. I just hope our roof is not already in Galveston."

Chuckling, Audra settled closer to Bertice, supporting her injured arm in her lap. They remained huddled in the pantry, nodding off to sleep through the long tense night as the vicious storm wore itself out.

Daybreak emerged eerily calm, and they cautiously came out of hiding to inspect the damage. Most of the windows on the second floor had been blown out, but those along the back of the house that Audra had covered with masking tape were still firmly intact.

At the sight of the gaping hole in the roof above the entryway, Bertice moaned, then shrugged her shoulders. With a grimace on her face, she said, "What a mess."

Audra eyed the cloudless blue sky above their heads, then broke into a wide grin at the sight of Neal's Jeep coming up the drive. Waving, she ran across the soggy grass to greet him and Jason, who had his small brown face pressed to the window.

Stopping abruptly, Audra turned and called back to Bertice, "I know someone who is pretty handy with a hammer and nails."

"Good," Bertice said, coming to link arms with her sister as they walked toward the car. "If we plan to have this family reunion tomorrow, Neal's got a lot of work to do."

HOMECOMING

by Sandra Kitt

Chapter One

"How come it's taking so long?" Shay Saxon complained.

"I guess the plane was late landing. Don't worry. It will get here."

"Can't we go stand over there, by the door? Then she can find us when it opens."

"We're fine just where we are," Gena Saxon remarked to the twelve-year-old girl in a voice that discouraged any additional debate.

"Well, how come all those people get to stand by the door?"

"They're reporters and airline officials."

Shay glanced up at Gena with a frown. "Yeah, but we're her family."

Gena Saxon sighed. She gently rubbed her hand across the back of Shay's shoulders and gave her an understanding pat. "I know, hon, but after the business stuff is over, then we get to have Renee all to ourselves. Be patient. See. There's the plane now. It'll only be another moment . . ."

"Can I go and . . ."

Gena grabbed the young girl's arm as she was about to rush through the crowd of people to get a view of the arriving plane through the large window. "Shay, stay here with me, please. I don't want you wandering away. There are too many people, and we might get separated."

Shay sighed, aggrieved, but did as she was told. She stood patiently and stared at the door through which passengers arriving from Los Angeles would come.

Two airline representatives soon opened the arrival gate doors and stood back on either side. In their crisp navy blue uniforms and military-style hats they looked like sentries awaiting royalty. A buzz went up in the waiting room area, and dozens of people suddenly stood up and bunched together, staring at the doorway. Gena realized that many of them had no idea who they were expecting to arrive through the gateway, but anticipation had spread. They recognized notoriety, fame, and importance. Reporters and photographers with press tags around their necks stood grouped to one side in the best position to see and greet the first passengers departing from the plane. Several other men and women with two-way radios, badges, papers, and an air of authority were also allowed to stand closer.

Shay, with her pecan-brown features fixed in a know-it-all smile of excitement, glanced at Gena. "She's going to see us first, right?"

Gena returned the smile. "I hope so."

But she wasn't so sure. She had learned, after many years of similar arrivals, that it was a question of priorities. And opportunity. It was a question of making the most of the moment.

Gena remembered one year when her sister Renee Saxon, ingenue actress, had been nominated for a Golden Globe Award and had flown to New York for the announcement and awards dinner. Three-year-old Shay had been jostled and nearly knocked to the floor by an overeager, adoring public, paparazzi, and the press. In anger and horror Gena had grabbed Shay, determined to get out of the frenzy and return home. But Renee's business manager, CJ, had rescued them and kept a watchful eye on them through the rest of the evening.

Gena knew she could wait until her sister had finished with the protocol of greetings and of being interviewed, photographed, and fawned over. Shay was a different matter. She was a child and was not going to understand being placed second. Gena didn't think the girl should have to.

Gena took Shay's hand and felt comforted by the way the small hand closed warmly and trustingly around her own. The anxiety she always felt under these circumstances abated for a while as Shay leaned against her and rested her head on Gena's arm. That unconditional love was reassuring. It was the one thing Gena was absolutely sure of. Renee's visits home to New Jersey were less about family anyway than they were another form of showcase. Business as usual. A brief appearance to receive an award, to appear on a string of talk shows. To be seen at several social events and remind the locals that she was still a hometown girl. She'd done good, and she'd made them proud.

And then Renee Saxon, current reigning African-American actress, would fly away back to the alternate universe of Hollywood, stardom, and fame. Gena reminded herself, finding a guilty peace in the thought, that she and Shay could then get back to their normal routine. Life, as they had always known it, would go on.

A small sound of expectation went through the crowd as the first-class passengers began filing out. Mostly men with attachés and clothing bags, dressed in jeans and West Coast ease. Women in leggings, oversize sweaters, and dark glasses. Not one of them prepared for the frigid February temperatures of New York. The crowd in the waiting area began to close in, and the officials tried politely to keep everyone at bay, except for those folks legitimately waiting for arriving friends, colleagues, or family.

Shay began to bounce childishly on the balls of her feet.

"I can't wait," she said, her bushy ponytail bobbing with her excitement.

Gena continued to hold the girl's hand, and to feel her own stomach tighten with the first warning of apprehension. Her enthusiasm was much more tempered, and since she felt ambivalent about her sister's visit, Gena remained silent. Renee's infrequent trips east were *never* just visits. They were often a total invasion, complete with her own entourage, agenda, and schedule.

Gena squeezed Shay's hand. But as the excitement began to bubble up around them, she felt her own turn to dread. It wasn't until this instant, as Renee was about to step through the entrance and into the spotlight, that Gena fully realized just what they would be put through over the next several days. Not that she wasn't happy to see Renee. She was proud of her sister's success and enjoyed listening to her spin on life as a celebrity. Yet, while being around Renee could be lots of fun, Gena knew from experience it was also exhausting and disruptive.

A flashbulb suddenly went off, and Gena blinked at the shocking light. Then there was another. And another. Shay pulled on her hand.

"There she is! There she is," she pointed.

The onlookers closed in around Gena and Shay, pushing them forward but obscuring their vision as a group of five or six people came through the arrival gateway and were immediately surrounded. Gena stood her ground as people swarmed around her and Shay. Shay tried to join the advancing mob but was stopped short by the hand firmly holding on to her.

"Everybody's getting in front of us," Shay complained.

"I don't feel like getting pushed and shoved. Let's

just wait here. She'll find us," Gena tried to reassure the child, but could feel Shay's battle between impatience and obedience.

Over the heads of the crowd Gena could see a bright light go on and microphones on boom poles appear out of nowhere. The cluster of people surrounding the arriving actress grew as questions were thrown out and more pictures taken. Occasionally the answer would spark laughter.

"I can't see anything."

"Calm down. There's nothing to see yet," Gena said quietly, even as her gaze swept over the gathering, searching the faces.

She couldn't see Renee, who was dwarfed by taller people. There was a young woman holding a fur coat and a pile of magazines. That was Laura, Renee's assistant. Renee had said she was a godsend, but then she'd said the same of her last three assistants until, in turn, they'd each done or said something to get on her nerves and were fired. There was a short, thin young man with blond hair who was probably the publicist from the studio. There were several representatives from African-Americans, Inc., the imaging group affiliated with a popular black publication that was giving Renee an award for her film work and for being a positive role model in the black community. And there was the business manager.

"Look, I see CJ," Shay exclaimed with enthusiasm.

Gena's stomach suddenly twisted in alarm, and a surge of emotions flooded through her, making her feel overheated, and then quickly a sensation of light-headedness. The swift juxtaposition of emotions took her by surprise, and she drew in a deep breath to compose herself. But her eyes were bright and attentive when CJ unexpectedly looked in her direction. He gave her an almost imperceptible nod of acknowledgment.

"Mommy . . ." Shay quietly whined, her impatience growing.

Gena glanced down at her but could not respond as another emotion swept over her. When she looked up again, it was to meet CJ's intense scrutiny. She felt like he was looking right into her . . .

CJ watched Shay wave at him, her face wreathed in smiles. He winked at her and hoped that she could see it, even though he couldn't greet her and Gena yet. It was impossible for them to get closer. Shay had grown since he'd last seen her. A lot of the round baby cuteness was gone, and he noticed she was close to being a teenager. Shay was going to be very pretty, like the other women in her family, he observed.

And then CJ shifted his gaze back to Gena Saxon. Her features were composed and her expression totally private, hiding her feelings as he knew she was wont to do. She wore her hair differently now, in a softly sculpted pageboy, the hair all one length and combed to one side. It gracefully curved to her cheek, emphasizing the delicate shape of her face and complementing the smooth brown of her skin. And, as always, there was that quiet caution about her, a personal control that CJ recalled granted trust selectively.

He took his time reacquainting himself with her and was instantly reminded of how different Gena was from Renee. Gena was taller and more slender. She was a little darker in complexion and had a more sensuous mouth. But it was more than just physical. It was something grounded. Mature. Gena lived in the real world. She was not a personality invented by an industry that believed in fantasy. He envied her.

The gathering around Renee Saxon shifted like some nebulous glob as she tried to follow the directions of both the airline staff and CJ. She was enjoying the attention, as usual, but CJ wanted to move her along through the rest of the arrival process. He took charge.

"Okay folks. That's it for now. Ms. Saxon doesn't want to spend her week here in the airport." There was chuckling among the audience of reporters and curious onlookers. "There'll be plenty of opportunity for interviews and a press conference. Now, if you'll excuse us. Thank you . . ."

Gena watched as CJ insinuated himself between Renee and the continuing questions. He helped her into her fur coat. Slowly the reporters backed off and began drifting away. Gena watched as CJ turned to her with a sharp questioning look. She was sure she understood his silent inquiry but could do nothing in response other than to stare back. Shay suddenly pulled her hand free and ran forward, ducking through and around the crowd of other passengers and luggage, which slowed her progress.

"Shay, wait . . ." Gena called out futilely after the girl. Clutching their heavy coats, she adjusted the strap of her shoulder bag and followed behind.

By the time Gena reached the selective group of people around her sister, Shay was being hugged and kissed and exclaimed over by Renee. Laura was talking with the airplane people about Renee's luggage being taken directly to the street level, where a limousine was supposedly waiting. The publicist was attempting to recite a complicated and lengthy PR schedule as CJ shepherded them all down the corridor in the direction of the terminal.

Gena found herself more or less forgotten.

"Where's Gena?" Renee called out.

The entourage immediately stopped as Renee reversed her movements and turned around to find her sister.

Gena smiled placidly in greeting as Renee's gaze found her. Renee flung her arms open dramatically, her thick, expensively designed faux fur nearly dwarfing her petite figure.

"Gen! Girl, what are you doing way back there?"

Laughing, Renee wrapped her sister in an awkward hug, forcing Gena to bend as their cheeks pressed together and Renee's perfume enveloped them.

It still surprised Gena that Renee was so enormously popular and was considered to be so glamorous. She had been cute as a teenager, although a bit overweight. She'd worn her hair in some god-awful style of the time, partitioned off in sections that had each been styled differently. Absurd, but just like all her friends. Red lipstick on her round, full mouth. Acne on her teakwood-toned skin. Gena thought about it now and wondered, what was it about Renee nearly thirteen years ago that had caught the attention of a casting director touring the local high school in search of new faces for a film?

Professional handling and care had turned Renee's potential into an attractively-packaged reality and sometimes Gena felt like her sister was another person. Only now and then, in behavior or conversation, did she catch sight of the Renee she'd grown up with, whom she'd alternately fought with and been protective of. And Gena wondered, as she stood back and looked closely at her sister, how all of their lives would been changed if Renee had never been discovered. If she'd never left Wayne, New Jersey, or had a second chance.

"You're looking good, Gen. Did you lose some weight? You know, that hairstyle isn't right for you. Makes you look too old. It's so good to see you. I can't believe Shay. She's as tall as I am. Lord, it's nice to be home. How you doing? Are you still dating what's his name? Ooops, I think I lost my earring . . . no, there it is. Laura, pick that up for me, baby . . ."

"I'll get it," CJ quietly announced.

He walked back toward them with a kind of laconic, predatory grace. Gena felt like she was being stalked. She allowed her attention to focus on him briefly as he stooped for the earring and then stood to face her and Renee. CJ silently handed the jewelry to Renee but glanced at her. Gena couldn't help staring back at him, looking for changes since she'd last seen him.

CJ wasn't quite six feet tall, but he gave the impression of being taller. He had a solid presence that commanded attention and respect. It was partly physical, but mostly attitude. A deceptive stockiness hid a muscular and firm body. He didn't sport sunglasses or pierced earlobes or gold bracelets and chains. He was dressed in khaki slacks, Dockers, a brown leather bomber jacket that added a distinctly masculine air, and a leather knapsack casually slung over his shoulder. The one addition Gena noticed, which hadn't been present the last time she'd seen CJ, was a beard. Or rather the beginnings of a beard and mustache, flat and dark, and neatly trimmed. It added a ruggedness to his good looks that took Gena by surprise. She felt herself becoming defensive under his hard gaze, but she was unable to withdraw from the silent attention he focused on her. She stubbornly wanted CJ to blink first. He didn't.

"Good to see you, Gena," CJ murmured smoothly.

No effusive greeting. No smile or questions. No handshake or hug.

"CJ," Gena returned quietly with a nod, and then gave her attention back to her sister. "How was your flight?"

"Terrible," Renee moaned. She linked one arm with Gena's and put her other arm around Shay's shoulder. Together they walked toward the main terminal building, with the entourage of almost ten people taking up the rear. "I always say I'll never take the red-eye again as long as I live, but it's so convenient and you don't waste as much time. It's a good thing I'm small. CJ got the stewardess to let me switch my seat around in first class so I could have two together. I made a bed out of it. It was better than nothing, but I didn't get any real sleep." Renee fussed with her hair. "I know I must look like something the cat dragged in," she chuckled self-consciously.

"You look beautiful," Shay said enthusiastically, grinning with adoration.

"Thank you, sweetie. And just look at you! You're almost as tall as I am. Gen, who do you think Shay favors? Remember how we thought she looked just like Mama when she was a baby?"

Gena declined answering. For one thing, she was momentarily startled by her sister's use of the nickname for her. Why had she started that? For another, Gena didn't want to get into her sister's speculations in public. And she didn't have to. Already Renee's attention had turned to other things, trying to answer the rapid-fire questions from Shay while listening to the instructions of the caretakers around her. Gena became distracted as well. She was so aware of CJ walking behind them that she felt uncomfortable. She was sure that he probably knew all of the Saxon family business, but Gena didn't want to know what he thought about any of it.

The rest of the arrival procedure was continually interrupted as people recognized Renee, and she insisted on chatting agreeably with total strangers while waiting for her luggage to be collected. She signed autographs and postured for effect, satisfying her audience's need to see that she was special. Gena watched her, smiling at how comfortable her sister was in the role of celebrity. Gena was also aware of Shay's withdrawal as the child stood apart watching Renee's performance. Gena was about to go rescue the girl when she felt a light touch on her arm. She turned to face CJ.

"We're ready. There are two cars waiting outside."

Gena glanced around at the number of people and things. "There's not going to be enough room for all of you."

CJ arched a brow and stared at her. "I know." Then he abruptly moved past her toward Renee. He solicitously took her arm. Nodding to the bystanders, CJ clearly indicated that it was time to move on.

As they walked ahead of everyone else, CJ bent to whisper something in Renee's ear. His hand on her back gently guided her forward, leading her effortlessly through the pedestrian traffic. Renee listened attentively, groaned at some unwelcome information from CJ but consented. She began to laugh lightly, shook her head and put her arm around CJ's waist. They walked companionably toward the terminal exit, arm in arm.

Like lovers, the thought went unbidden through Gena's mind.

"I didn't even get a chance to talk to her," Shay complained softly, slipping her hand once more into Gena's.

Gena squeezed the child's hand and smiled reassuringly. "This is not exactly the place to have a family reunion. Wait until we get home, hon. Then we can have her undivided attention."

Shay turned startled eyes to Gena. "But she just told me she was staying at a hotel in Manhattan."

Gena was equally surprised. She frowned, quickly thinking of what to do with the announcement. "I'm sure you're wrong. Don't worry about it now. I'll talk to Renee and get it straightened out."

On the sidewalk outside the terminal, Gena stood watching the organized bustle as a mound of luggage and boxes were being loaded into two waiting black limousines. She was grateful that they weren't those ostentatious stretch limos, but they were still obvious enough, automatically drawing attention and granting an air of prominence and importance to those waiting to ride inside. Gena stood to the side, feeling peripheral and unimportant. This was definitely going to be The Renee Saxon Show.

She saw that Shay had managed to get Renee's attention again by making herself useful. She had taken charge of Renee's carry-on, a red Coach tote that looked like a fashionable feed bag. Gena approached her sister while CJ and Laura supervised the distribution of things into the two cars.

"Renee, I have to talk with you a moment," Gena said in a low quiet voice.

"Sure, what about?" Renee responded distractedly, watching as those around her took care of the details of her arrival.

"This weekend."

"What about it?" Renee asked with a frown. "What are you talking about?"

"Shay told me you're planning on staying at a hotel while you're here. I thought you were going to spend some time with us at the house."

"I thought I'd come out on Sunday. You know, I really need some time to recover from that flight, and I need to have my hair done . . ."

"Renee, you have to come home. At least for the weekend. Shay and I haven't seen you in almost a year."

Renee managed to look contrite and impatient at the same time. "Yes, I know that, but I can't help it. I get so busy, and everybody needs me for something."

Gena leaned closer. "Well, so does your family. What's more important?"

Renee grimaced, pouting her mouth in annoyance and shifting her weight to one hip. "Look, I have all these things I *have* to do. I . . ."

Gena shook her head in disbelief. "Which part of the week do we get?" she persisted.

"I think Gena has a good point," CJ piped up in his quiet but authoritative voice.

"How's that?" Renee asked.

"Because nothing is really going to happen until Monday morning. Why don't you take tonight and tomorrow and spend it with Shay and Gena? You won't have to answer the phone, get dressed up, or wear makeup. You can visit with your girlfriends and just hang out."

Gena glanced covertly at CJ. She suspected a sly observation laced with humor but knew that Renee didn't get it.

"What about you? Where will you be?"

CJ kept his gaze focused on Renee. "I'll be doing what I'm supposed to do. Running interference and getting everything set up. Don't worry. You'll be where you're supposed to be next week. You'll get seen."

Renee relaxed and smiled charmingly at CJ. She gave him an affectionate impromptu hug. "CJ, you're the best. I'm so glad I have you to take care of me. You can stay with us, too," Renee invited magnanimously.

"No," CJ responded emphatically before Gena could even open her mouth. "I have to be in the city. I have phone calls to make. I want to stop by the studio and make sure everything is in order for the presentation next Wednesday night. I'll send a car for you Monday."

"Are you staying with us?" Shay asked, looking at Renee with a hopeful expression.

Renee turned, patted her cheek. "Yes, sweetie. Are you happy now? I'm all yours until Monday."

"Good," Shay answered joyfully.

"Then, it's settled," Gena murmured to no one in particular. She dug for her keys in the pocket of her white sports parka. "I'll be right back." She was half-way across the pedestrian walk when she heard her name.

"Gena, wait up."

Reluctantly she glanced over her shoulder. CJ was advancing upon her with easy strides. "Where are you going?" he asked.

"To get my car. How do you think I got here?"

He ignored the barbed question. "If you hang tight a moment, I'll go with you."

"You don't have to. I can find my car by myself. Besides, Renee might need you." CJ put out a hand to stop her, but Gena turned away and continued walking.

She took a deep breath as she unlocked the Toyota Camry and climbed into the driver's seat. Then she sat for a few moments reflecting on her bad mood.

Gena had promised herself she would keep her feelings to herself. But she was ambivalent about what her feelings were. Every trip her sister made home created the most awful stress in her. Gena knew her fears were of her own making and had, so far, proven to be groundless. But the anticipation of her sister's moods and possible change of heart . . . the capriciousness of her behavior was enough to set Gena on edge. She also didn't like how Renee's presence always affected Shay.

Whether Renee realized it or not, to some extent she controlled all of their lives.

Gena started the car engine and drove toward the parking lot exit. In her mind she again saw CJ coming through the arrival door just behind Renee. Standing protectively close, but managing to appear unobtrusive at the same time. He'd been watchful of all the strangers approaching Renee and had carefully monitored her answers to the reporters' sly questions. It was her own reaction to him that Gena replayed, and that moment when he'd stared right back at her.

What had she imagined she'd seen in his look?

Gena drove across the short roadway and swung around to pull up in front of the baggage claim entrance. Both limousines were gone, and CJ stood alone on the curbside waiting for her. The tension which had begun earlier that morning with the awareness of Renee's impending arrival suddenly grew in direct proportion to her personal fears. Her stomach seemed to somersault, and her heart lurched into a double-time beat. She quickly broke out into a prickly sweat that almost made her feel nauseated. She gripped the steering wheel.

As CJ was approaching the passenger side of her car, she was halfway out of her door, talking to him over the hood.

"Where's Shay?" she asked, her voice louder than usual.

CJ noticed the strident tone, very close to panic. He opened the door.

"Don't worry. She wanted to ride in the limousine with Renee," he responded easily. For a second he stood staring at her. "She was concerned about what you'd think, but I told her it was okay. I told Renee we'd catch up to them at the house."

With that CJ got into the car and closed his door. Gena took a deep breath and calmly seated herself behind the wheel, but CJ's announcement made her feel tight. She put the car into drive and stared out the windshield at the traffic and signs before slowly pulling away from the terminal. She wouldn't look at him. She didn't know what to say to him.

"Are you going to tell me it wasn't any of my business?" CJ asked smoothly.

The thought had crossed her mind, but seemed too petulant and childish. "I would have appreciated being included in the discussion, that's all."

"There was no discussion. Shay asked Renee, Renee said sure, and I said I'd let you know."

It was perfectly reasonable, yet Gena had to curb her anger and keep her anxiety hidden. She felt herself wanting to blame CJ for the way she was feeling. Maybe just because he was there.

"Put on your seat belt, please," Gena murmured, merging with the flow of cars toward the airport exit.

CJ complied, but chuckled at her request. "Concerned about my safety, or are you that bad a driver?"

"I'm used to driving with Shay, and I always make her put it on. It's for your own protection, and it's the law."

"Yes, ma'am," he drawled quietly.

There was just a moment's silence, but Gena knew that CJ was grinning at her. She signaled to enter the turnpike and increased her speed to match the traffic, driving competently while trying to ignore the man next to her. CJ settled into his seat comfortably, spreading his knees the way men do, making the front seat of the compact seem much too small for the size of him. Gena realized how she'd grown out of the habit of a male presence in her car. It was a pitiful admission, and she smiled grimly to herself. The awareness, however, stirred up a memory and kept her silent and pensive.

She paid attention to the signs until she settled into a steady speed and her driving became automatic as she headed for a familiar route home. Gena tried to keep her mind focused, but she couldn't pretend that

CJ wasn't with her. His every movement and gesture made her nervous.

"I really wish you wouldn't do that," Gena spoke into the silence.

"Do what?" CJ asked.

"You're staring at me."

"Does it bother you?"

"Of course it does."

"Why? Because I find you more interesting than the New Jersey Turnpike and passing warehouses?"

"That's hardly a compliment," Gena responded.

He chuckled again. "Just wanted to see if you noticed or cared." When Gena refused to rise to his baiting, he glanced out the window. What remained of a snowfall from two weeks earlier still spotted a lot of the suburban ground. Now it was all ice because the temperatures hadn't reached high enough to melt it away.

"Man, it's cold here." He rubbed his bare hands together.

"Maybe you should have stayed in California."

He chuckled quietly. "I thought about that, but . . ."

"Renee couldn't manage without you?" Gena interrupted. And then she regretted the sarcasm.

"She manages better without me than she thinks. No . . . I had some other business to take care of." CJ turned and reached for the heater button. He pushed it on. "If you don't mind."

"I don't care," Gena said indifferently.

CJ turned to her. "I guess you're still upset with me."

"You should have waited and asked me first," she said tightly.

CJ frowned. "You mean about Shay? Why?"

"She's not your responsibility."

"Or Renee's?" CJ asked quietly.

Gena's hands tightened on the wheel. "I . . . didn't mean that."

"They don't get to see each other that often. Think about that. Don't you think that's important?"

"Whose fault is that?"

"It's nobody's fault," CJ said quietly. "It's just the way it is."

"I'm just very concerned that these short quick visits of Renee's are upsetting to Shay. For a week her life is turned upside down with all the excitement. And then afterward . . ." she let the thought drop.

"Are you talking about Shay . . . or yourself?"

Finally Gena turned to him with a quick, startled glance. "Why would you say that?"

CJ spread his hands and then clasped them again to dangle between his knees. "Shay's growing up. She's going to want to know what's going on. Things could change real fast."

Gena blinked rapidly. Her stomach twisted again, and now her mouth felt dry. "I don't want to talk about it," her voice was soft and low.

"Then, we won't," he shrugged. "Besides, I have other things on my mind."

She moistened her lips and resolutely continued to focus out the windshield into traffic. "Do you?"

"Yes . . . I do. The last time you came to LA . . ."

"We have nothing to discuss, CJ."

Then Gena was pulling up to the tollbooth, and all conversation ended. She gave her attention to the tollbooth attendant, handing her the ticket as CJ twisted and dug in his pocket for money. They drove through and onto the exit to Route 46.

"I could have paid for the toll. I don't want your money."

CJ looked at her stubborn profile. "You've got to be the first woman I've ever met who's said that," he commented dryly.

Gena was appalled. Her attention swung briefly to CJ. "Do women take money from you?"

CJ laughed, and the deep-chested roar filled the car. "All the time. But not the way you're thinking. Anyway I was only teasing. I just meant that . . . you can take care of yourself. You're very independent." He grew serious. "You're a pretty strong woman, Gena. You don't seem to need anybody."

Gena's brow wrinkled into a frown. Where did he get that idea?

CJ bent forward to try and peer into her face. Gena's expression wiped away his amusement. "I'm sorry if I made you mad," he finally said in a conciliatory tone. "We got off to a bad start again. It's getting to be a habit."

Gena blinked at the traffic lights through the windshield. CJ's apology should have taken the edge off her prickliness with him, but instead forced more memories to come rushing at her. She didn't even feel annoyed with him anymore. Just sort of bewildered and sad.

"We don't know each other well enough for anything to be a habit," she said softly.

He shrugged. "You're right. That's why I want to talk to you."

"No," she said, and quickly put the radio on. The music was a harsh intrusion, but she preferred it to anything CJ might say.

He turned it off. "Yes," he shot back at her.

She stared straight ahead, considering the consequences of telling CJ Brock to get out of her car. But her resolve was already failing. And it was cold outside.

"I'm not interested in anything you have to say . . ."

"I liked your hair when it was short and curly," CJ suddenly murmured thoughtfully.

"Are you listening to me?" she asked in irritation.

"Every word."

She let out a deep breath. "Look, CJ . . . you're only going to be here a week."

"Maybe,"

"I don't want to spend it dodging you."

"Good. I don't want to waste time, either."

He turned in his seat a little toward Gena. He stretched out his hand to rest it on the back of her head. "Gena," he began, his voice patient and low.

"I didn't have to come with Renee for this awards dinner. Can't you figure out why I'm here?"

Gena was acutely aware of his hand. It was big enough to almost cup her head. She was angry at the slow-stroking motion of CJ's thumb. It reminded her of a moment in the dark when she'd been persuaded that his touch was special, and she'd given in to it.

"June was a very long time ago."

"I was foolish," she whispered in response.

"Then, we both were. And I liked it just fine."

When she made no further answer, CJ sighed and faced forward again, clasping his hands loosely between his knees.

In another few moments Gena had turned off the parkway onto a service road. Three miles later she pulled into the driveway of a split-level wood-frame house with modest Victorian details. The two limos were parked curbside while the drivers removed the luggage and walked cautiously through the layer of packed snow to the house. Shay and Renee were nowhere to be seen, but neighbors were already slowly passing by to gawk at her arrival.

Gena turned off the engine. Then she just sat, sensing that her life, her world, had been taken over once more. She turned to look at CJ. She was going to say something flippant like it looked like Renee was planning on staying a month. But then she saw more in his dark, understanding eyes than she wanted to.

"I suppose you're going to try and convince me that we're all going to have a good time this week."

"I'm only interested in convincing you that I'm glad to be here," CJ said seriously. "And I want to know why you never answered my letters."

Renee laughed like she used to. As if she'd never left home. She laughed the way girlfriends do when they talk on the phone together. She made more promises than she ever intended to keep.

As Gena listened to her sister's skillful handling of dozens of former childhood friends, she realized that Renee *was* a good actress. She could be whatever anyone wanted her to be. And when she left for California again, no one would be the wiser that she had created a brief fantasy of which they had been made a part. Yet Gena worried about whether Shay could tell the difference between the many women Renee was capable of impersonating. Which one was the real one, now that she was home?

Shay left the living room and wandered into the kitchen. She took a glass from a cabinet to pour herself some orange juice. Gena watched her covertly.

"Are you okay?"

"Yeah," Shay shrugged, reluctant to complain.

"Have you called Kimberly back yet?"

"I can't."

"When Renee finishes this call, you should."

"If I can get to it before it rings again," Shay observed dryly.

There was a loud guffaw of feminine laughter from the living room. Shay winced.

"Why don't you read in your room for a while? Things will quiet down soon, I'm sure."

"I can't concentrate."

"It does get a little . . . lively when she's around, doesn't it?"

Shay sighed. "It sure does."

"But I know you're glad she's home again," Gena said reasonably. She watched the girl take her time before answering.

"Well . . . I don't know if she's here to see us or just her friends."

Renee finished the current conversation, cackled an amused good-bye and hung up the phone. Before it could ring again as they knew it would, Gena quietly lifted the receiver from the base and laid it on its side.

"Whew!" Renee exclaimed in mock exhaustion. "I can't believe so many people know I'm home. Haven't been in the door two hours and the old network is in place. Did you tell people I was coming?" she asked brightly, her intonation a combination of disbelief and merriment.

Gena smiled at her sister and arched a brow. "If it was up to me, I'd disconnect the phone until you left."

"We never get this many calls," Shay said, standing next to an easy chair where Renee had taken up center court in the living room.

Renee chuckled quietly, curling her petite frame into the chair and glancing slyly at Gena. "You mean Paul doesn't call you every night?"

Shay stifled a giggle. "He doesn't call at all anymore."

Gena gave Shay what she hoped was a stern, censoring glare, reminding her not to be rude or impertinent. "Why don't you put those things away before they get soiled," she said, referring to the sweater, the three pairs of jeans, and the leather coat, which had been gifts from Renee to the girl.

Renee remained quiet until Shay had gathered up her new clothing and carried them off to her room on the second floor.

"Sorry if I asked something I shouldn't have," Renee shrugged lightly. "I've been expecting an engagement any day."

"I guess you don't remember I told you last summer, Paul and I broke it off," Gena said smoothly, her indifference successfully masking any lingering feeling she may have had about the failed relationship.

"CJ said Paul wasn't the right man for you."

"What would CJ know about it?" Gena asked tartly.

"Why don't you ask me?" he said as he exited the small den off the kitchen, where he'd been using his cellular phone. He picked up his jacket from the back of a chair and shrugged into it. He looked directly at Gena but wasn't surprised when she turned away from his question. She'd hardly spoken to him since they'd arrived at the house. And she'd never answered his question.

"Gena is very close-mouthed," Renee quipped. "You're not going to get anything out of her. She acts like she's everybody's mother."

"I bet Paul didn't want a mother . . ." CJ murmured.

Gena crossed her arms over her chest. "Maybe I should have let you stay at a hotel after all," she said to Renee.

"What about me?" CJ asked.

Gena felt the challenge from him grip at her chest. Nonetheless she kept her tone light, determined not to let him rile her. "You control Renee's life, not mine."

"Oooooh," Renee breathed. "I'd watch out if I were you, CJ. My sister won't stand for nonsense from anyone!"

"Is that right?" he drawled as he zippered the front of his coat and stuck his hands in the pockets. He stared at Gena, watching the way she struck a pose of haughty composure, as if nothing he and Renee said about her mattered in the least. But he could detect the way her nostrils flared and her bottom lip pursed. CJ slowly grinned. "We're going to have to do something about that."

"She's so serious. Gena's going to be an old lady before her time if she keeps on like this."

"Tease if you want," Gena said quietly to her sister,"but if one of us hadn't taken things seriously, some of us would have been in trouble a long time ago."

"*I* wasn't in any trouble," Renee countered sharply.

"Come on. It's been a long day," CJ said, putting a swift end to the petty argument.

Gena turned away, absently gathering the things carelessly left about the room. Empty glasses, paper with scribbled messages, lists, shoes, and accessories discarded as Renee got comfortable and settled into the surroundings, making herself at home once more.

"I'd better get going. The limo is still waiting outside. Remember what I said," he instructed Renee. "No interviews over the phone. No appointments without checking with me first. Don't accept any invitations. Otherwise have a good weekend."

Renee grimaced. "Why don't you just tie me to the chair and put a sack over my head, CJ?"

Shay came quickly down the stairs again, and looped her arm playfully through CJ's as he stood ready to leave. "Are you coming over tomorrow?"

The question was innocent, but still Gena found herself anxious over CJ's answer, as if all of her plans for the next day rested squarely on what he and Renee were going to do.

"Probably not, baby. There's an interview I have to set up for Fox TV. I'll send a car to pick Renee up."

Shay's eyes widened. She turned to the two women

and blurted out, "Mommy, can I go to the studio, too?"

The reaction was swift and absolute. No one said a word.

A strange, deep silence followed the question. It was a long moment before Shay realized why everyone was staring at her. She hunched her shoulders and quickly covered her mouth. It was CJ who broke the spell, glancing down at the girl and pulling her hands away from her face. "If you do, you might get to meet Salt N' Pepa. They're supposed to be on the same program."

But Shay was still waiting for another response. Her bright eyes switched back and forth between Gena and Renee, aware of the uneasiness she'd created with one simple question, but too startled and inexperienced to know how to reverse the course of events now.

Gena and Renee exchanged glances as well and held each other's gaze for a fixed moment. Each was expecting the other to answer first, but only one of them could.

"Sure you can come with me," Renee said as her daughter stared poignantly at Gena.

Gena knew Shay wanted to apologize, but there was nothing for her to be sorry for. The circumstances were not of Shay's making, and Gena realized it was up to her, as always, to make things right. CJ had somehow made himself scarce, moving away into the shadows, where he was not a witness to the awkward scene. Gena didn't know whether to be grateful for his insight, or embarrassed. She smiled gently at her niece, to put her at ease and reassure her.

"It's okay, hon. That sounds like fun."

"No wonder no one else has tried to call. The phone's off the hook," Renee announced, replacing the receiver.

The telephone promptly rang. She answered cheerfully, as if knowing the call was for her. She turned to CJ and waved at him as he stood at the open door ready to leave. "Regina, is that you? Hey, girl . . ."

Gena found herself the only one left to see CJ off. Shay had quietly retreated to her room to watch a video of her mother's latest film, not even released yet. Gena turned from the girlish chitchat of her sister's conversation and faced the tall manager.

Gena hazarded a swift glance at CJ's face, but his brown features and the dark beard hid any real emotion. Yet she could see empathy in his eyes, and it took her by surprise. She didn't want to be grateful.

"Well . . . good night, CJ. I hope you get more rest than any of us will," she murmured awkwardly.

"I doubt it," he smiled slowly, stepping out of the door onto the small porch. "I've got a lot of running around to do. Don't let Renee wear you out. Don't let her forget she's home, not in Hollywood, where everyone is at her beck and call all the time."

She looked thoughtfully at him, noting the strong

masculine structure of his face. The square chin and jaw. The deep-set eyes with their very dark brows. The parallel furrow of lines on his forehead, which she'd never noticed before. They suggested concentration. Seriousness. "Is that what you do? Run when she calls?"

"That's my job. I'm supposed to make it easy for her to do what she does."

Gena shook her head, considering the extent of CJ's commitment. Where, exactly, did it end?

"I hear what you're thinking," CJ whispered suddenly.

She stared at him. His expression was neither insulted nor annoyed. It occurred to her that CJ Brock was a very observant man. "I only meant . . ."

"There are followers, and there are leaders. I prefer the latter. I do it well."

She believed him. Gena shifted. She hugged her arms around her body as the evening winter chill began to seep into her bones. "I bet. Does Renee know she's being led?"

"I don't think she cares, as long as everyone loves her and thinks she's wonderful. Shay certainly does. She's the one that matters the most, right?"

The reminder struck a nerve. Gena turned from him. CJ reached out and grabbed her arm. It was a firm but nonthreatening move. She stared suspiciously into his face as his fingers slid down her arm, pulling it away from her body, the way he'd taken Shay's hands from covering her mouth. CJ didn't stop until his hand was clasping hers. Gena glanced down at his large hand, astounded at how very warm it was, how it made her feel protected. She was too surprised to even pull away.

"I know it was rough, Gena," CJ said earnestly. "But you just remember one thing . . ."

"What?" she asked, mesmerized by his voice despite herself.

CJ squeezed her hand and stepped off the porch as their fingers separated. "Take care of yourself, too."

Gena frowned at him, and watched as he jogged with athletic grace toward the waiting limo.

Chapter Two

Gena walked into the quiet living room. It seemed eerie and strange after the previous day's hectic activities. The phone had continued to ring incessantly. Old neighborhood friends, or those who claimed to be old friends, stopped by to visit with Renee. Some of her girlfriends were gawking and adoring, and some displayed overfamiliarity. Gena didn't understand how Renee could stand all these people she hadn't seen in years, many of whom she used to complain about as being two-faced or insincere.

Now the house was still, like those Sunday mornings when she and Renee were young and everyone was still moving kind of slow as they prepared for church and Sunday school. There was sunlight pouring through the curtained windows, warming the rooms and belying the winter weather outside. But Gena's Sunday-morning routine of a first cup of coffee while browsing through the papers was stymied by the disorder around her. She blinked at the disarray, remembering how if their mother had come upon such a scene, she would stand with her hands on her hips and say sternly, "*I didn't raise any wild children. Come in here and straighten up this mess.*"

Gena sighed as she stood shaking her head in exasperation, her gaze sweeping over Renee's carelessly dropped possessions. She still had the ability to come into a place and take it over, fill it up with her presence. Her open tote bag was in the middle of the sofa, with its fat appointment book and a cosmetic case sticking out the top. The chairs were askew, and the coffee table was piled with newspapers and magazines. Gena ignored the mess, controlling the urge to pick up things. She wasn't going to allow Renee to get away with thinking others would clean up after her.

She glanced suddenly at the bookcase. One shelf was emptied of its photo albums and scrapbooks. Her stomach lurched suddenly in alarm as she noticed that her own books and things had been shifted aside and lay in different places. She reached out quickly and grabbed a flowered box. She opened the box, and her eyes swiftly scanned the contents. Inside she kept loose photographs and keepsakes. Personal things that only had meaning to herself.

"Good morning."

Gena gasped and swung around, clutching the box. Her sister was slowly coming down the stairs. Renee's hair was partially in rollers, and she was dressed in an inappropriately sexy negligee visible under an open white terry cloth robe, which Gena recognized as her own. The nightgown was mostly lace and spaghetti straps, and she wondered absently how her sister managed to sleep in something so skimpy. It was a garment meant to be worn *for* someone. A man. Someone who would eventually remove it. Gena forced her mind away from an obvious choice.

Renee's face was devoid of makeup, showing the naturally uneven brown areas and texture of her skin. Her mouth was pouty and full, and she looked slightly older than her carefully airbrushed publicity shots indicated. Right now she looked not like a glamorous actress, but a thirty-something black woman who had had too much of a good thing the evening before.

"Guilty conscience," Renee said in a gravelly sing-song voice as she descended the stairs, yawning.

"You scared me, sneaking down like that," Gena murmured, holding the box covertly.

Renee sighed sleepily as she surveyed the living room. "Well, you certainly can tell I'm home," she chuckled. "I don't know how people live without housekeepers."

"People do all the time. Especially black folks. *You* used to." Gena walked past her sister and placed the box on a chair near the living room entrance. She would take it upstairs with her later.

Renee shoved aside things on the sofa and plopped down heavily. "Well, I got over it. I'm sorry, but I enjoy having people do things for me and now I can afford it."

Gena stood staring at her sister. She wondered if all younger siblings developed this extraordinary sense of entitlement. Her sister had gotten older, but there was still an unapologetic attitude about her. She had never known Renee to be repentant about anything. There was something carefree and even innocent about her outlook on life. Unrealistic. And she consistently got away with it. There had always been someone else to take care of the details, clean up after her mess, correct her mistakes. Big sisters . . . and business managers.

Renee stared back at Gena, looking her up and down as she slouched against the sofa cushions, her pedicured bare feet curled beneath her. "You going to church?"

Gena nodded and sat on the edge of a chair. "You coming? You can see everybody in the town if you do. Maybe then the phone will stop ringing off the hook."

"Uh-uh," Renee shook her head and yawned again. "I'm not up to that this morning. The pastor telling us we got to save our souls. Everybody carrying on and getting the spirit . . ."

Gena couldn't help grinning at her sister. "What's wrong with that? You used to like to get all dressed and show up the other girls. You'd listen to the service, and then come home and promise Mama you were going to be good and never give her any trouble. For about a fast New York minute. The next Sunday you'd start all over again. You've had your soul saved more times than anybody else I know."

Renee chuckled at the memory. "Hasn't helped, right?"

Gena shrugged. "You turned out fine. You have a great career, people love and admire you. You're talented and attractive . . ."

"But I'm a lousy mother," Renee whispered.

Gena pursed her lips, but didn't respond.

"This comes up every time I'm home," Renee remarked in a tone of mild annoyance. "You know I love Sharon Lee. You know she means the world to me . . ."

"You're like a visitor in her life. Maybe you could get away with that when Shay was a small child, but by August she's going to be a teenager. It's confusing to her."

Renee sucked her teeth and shifted on the sofa. "Gen, why do we have to talk about this now? It's too early in the morning."

"Yesterday afternoon should have told you something," Gena insisted quietly. "How do you think I felt?"

Renee looked sharply at her sister. Her attitude changed from being offended to being contrite. "Gen, I'm sorry. I really am."

Gena felt a swirl of warmth through her body, a subtle embarrassment and sadness. An odd sense of floating out of herself; disoriented. "You know, she looks so much like you. Only prettier."

Renee laughed and made a dismissing gesture with her hand. "As long as she doesn't follow in my footsteps."

"There's nothing wrong with you," Gena murmured softly. "But Shay is different. She's really smart. Already she knows what she wants to do with her life."

"Tell me she wants to be an actress." Renee rolled her eyes.

"She wants to be an astronaut."

Renee blinked in confusion and frowned deeply at Gena. "A *what*?"

"She wants to fly. She wants to be a scientist and go into space, like Mae Jemison."

"An . . . astronaut?" Renee repeated in disbelief. "Where on earth did she get that idea?"

Gena stood up. "She reads a lot. You should sit and talk to her. You might be surprised at what you find out about your daughter."

Gena headed into the kitchen, suddenly feeling the space around her closing in. A tension tightened within her and started a headache that throbbed at her temple. In the kitchen she got the coffeemaker started, checked the time on the oven clock, and began the Sunday-morning ritual of breakfast. She could hear Renee enter the kitchen behind her and settle into a chair at the round oak table.

"So what's this business about you and Paul?"

Gena pulled the refrigerator door open and bent over to peer inside. "I told you we broke off. It was so long ago, it's not worth talking about." She took out eggs and sausages and placed them on the counter.

"How come?"

Gena sighed deeply and turned on her sister. "Renee, let it alone. You never liked Paul anyway. You said he acted like he was the only black man who ever got an education and owned a business."

"He was stuck up. You deserve better."

"There isn't any better. Not when you work the kind of hours I do, and . . ." Gena abruptly stopped.

"Go on. And what?"

"He thought I spent too much time worrying about Shay. He said I loved her more than him." Gena turned to look at her sister. "He reminded me that she wasn't my own child . . . and he didn't want a ready-made family."

"Fool," Renee muttered under her breath. She shifted uncomfortably in her chair but had no other comment on the issue of her sister's commitment and responsibilities.

"He was right about one thing."

"What?"

"I do love her more than him. It wasn't that he didn't like Shay, either."

"He was okay," Shay said quietly as she slipped into the kitchen.

Gena and Renee were surprised at her sudden appearance. They glanced briefly at each other with a silent understanding that the conversation end there. "It's rude to eavesdrop."

"I wasn't eavesdropping. I just heard Paul's name. I like CJ better."

Renee cleared her throat. Gena turned back to the stove, settling a frying pan on the front burner.

"Good morning," Shay belatedly murmured, kissing her mother and then Gena on their cheeks.

"Morning, baby," Renee looked her daughter over. "Don't you look cute. That's a pretty dress you're wearing."

Shay wrinkled her nose. "I wish I could wear jeans to church."

Renee groaned and shook her head. "Your grandmother, God rest her soul, would have had a fit if Gena or I *ever* said that."

Shay began to set the table, putting out the orange juice and making a glass of chocolate milk for herself. "Well, I don't think God is going to mind if I wear jeans, so long as I come to church. CJ doesn't go to church. He says he just prays in his head and his heart."

Gena and Renee again exchanged looks. "CJ said that to you?" Renee asked, astounded.

Shay nodded. "He's pretty cool. We talk about a lot of things."

"Is that right?" Renee remarked.

Gena stared at her niece. "Like what?" she asked in a soft voice.

"Oh . . . we talk about school and what I want to be when I grow up. CJ said he wished he had thought about becoming an astronaut when he was my age. He knows how to fly helicopters . . ."

"CJ?" both Renee and Gena voiced together.

". . . And he likes to cook. And he told me a lot about his son, Nicholas."

Gena turned back to the stove. She cracked two eggs into the hot skillet, and they sizzled. She didn't know what to make of the fact that Shay knew so much about the man. She wondered what else they'd talked about.

"Yeah, Nicholas is only a year older than you are," Renee added. "He lives in Philadelphia with his mother."

"I know," Shay said, putting out butter and jam for the English muffins. "You know what I liked best? When I came to visit with you and CJ took me and Mommy . . ." She stopped, quickly covering her mistake. "I mean, Aunt Gena to Disneyland. I had such a good time. Right, Aunt Gena?"

Gena slid the eggs onto a platter and placed it in the warm oven. Then she began two more eggs, and added the sausage to the side of the pan. "Yes, it was a lot of fun, wasn't it?"

"Are you coming to church? You're not even dressed yet," Shay commented to her mother.

"Not today, sweetie. I'm so tired from the flight yesterday and all that running around we did at the mall. I want to rest up for that TV interview this afternoon."

"Can I stay home with you, then?"

Gena frowned at her niece. "No, you may not. You're supposed to help serve snacks to the children's group after Sunday school this morning."

"What do you mean she can't?" Renee asked, her puzzled tone disguising an edge of resentment. "What's the big deal if she stays home with me today?"

Gena wiped her hands slowly and carefully on a linen towel and took a deep breath. "Look, I'm just trying not to let the things that Shay and I normally do get pushed aside. Yesterday she was invited to go to the movies with some of her friends. Instead you took her shopping for clothes she really doesn't need. This afternoon she should be working on a book report for school, and cleaning her room. Now she's going to be in Manhattan for your taping. Instead of being able to just relax this evening, Shay will still have to finish that report."

"Can't she miss one day of school while I'm here? She can hand in the report late. After all, I haven't seen the child since last summer."

Gena glared at her sister, trying not to let her annoyance or frustration make her voice brittle. "And whose fault is that?"

"I think the eggs are burning ..." Shay murmured awkwardly.

Gena removed the skillet from the flame and began

to silently portion out the food onto three plates. She poured coffee for herself and Renee, and finally sat down at the table. The three Saxon women looked furtively at one another. Renee absently picked at her plate with the fork. Shay liberally spread apricot jam on her English muffin halves and demonstrated that there was nothing wrong with her appetite. Gena spread a napkin over her navy blue two-piece knit ensemble.

"I don't think Shay's routine should be tossed out the window because you're here for a week, Renee. She can stay home from church today, or from school tomorrow. But not both," Gena offered with a quiet dignified authority.

Shay stole a sideways glance at Renee. She shrugged and then stared down into her plate. "I'd rather stay home tomorrow from school."

Gena kept her features blank of any particular expression. "Fine."

"I thought so," Renee chuckled. She winked at her daughter. "You go on to church with Gena like you always do. Say a little prayer for me and CJ."

"I will," Shay agreed around a mouthful of sausage.

"We'll have *big* fun tomorrow," Renee predicted generously.

"Sharon Lee . . ." Gena quietly warned the girl.

Shay stole a glance at her aunt. "I know . . . don't talk with my mouth full."

* * *

CJ looked at his watch and walked past the studio entrance. Out on the street there was little traffic and no sign of the limousine. The muscles in his jaw tightened. Pensively he scrubbed his hands along the side of his jaw and chin. He was tired and annoyed. He always forgot that he could never depend on Renee to show up any place on time unless he was with her. The limo had been dispatched out to New Jersey to pick her up and return her to the Manhattan studio with plenty of time to spare. But, CJ acknowledged with a sign of exasperation, that didn't mean Renee would have been ready when the car got there. Or that it would leave New Jersey on the schedule he'd outlined.

The phone on the security guard's desk rang, and CJ knew who it was. He cursed under his breath as the guard held the receiver out to him.

"Has she gotten here yet?" the executive producer asked briskly in his ear.

It was a subtle hint to CJ that there were other things and people planned for the program and, if need be, Renee's appearance and interview could be preempted altogether. CJ lied smoothly. "Just this instant. She's on her way up."

"Good. I'll have someone take her right to makeup. The director will want to speak with her briefly before they go on the air, just to make sure they have their stories straight."

CJ silently nodded as the woman hung up. He checked the time once more. There were twenty minutes before the show went on. "This is it. I've had it," he muttered darkly, wishing belatedly that he'd let the publicist here in New York handle all the details. Wishing that he'd stayed in Philadelphia with Nicholas, or that he'd thought to let his son come with him to New York. One day was not enough time to bridge the time and distance imposed by the sanctions of a divorce.

CJ turned abruptly at the sound of the door opening, and a noisy flow of people and voices entered the studio. In front, regal and imperial, was Renee. She was beautifully dressed in a mauve pantsuit with a pale pink silk shell top underneath. She hadn't bothered to fuss with her hair, but instead wore one of the half dozen or so wigs she'd had designed in varying styles. She wore makeup, and CJ knew she was not going to permit the studio artist to do much more than powder her face and add lipstick.

CJ's expert eye took just a few seconds to check Renee over, to make sure that everything was in place and that her colors suited the studio setting. His gaze then swept past Renee to Laura, who'd also accompanied the limo from New Jersey. There was Shay, looking shy and small in the mad flurry of people surrounding her mother. CJ knew that ordinarily there was a kind of dispassionate aloofness to the way people were treated by station staff, except for the biggest stars. Renee was pretty much being given the royal treatment. So CJ winked at the girl and gave her a brief hug to let her know she was still special, too.

It was only as he was about to turn away, to guide Renee toward the elevator and the studio on an upper floor that CJ noticed Gena. He did a double take, and blinked in surprise as she took up the rear of the entourage. A slow smile spread across his face at her cool, quiet presence. She and Shay seemed the only normal part of this whole proceeding. His smile broadened.

"Hey. I didn't know you were coming."

Gena grinned in a self-deprecating manner. "I didn't know I was, either."

"So, how come?"

Gena didn't want to admit she was curious about what was going on. And she certainly wasn't going to admit that she didn't want to be left out and at home alone all afternoon. Despite her best argument on the benefits of routine and order, on reason and good sense, she realized that this was an adventure.

"I thought I could lend moral support or something."

CJ arched a brow, and his grin was lopsided. "Renee's got this routine down cold. She doesn't need moral support. But I could use a bunch."

For a very brief moment their gazes met, and Gena found that she was hard-pressed to turn away, to avoid the intense questioning in CJ's eyes. His confession was light and charming. She found herself staring at his mouth, the way it was circled by the dark hair on his cheeks. She was fascinated by its movement as he talked or smiled. In that quick instant the memory of another meeting between them made Gena catch her breath.

CJ recovered first. "Come on," he said, reaching out his hand to urge her forward. "Everybody's waiting upstairs."

She felt CJ's firm hand on her shoulder as they rushed toward the waiting elevator. They got on and found themselves facing one another. The position was unintentionally intimate. Gena felt embarrassed and wondered if anyone else noticed. But Laura was answering Renee's questions about how long the segment was, and what kind of questions the show's host would ask. Shay wanted to know if she could watch from the set.

Gena had never imagined an elevator ride could be so long.

She was so conscious of CJ that she was afraid to move, lest they touch. Her eyes were at his chin level, and Gena stared at the short-trimmed beard that lay so smoothly against his brown skin. She'd never known another black man with a beard, and Gena wondered if it was bristly like it looked, or soft to the touch.

His jacket was opened, and Gena could see the steady pulsing of the vein in the side of his neck. She'd forgotten how wide his neck was, and his shoulders . . . and the automatic sense she had of being safe and protected with him. CJ's hand slowly rose along their sides, and he took hold of her upper arm. For a moment Gena was afraid that he would actually take advantage of their closeness. Instead he merely squeezed her arm, as if to catch her attention.

It worked.

Slowly Gena raised her gaze until she could see CJ's eyes. His attention was fixed on her face. Pride made her refuse to look away first, to acknowledge the questions in his intense study of her. Afterward she had reason to be cautious. The standoff continued between them until the elevator came to a stop and the spell was broken.

The executive producer of the program was waiting for them with nearly a half dozen or so staff people. Gena was surprised at the reverence given to her sister, simply because she was well-known. Everyone clustered around Renee, greeting her and asking solicitous questions, prepared to cater to any need. Shay tried to stay next to her mother, but it was clear that Renee's attention was focused on the moment. Gena reached out and took Shay's hand, and the girl fell into step beside her. She turned to find CJ standing next to them.

"They're going to take Renee to makeup, and she's going to meet the host of the show for a preliminary chat."

"Where should Shay and I go?"

"You can sit in the green room until it's over. It should only take about twenty minutes or so."

"Can't we watch?" Shay asked.

"We'll be in the way, sweetie," Gena said.

"No you won't. As a matter of fact, let me see about getting you both in the studio during the taping."

Before she could protest, Gena watched CJ walk away, signaling to get the attention of one of the assistants. Renee's assistant, Laura, joined Gena and Shay in the reception area.

"The taping is going to be live, and there will be call-in questions from the home viewers. You can watch the whole program from the green room . . ."

"CJ said we can watch the taping," Shay interrupted in a tone of importance and excitement.

"Great. Follow me, and I'll show you were it's all going to happen."

Gena, still holding onto Shay's hand, followed Laura as she made her way with familiarity through the labyrinth of hallways to a studio. As they were about to enter, a tall dark-skinned man in shirtsleeves appeared from an office. He was quickly looking through papers in his hand and nearly collided with them.

"Ooops. Sorry 'bout that," Laura chuckled.

"Where are you off to in such a rush?" he asked good-naturedly, glancing briefly at Gena and Shay.

"They're here with Renee Saxon. This is Gena, her sister. And Shay Saxon, her niece."

Gena could feel Shay's surprised reaction in the reflexive tightening of her hand. The little girl glanced quickly at Gena, her face frowning and confused.

"But . . ." Shay began with a short shake of her head.

"It's nice to meet you," the host said pleasantly, already turning his attention back to his notes. "You'll have to excuse me. We go on in about ten minutes . . ."

"But she didn't get it right," Shay whispered.

Gena put her arm around Shay's narrow shoulders and hugged her to her side as they continued to follow after Laura. "I know, but it's not important right now. We don't want Renee to be late for her part in the program, and you and I don't want to get in the way. We'll discuss it later."

Shay nodded silently, but Gena could see that she was upset by the mistake. Something CJ had said to her the day before, when they were on the ride from the airport, came to mind. That sooner or later Shay was going to start asking questions about their family dynamics. It was definitely going to be sooner, and Gena suddenly realized, with a bit of apprehension, that neither she nor Renee had prepared themselves with many answers.

Gena decided not to say any more about it just then as they were led onto a dark open set that had just a small scene setting, meant to look like someone's comfortable den or family room. It was complete with artificial plants and shelves of books.

A friendly cameraman engaged Shay in conversation, and Gena smiled gratefully at him for unwittingly providing a momentary distraction. He put his headphones over her ears so she could hear the chatter from the control room. She peered through the camera lens, which was focused on the chairs where Renee and the host would sit.

"Has Shay changed her mind about being an astronaut already?"

Gena turned casually to CJ as she watched Shay. "How did you know about that?"

He grinned. "Shay and I are buddies. She told me all about it."

"I suppose the same way you told her you flew helicopters?"

CJ's gaze swung to Gena's face. He pursed his lips and nodded. "That's right."

"Is it true?"

He arched a brow. "I can lie about a lot of things when I have to. That's the kind of business I'm in. But I don't do that to friends, or people I care about. Yeah, it's true."

Gena felt chastened. "I'm sorry. I didn't mean to suggest . . ."

"Don't worry about it," CJ said distantly. "There are a lot of things about me you don't know. There's probably even some real reason why you don't want to trust me." His eyes then seemed to soften as his attention wandered over Gena's face. "But I've never lied to you, either," CJ finished in a low quiet voice.

Gena took a deep breath, disconcerted by the look

in his eyes, which made her feel vulnerable. She nodded in the direction of her niece. "As far as I know, she still wants to go into science. But she'd probably make a better living if she did something more practical."

"Money isn't everything," CJ quoted. "Certainly can't replace being happy doing what you like to do."

"You sound very philosophical," Gena teased.

CJ grunted. "The voice of experience speaking from the school of hard knocks."

"I thought you liked what you did?"

CJ didn't answer right away, taking a moment to watch as Renee was led onto the stage from a side door, again followed by Laura and other minions at her beck and call. "I used to," he finally murmured absently.

Gena was intrigued and waited for him to say more. But CJ simply excused himself as he went to see to the final preparations for Renee's interview before the cameras were turned on. Shay wandered back to her side, and the two of them watched the routine. A mike was attached to Renee's jacket by one of the sound technicians. Someone brought her a glass of water. Renee whispered to Laura, who then checked her hairstyle and declared it wonderful . . . and in place. The makeup artist appeared to dab at Renee's forehead and chin with a sponge, to add just a bit more lip gloss.

The host took his seat and joked with his crew.

And then, at some silent signal, everyone suddenly vanished from the set, leaving Renee with the host.

Gena watched her sister's face. Watched the subtle transformation as she settled into a professional posture of someone of importance . . . who was trying not to appear too important. She had a gracious smile on her face, and her eyes were bright and focused on the host, as if he was even more important than she was. Gena smiled to herself. Renee was good at this. She was *very* good.

Gena turned her attention to CJ, who also watched and monitored, paying attention to every single detail happening on the set and in the studio. At one point he whispered to one of the camera operators, who nodded and made some sort of minor adjustment to what he was doing. Then CJ stepped back and out of the way.

Shay went to stand next to him, and he stood whispering explanations of what was going on. The little girl listened attentively, whispering back questions and comments.

Gena found herself fascinated with the interplay between her niece and CJ. And then she wondered, with a flash of memory, why she should be. She suddenly had a recollection of CJ accompanying them around Disneyland nearly a year ago, cheerfully agreeing to Shay's demands to try every ride in the theme park. He'd had the most incredible patience, standing on endless lines, entertaining and distracting the girl when she became impatient or started to get tired. Filling her with ice cream. Willing to buy just about anything Shay had set her mind to, until Gena had to put a firm stop to such overindulgence.

Overindulgence . . .

Gena stared at CJ, noting his masculine profile, the attractive grooves that appeared when he smiled. She was even more curious about the beard and why he'd decided to grow one. And she realized now that CJ smiled a lot. Gena admitted to herself that it was devastating. She experienced an internal tension, an awareness. It was piercing and evocative. A startling sensation of déjà vu as other memories came rushing back to her. Memories that made her sigh softly. Her cheeks flushed with a warm glow Gena hadn't allowed herself since the previous June. Watching CJ now, she admitted, finally, how much it had meant to her at the time.

The taping was over.

It had gone smoothly, Renee demonstrating the skills that had made her famous as a sympathetic and appealing black woman to millions of people across the country. Shay walked across the studio to stand next to her mother, waiting to be acknowledged.

"I've met your sister and niece," the host said, smiling at Shay.

She looked expectantly at her mother.

Renee hesitated for a heartbeat before smiling at the TV host. "Did you? Isn't she pretty?"

"I can see the family resemblance. All the Saxon women are good-looking."

Renee laughed lightly at the remark, but when Shay leaned to speak into her ear, she quickly whispered in return, "Not now, sweetie. I have to finish up here."

Gena, witnessing the exchange, was on the verge of speaking up when the host shook hands with Renee and walked away. Shay made her way back to Gena's side. Over the child's head she caught CJ watching them. They exchanged a look of mutual concern before he hurried to Renee's side.

Shay had recovered by the time they were ready to leave the studio. But she'd also lost much of her enthusiasm for the many details and delays of her mother's affairs.

"Are we going back home now?" she asked Gena.

"I've arranged for Renee to make a surprise appearance at an Urban League luncheon event. Part of it is being taped by ET," CJ said regrettably.

"I don't have to go, do I?" Shay asked quietly.

"That's right! A director I'm dying to work with is going to be there. We've never met, and I really want to work on him for a role in his next film," Renee said, oblivious to anyone else's wishes.

Gena could see that Shay wasn't going to make a fuss, but was simply withdrawing in silence from the adults. "Well, maybe Shay and I can meet you all later. We can go get something to eat or window-shop a little bit. How does that sound, hon?"

Shay shrugged.

"I tell you what," CJ spoke directly to Renee, "Laura can take you over to the Waldorf and walk you through what has to be done. I'll call ahead and let them know to expect you. The studio publicist was supposed to be there, too. You know what to do."

Renee frowned at CJ. "You mean, you're not coming with me?"

CJ smiled at Renee reassuringly. "You don't need me there."

"But what if something goes wrong?" she asked petulantly. "You know what some of these assistants are like, and I hate it when you're not there with me."

"Everything's going to be fine. I'll catch up with you."

Renee made an impatient sound. "Well . . . where will you be?"

"I promised Shay I'd take her to ice-skate at Rockefeller Center," CJ said, glancing at the young girl and raising his brows.

"You've got to be kidding," Renee uttered doubtfully.

Shay brightened and giggled. "You don't know how to ice-skate," she challenged with delight.

"Well, I'm counting on you to teach me," CJ winked at her and turned back to Renee. "We'll come with the car to pick you up afterward."

"All right," Renee finally consented. She stroked

her hand down Shay's ponytail and tugged playfully on the end. "My thing is going to be so boring anyway, I bet. Maybe later we can all go to Rumpelmayer's for ice cream."

"If they still exist," Laura interjected in passing, approaching with a tape of the just completed interview in hand.

Shay grimaced. "Rumpel who?"

"Laura can check it out. If they're not, we'll go someplace else," CJ said.

"If not, we'll just go home," Gena countered smoothly. "I'm sorry, but some of us normal folks have to work tomorrow."

Gena laughed gently as she watched Shay's slightly shaky movements around the ice rink. Her arms flayed out a bit to keep her balance, and her gliding steps were short and jerky. Whenever she got going too fast, however, she allowed herself to run right into the hard rubber railing in order to slow down.

Shay continued to concentrate on her balance, even as she exchanged conversation with a young blond boy about her own age who skated next to her, did a graceful pivot, and began to skate backward as they talked.

"Well, I'll be. He's trying to pick her up," CJ said in throaty amusement.

"No he's not," Gena shook her head. "I bet he's just asking her if she wants some help."

They watched silently as Shay came to a halting stop and watched and listened to the boy. He performed some very simple maneuvers several times to demonstrate his skills. Then he stood aside to watch her repeat what he'd done. Shay's first attempt was awkward, but after only a few more tries she'd mastered the step.

"See," Gena nodded, vindicated.

Shay tried another step and then promptly fell. The boy came to her rescue, gallantly offering a hand to help her up from the ice. When she was up again, they made another circle of the rink . . . hand in hand.

CJ chuckled. "What did I tell you? He *is* trying to pick her up."

Gena laughed. "Don't be crazy. They're both too young for that stuff."

CJ continued to watch the two silently for a moment before turning his attention to Gena and staring at her. "No," he said, shaking his head and taking a sip for his coffee. "I think another Saxon woman has just made a conquest."

"I don't know what you mean by that," Gena murmured.

"It means the boy's got good taste," CJ said in a soft teasing tone. He leaned across the table to whisper to her. "Want to go back on the ice for a while before we turn our skates in?"

She chuckled and shook her head. "No thanks. I think I've embarrassed myself enough for one day."

"You did good."

Gena allowed herself a private smile and looked over at CJ.

He had surprised her again. He had rented skates not just for Shay but for the two of them as well. He didn't have the smooth grace of the male rink attendants, who, when she, CJ, and Shay had first gotten on the ice, had politely followed them around in case they'd needed help. CJ simply had shown an athlete's natural sense of balance and a good feel for his own body's capabilities. He had a fearlessness that was breathtaking, a willingness to try anything that Gena couldn't help but admire.

All through their subsequent lunch, she also couldn't help recalling the secure strength of CJ's hands as he'd guided her around the rink, promising he wasn't going to let her fall. And he hadn't. CJ had given her confidence with his quiet reassuring words. He held her hands, or partnered her with his arm around her waist, his own body warmth wrapping itself around her on the cold rink.

Gena had enjoyed herself just as, she now realized, CJ had intended. His gentle guidance and care had gotten to her.

Just as he'd intended . . .

"That's it . . . that's it. You're doing great . . ." he had whispered with encouragement.

And Gena trusted him all over again.

She cast another glance out the large viewing window of the restaurant to make sure Shay was okay, and then turned her attention to CJ with the intentions of ignoring his provocative comment.

"I guess I should thank you. You're very sweet to Shay."

He lifted his shoulder negligently. "Shay's a nice little girl."

"As much as I know she wants to spend time with Renee, all those interviews and running around and people wanting Renee's attention makes her feel left out."

"I know. I mentioned it to Renee."

Gena raised her brows. "Did you?"

CJ nodded thoughtfully. "One year my son Nicholas came out to spend six months with me. I thought he'd enjoy meeting some of the stars and hanging out on sets or seeing how some of the special effects are done in movies. All he really wanted to do was hang out with *me*. I finally figured it out when it was time for him to return to his mother in Philadelphia. Too late to do anything about it. I'm hoping Renee won't wait as long as I did."

Gena stared at him. "That's very observant of you."

He grinned sadly. "Didn't think I was capable of deep thought?"

She flushed. "No, it's not that. It's just that . . . everything in Hollywood is so . . . unreal. That's how I feel whenever I'm out there."

CJ looked right at her, his expression intense and curious. "Is that how you felt last June?"

"I wish you wouldn't bring that up. I want to forget it ever happened."

"Do you?" he asked earnestly. "I don't." CJ reached across the table and carefully took her hand. "I think about it a lot."

"Don't, CJ . . ."

"Gena, what do I have to do to convince you I'm not running a line on you? Can't you tell I'm serious?"

"Maybe you think you are. But you still belong to my sister."

CJ squeezed her hand tightly, causing Gena's eyes to widen as she watched a frown spread across his strong male features.

"I don't belong to anyone. I'm Renee's business manager. I watch out for her and take care of details. I'm the advance scout and the cleanup man. But I'm not her companion . . . or her lover. Never have been," he finished in a low growling voice.

Gena pulled her hand free. "You treat Renee like she's totally helpless."

"Doesn't everybody? Don't you? Look how much you've conceded so that Renee can be who she is. You've raised her daughter like she was your own. You told me last year that you liked being an editor for that magazine in New York. But you gave it up so you could be with Shay more." CJ leaned across the table to stare into her eyes. "How's *your* love life?"

"CJ . . ."

"Mine is lousy. Look, I didn't start out to manage *anyone.* I was doing a favor for the producer of Renee's first film, because I was one of the few black people he knew in Hollywood at the time. I was managing black stunt crews when Renee was turned over to me. I haven't done so badly by her. She hasn't done so badly by me. I've made a lot of money, and I have a reputation that people trust. Except that it drove my wife away out of jealousy. And now I don't see my son as much as he or I want."

Gena was surprised by CJ's confession, and mesmerized by the insights she was suddenly gaining about him. There'd been no time for that the previous June.

"So why don't you do something about it?"

"I will. I am." He took her hand again. "But I want to do something about you and me, too."

She was shaking her head.

"I don't understand what happened last year, Gena. We were having a good time. I thought you were so beautiful. When we were together . . ."

Gena felt like she couldn't catch her breath. "Renee saw too much. She told me she needed you. She told me . . . men in Hollywood were used to affairs. You were nice to me . . . but it didn't mean anything. And I was leaving to come back to New York."

"Why didn't you ask *me?*" he frowned at her. "I could have told you I don't do affairs . . . like I don't do lunch because they're a waste of time."

"It doesn't matter. That was last year. I had to

come back home to my life with Shay. Yours is clearly in LA with Renee."

"Gena, give me a chance . . ." CJ said in a low sexy tone.

She was moved in spite of herself. She was tempted. She realized that it certainly would be a lot easier for CJ to get involved with someone more ready, willing, and available than she was. She had given them both a chance on her last visit out west. But it wasn't her playing field, as Renee had suggested. There certainly was no question that in Hollywood CJ had more choices than she did. But he wanted her, as he'd made perfectly obvious. She wouldn't tear her gaze away, remembering . . . *remembering* . . . that afternoon and evening with him.

After they'd returned to Renee's house from Disneyland with Shay. After Shay had gone to sleep, exhausted but happy. After romantic music from the stereo and wine drunk around the pool. She remembered an incredible sense of well-being and care. Of what love could be like.

Of passion in CJ's arms.

Gena sighed and lowered her gaze. "Nothing has changed. We both still have responsibilities."

"But you haven't said you're not interested. You haven't said you don't feel the same thing I do."

She shook her head again, this time in confusion. "CJ, I don't . . . I . . . I don't know how I feel."

"Fine. Fine. That's better than turning me down cold."

There was a tapping on the glass, and they both looked up to find Shay at the window trying to get their attention. Her young companion was still at her side.

CJ looked at his watch. "We'd better go. Otherwise Renee will pout," he said dryly.

Gena sighed deeply, relieved at the break in the intensity between them. But at the same time sorry that they had to end their private conversation. She gathered her things and Shay's coat. CJ indicated to Shay that they would meet her by the rental booth. He paid the bill, and he and Gena started for the elevator that would take them to the street level.

They were silent as they boarded the elevator with two other chatty couples, tourists from all appearances. The visitors got off first. Suddenly CJ grabbed Gena's arm, preventing her from getting off. She turned a questioning gaze to him, but CJ was coaxing her toward him until she was in his arms, and his mouth had descended to cover hers.

Gena was too stunned to protest, and CJ was too quick for her in any case. Pure surprise kept her still and unresponsive, but that only lasted a moment. The memory came back again. Her eyes drifted closed, and she let her body go limp against CJ, as if he'd found the key to her resistance. As if she couldn't pretend any longer. As if she'd been waiting for this.

CJ coaxed her mouth open, and the gentle assault of his warm tongue was like an electric shock to

Gena's system. She felt like she was sinking into an abyss.

The memory . . .

It had been wonderful between them before. Nothing, apparently, had changed, and Gena felt fearful and astonished at the realization. CJ knew how to hold her, where to place his hands. He knew when to be tender . . . and when to be aggressive. He had not forgotten a *thing* from the previous June. And she was remembering . . . all over again.

CJ slowly ended the kiss, drawing it out with excruciating expertise. He kissed just her lips once more briefly while his large hands held the side of her face.

And then CJ said the words that made all the difference, the words which closed the distance between fantasy and possibility.

"Gena . . . I remember *everything*," CJ whispered against her parted lips.

Gena closed her bedroom door and leaned back against it. Immediately her gaze sought out the flowered treasure box, retrieved from the living room bookshelf just that morning. There'd been no time to examine it earlier. She'd been thinking about it all day, agonizing over whether or not Renee had found it and looked inside. Wondering if *she* wanted to open it now. But CJ had answered that question for her that afternoon. She could still feel the pressure of his lips moving on her own. Now Gena was consumed with curiosity of another kind. She suddenly wanted to know what it was CJ had been trying to tell her since last June.

They'd stood staring into each other's eyes, until the elevator doors had opened again and there was another group of people waiting to get on. Embarrassed, Gena had sprung away from CJ, but he was in no hurry and didn't seem to care what the strangers thought might have been going on between them.

The rest of the afternoon had been anticlimatic, and Gena had been unable to meet CJ's gaze again. Afraid that he would once again see beyond her eyes . . . or that she would give away too much before she was ready.

Gena sat on the side of her bed and rested the box on her lap. Abruptly she flipped the top open and stared inside. Everything was there in place, exactly as she'd left it. She felt relief. She drew her legs up onto the bed and settled back against the pillows. She picked up the first of the three letters that CJ had written her between June and November of the previous year. Slowly, carefully . . . and with particular attention to details and tone . . . Gena read each one in turn for the first time. The first letter propelled her back to that summer visit, outlining in detail that day together . . . that night. The second one made Gena feel doubt and regret about her decision to try and wipe the memory from existence because of what her sister had told her. But the third letter, filled with the most open sincerity and desire, with plans and dreams and even fear, made her cry.

Chapter Three

When Renee came downstairs to the kitchen on Monday morning, she found her daughter at the table eating cereal and reading a book.

"Hi, baby," Renee murmured a greeting in a voice still thick with sleep. "What are you doing up so early?"

Shay put her book down, perking up a bit. She turned a bright gaze on her mother. "Waiting for you. Besides, it's not that early. It's almost nine-thirty."

Renee shook her head and sighed. "That's what I mean," she said dryly, heading to the counter to pour herself coffee. "Gena's already gone?"

Shay giggled. "She's already at work. I've been up since seven. That's the time I get up to go to school."

"Hummm," Renee uttered distractedly. She turned from the counter with a mug in hand, stirring sugar into the black brew. She came over to the kitchen table and sat adjacent to Shay, frowning at the book in front of the young girl. "What are you reading?"

"*The Bluest Eye* by Toni Morrison."

"What's it about?" Renee yawned, picking up the book to squint at the cover.

"It's about this little girl who's abused and wishes she was white so that bad things wouldn't happen to her. Then she goes crazy."

Renee was appalled. "You shouldn't be reading stuff like that. You're just a kid."

Shay shrugged. "So's the girl in the book. I feel so sorry for her. It's a good story, but very sad."

"Then, why are you reading it?"

"I have to do a book report. I have to first write a synopsis of the story. You know . . . like an outline?"

Renee nodded vaguely. "Synopsis . . ."

"And then I have to write what I think about the story and if I learned anything from the characters."

"Well, it certainly is depressing."

Shay made a childish face of astonishment. "You should read this other book she wrote called *Beloved*, about this woman who kills her baby so she won't grow up to be a slave."

"When I was your age, I was still reading children's books," Renee chuckled, blowing on her coffee to cool it.

"But I'm in an advanced reading class."

Renee finally turned her full attention on Shay and smiled with pleasure at her. "Gena said you're very smart. She said that you wanted to be an astronaut. An *astronaut!* Why?"

"I want to learn how to fly, first. Do you know

there's this black woman in the navy who flies planes from an aircraft carrier? That is *so* great!"

Renee's gaze softened maternally, and she reached out to caress her daughter's cheek. "You're going to grow up to be a beautiful young woman, you know that? I'm glad you're doing well in school. Gena said the school wanted to skip you past the rest of seventh grade. Then, you're practically a high school freshman. You *are* too young for that."

"The work is a lot harder," Shay acknowledged with a grimace and sigh.

"An astronaut," Renee murmured with a bemused shake of her head. "Just don't be an actress. It's a tough life."

"But you're an actress," Shay pointed out to her mother.

"It was the only thing I was good at," Renee said reflectively. "And . . . it was a way out of the mess I . . . well . . . never mind." She smiled lovingly at Shay and stroked her daughter's hair. "You just make sure you finish school, and always take care of yourself. And don't let anybody try to make you do anything you don't want to. And don't worry about boys until you're much older. Like twenty or something."

Shay became bashful and used her spoon to play with the rest of the cereal in the bottom of her bowl. She was rocking her leg back and forth beneath the table, and the motion caused her body to bob up and down. "You mean, don't let them fool around with me?"

Renee raised her brows in shock, and then frowned. "Do you know what fooling around is?"

"Sure. Aunt Gena told me."

"Now, why would she do a thing like that? I tell you, you're too young to even be thinking about that."

Shay remained silent for a moment, refusing to look directly at her mother. "No I'm not," she finally said quietly. "I know girls in school who got in trouble that way."

Shay lifted her gaze to look searchingly at her mother, and Renee stared back, wondering how much her daughter really knew. She got up from the table to refill her coffee mug. She took Shay's empty bowl and put it in the sink.

"I got in trouble that way. You know that, don't you?"

"Yes," Shay said, almost inaudible.

Renee turned around, and the expression on her face was sad and regretful. "I was a lot older than you, and *I* didn't know any better. Or maybe I just didn't want to. I was hardheaded. Do you ever wonder about your . . . father?"

There was a long silence. Shay leafed idly through the pages of the thin paperback book she'd been reading. "Sometimes." The voice was still very soft and quiet. "Not too much."

"He was a nice boy, Shay. We were just too young and stupid. He wasn't even around when you were born. I don't even know where he is now."

Shay looked over her shoulder at her mother. Her eyes were bright and thoughtful, but didn't hold any particular emotion.

"How come you left me when you went to California?"

Renee fidgeted and absently tried to push her flattened hair into some order with her hand. "Your grandmother thought it was best. I was very young, and I had this incredible chance to be in a film. I had no idea what I'd do with a baby while I was working."

"Day care," Shay answered with prim logic.

Renee took a deep breath. "Sharon Lee, it wasn't that simple," she said with some asperity. "There are still a lot of things you *don't* know about or understand."

"I thought you didn't want me," Shay whispered, her round dark eyes poignant with sudden longing.

"Oh, baby, *no*. That wasn't it at all." Renee came back to the girl and put her arms around her, hugging her tightly against her.

Shay shyly returned the embrace, her cheek resting on her mother's breast.

"But I was so scared. I didn't know about taking care of babies."

"Is that why Aunt Gena raised me?"

"That's right. And your grandmother, until she died. Are you mad at me for what I did?" Renee asked in a small worried tone.

"No. I don't think so. I just wished we could all be together. You, me, and Aunt Gena."

"You call her Mommy," Renee observed flatly.

"I know. But she is, in a way," Shay murmured uncomfortably. "She takes care of me like a mommy."

"Well, I don't want you to forget that *I'm* your mother. I know we don't live together, but there are lots of kids who go to boarding school who don't see their parents all the time."

"I know . . ."

"You know I love you, baby," Renee said, kissing the top of Shay's head and taking her seat again. "I tell you this . . . if I had it to do over again, I certainly wouldn't get pregnant," Renee chuckled nervously.

Shay absently traced a design on the tabletop with her finger. She peered at her mother. "What are we going to do today?" she asked, effectively putting an end to the subject of her origins. And what might have been.

Renee sighed in unconscious relief. "I don't know. What would you like to do?"

"Could you help me with my homework?"

Renee hesitated. "Like what?"

"Math. But I can do that. I have to quantify some values in algebra."

"Quantify?"

"That means I have to measure."

"Umm humm . . ."

"And then I have to read the next chapter in my

book on the Serengeti. That's in Africa. Then I have to draw and label all the organs in a frog. That's for science . . ."

"Forget that," Renee said emphatically. "I'm not looking at any frogs. Dead, on paper, or otherwise."

"That's okay. Aunt Gena can help me tonight after dinner."

"She's good at this, huh?"

"Not all the time, but she talks to my teachers about my work."

"I've been out of school a long time . . ."

"We could go to the Newark Museum."

Renee wrinkled her nose. "Not today, baby. Gena leave the car?"

"I think so."

"Good. Then, let's go shopping."

"But we went shopping on Saturday," Shay responded indifferently.

"Well, let's go shopping anyway. I'm tired of being in the house. We'll buy something for Gena. And maybe CJ, too."

Shay thought for a long moment, considering the options. "Okay," she reluctantly conceded with a sigh.

"I don't feel so good," Shay groaned, hugging herself around the middle and trying to draw her legs up. She was restricted by the car's seat belt.

"What's wrong?"

"My stomach hurts."

"Maybe it was something you ate," Renee offered with mild concern. "We'll be home soon. You know, I thought those hamburgers tasted a little gamey."

Shay whimpered softly and closed her eyes, her small face distorted with her discomfort. "I don't think it's . . . it's the hamburgers. It's something else."

Renee frowned, shifting her attention briefly from her driving to her daughter. "Are you in pain? I sure hope it's not your appendix."

Shay moaned. "Are we almost home yet?"

"Almost. Just a few more miles."

Her daughter's continued sounds of distress unnerved Renee. She abruptly pulled the car into the driveway, tires screeching as she slammed on the brakes. She turned a worried expression to Shay, who was still bent over, resting her forehead against her knees. Renee shook Shay gently by the arm.

"You're not going to be sick, are you?"

"I don't know . . ."

"Come on. Let's get into the house," Renee said, climbing out of the car.

Shay slowly followed suit, and when she stood up Renee gasped.

"Oh, my God. There's blood all over you. When did you hurt yourself?"

Shay turned around swiftly at the sound of dismay in her mother's tone. She saw the blood smeared on the vinyl car seat. She bent further to see it stained dark against the back of her jeans. Shay burst into tears of confusion and fright and ran toward the house.

"Sharon Lee, wait! Wait for me," Renee called after the fleeing child.

When Renee reached the house, she could hear the upstairs bathroom door being slammed shut.

"Shay?" she called up the stairs but got no answer.

Renee hurried up the stairs, dropping her purse and keys and calling out her daughter's name.

"It's all right, baby. I'm coming . . . open the door." Renee knocked softly and turned the doorknob. She slowly pushed open the door, sticking her head around the panel and peering into the bathroom.

Shay stood with her jeans down around her ankles, crying as she used a wad of facial tissues to wipe the blood from the inside of her thighs.

"Oh, my poor baby . . ." Renee said sympathetically. "You're not hurt. You know what this is?"

"Y . . . yes," Shay whimpered, her face wet with tears.

"Here . . . let me help you. Lord, you scared me, girl," Renee said on a long sigh. She scooped up the soiled jeans, holding them gingerly. "You knew this was coming. You're the right age. Clean yourself up. I sure hope Gena has some . . ." She searched through the bathroom cabinet and under the sink. "Oh, here it is." She took out a small box and sat it on the edge of the sink. "You go on and finish up here. I'm going to soak these pants in some cold water before the stain sets in."

Shay turned panic-stricken eyes to Renee. "Mommy, aren't you going to help me?"

"Sweetie, there's nothing for me to do. See, there's a picture on the side of the box, and it tells you everything. I'll be downstairs when you're finished, okay?"

"I don't feel good," Shay repeated sorrowfully.

"I'll make you some tea. Hurry up, now," Renee said as she closed the door and left Shay alone.

Renee made her way to the basement laundry room, where she filled the deep sink with water and attempted to slosh out much of the damage to the jeans. Then she threw them, still wet, into the washer and began a cycle. Back in the kitchen she put on water for the hot tea she'd promised her daughter, and looked around for something a little bit stronger for herself. There was nothing but a half-filled bottle of wine, and she grimaced at how long Gena might have had it in the refrigerator. *Probably since Paul,* she guessed, but poured herself a glass anyway.

Then Renee picked up the phone and tried to call CJ.

He was not at the hotel, so she tried paging him. Five minutes later he called her back.

"Oh, thank God I reached you," Renee got out.

"What's wrong?" CJ asked crisply, alert to the sound of stress in his client.

"Oh . . . Shay started her female thing today, and it was quite a mess . . ."

"How is she?" CJ asked, his concern not abating.

"She's fine. It kind of caught her off guard."

"Did you talk to her?"

Renee made an impatient sound. "What was I supposed to say? No one ever told me anything except I had to deal with it once a month."

CJ made his own impatient sound. "Stay with her, Renee. She's going to be confused."

"Shay knows what this is all about. She said so . . ." Renee turned around at the sound of someone in the living room entrance, and found Shay shyly standing in the door. She wore a fresh pair of slacks, and kept her gaze down. "Here she is now."

"Well, tell her what she needs to know."

"Oh, CJ . . . anything I say will probably scare the child to death."

Shay gasped and stared at her mother with a pained expression. "Is that CJ?" she asked on a high thin note.

"Yes. I was just . . ."

"Why did you tell him! Why did you tell him?" Shay wailed. She turned and fled back up the stairs, crying anew.

"Sharon Lee . . . CJ, I gotta go," Renee said swiftly and hung up the phone. She got up and stood at the base of the stairwell, calling her daughter's name. "Shay, it's all right. It was only CJ."

Renee heard the bedroom door slam, and this time Shay locked herself in.

* * *

"Renee? I want to talk to you," Gena said, knocking on her sister's bedroom door. She entered without waiting for a response.

Renee was comfortably ensconced on the queen-size four-poster bed, dressed in another of her endless supply of beautiful silk nightgowns. She was simultaneously watching the color portable TV and reading through a number of film scripts FedExed just that evening from her West Coast agent.

The space had been taken over. Evidence of Renee's excessive lifestyle had changed the formerly neat but functional bedroom that had once belonged to their mother into more of a boudoir.

Renee sighed and slanted a suspicious glance at her sister. "If this is about Sharon Lee . . ."

"You could have been a little more understanding with her."

"Yeah, I guess so, but it happened so fast. When Shay said she didn't feel well, I thought something else was wrong. I thought maybe it was something she ate."

Gena came and stood at the foot of the four-poster. She stared at her sister, seeing the soft transition of emotions cross her pretty brown face. Renee raised her brows and looked plaintive. She curved her mouth and seemed confused. She shook her head and was regretful. As Gena continued to watch the changes, she suddenly couldn't tell if Renee was genuinely contrite . . . or just covering herself very well with the body language of an actress.

"Shay understands what's happening. She just needed a reminder that it was time for this to happen to *her.* She just needed a little comforting. And why in heaven's name did you have to call CJ? Don't you realize how that embarrassed her?"

"Look, why is everybody dumping on me? Okay, so I didn't handle it well. I'm sorry. I'll make it up to her." Renee sighed and rubbed her temple wearily. "It probably would have been better for me to stay in the city."

"No," Gena said quietly. "It would have been better if you could just focus on Shay for a while and not yourself. She wants so badly to know that she's important to you, Renee. And you keep forgetting that *she's* the child, not you."

Renee drew back and suddenly reminded Gena of the feisty adolescent she once was. "Look, don't talk to me that way. I'm doing the best I can. When I tried to talk to her after dinner, Shay told me she was okay. So what else was I supposed to do?" Renee asked with an impertinent waggle of her head.

"Tell her that you love her," Gena responded at once. "Tell her this is part of life and not to be afraid of it."

Renee was silent for a long moment as she continued to leaf idly through a script. Finally she looked up. "You're right," she conceded quietly. "I guess I blew it again."

Gena grimaced. "Renee, I'm not trying to *blame* you. I'm only suggesting you pay a little more attention to what Sharon Lee needs. I know you love her. I don't doubt that for a single moment. But you have to show it in more ways than buying her things. Spend more time with her instead of spending money on her."

Renee frowned. "Is she mad at me?"

"No. For some reason she thinks you're mad at *her*."

"That's crazy," Renee murmured impatiently as she climbed out of the bed and pulled on the white terry cloth robe. "Let me go and talk to her. I'll tell her this isn't such a big deal . . . she only has to worry about it once a month, for heaven's sake."

Gena shook her head and sighed, not happy with her sister's cavalier attitude, but reluctant to interfere in Renee's efforts to communicate with her daughter. She returned to her own room to prepare for bed. Only now was she beginning to decompress after the events of the afternoon and evening. She had been scared out of her mind when she'd gotten the phone call from Shay, crying nearly hysterically, asking Gena to come home.

Gena hadn't even bothered to ask what was wrong. She'd simply made a hasty and breathless apology to her supervisor, claiming a family emergency, and left her office. She'd found Renee defensive and anxious, and Shay quiet and withdrawn and still hiding in her bedroom. It had taken Gena the whole evening to worm out of her niece what had happened between her and her mother.

Gena heard Renee return to her room but still she sat, feeling exhausted and uncertain. She wasn't sure what she could say to Shay, either. Gena recalled that when she was thirteen and her passage into adolescence had begun, she'd been a little better prepared, courtesy of her old girl scout troop, a couple of relevant films and brochures . . . and a lot of giggly and boastful conversations with girlfriends. She had tried to warn Shay in the same way . . . gently, but not too forcefully. After all, she didn't want to scare the child. She wanted so much to let Shay know that this change was nothing to be afraid of.

And she wanted to hint to her niece that some aspects and consequences of growing up could be wonderful under the right circumstances . . . with the right person. But Gena considered Renee's feelings, and recalled how anxious her sister had been when she'd arrived home. Perhaps now was not the right time to fix things, as it would leave Renee with little to say to her own child.

After a time Gena went down the hall to the small room that Sharon Lee Saxon had occupied all her life. She found the young girl in bed hugging a teddy bear, and listening to music through the headphones of her portable CD player. Gena sat down on the side of the bed, and Shay looked poignantly at her. Gena tried smiling at her.

She slipped the headphones from her niece's ears and hung them around Shay's neck. The distorted audio of the music sounded like aliens screaming from the circular speakers. Shay turned it off.

"How you feeling?" Gena asked, gently pinching Shay's cheek.

"Okay."

"Anything you want to talk about?"

"No."

"Anything you want to ask me?"

"Not right now," Shay murmured with a slight shake of her head. She absently picked at the fuzzy material of her stuffed animal.

"Then, there's something I want to tell you," Gena began as Shay looked shyly at her through the fringes of her dark lashes. "I know everyone tells you that this means you're a woman now. Well, you're not. You're still just twelve years old, and you should enjoy being twelve. Don't think you have to act like you're almost twenty. This simply means you're growing up, sweetie. Your body is changing like it's supposed to do. It happened to Grandma, and me, and your mother. This isn't unusual, but it is special. It means you're preparing to become a grown-up . . . but you aren't one yet. So I don't want you to be afraid. Everything that is happening to you is perfectly normal. Okay?"

Shay didn't meet her aunt's gaze, but she nodded. "Okay," she whispered quietly. "I guess I'd better tell my mother I'm okay. I'm not mad at her, you know."

"I know."

Shay shrugged. "She's just not used to dealing with kids and their problems, I guess."

Gena blinked at her niece, amazed at the depth of her perception. She thought it best not to respond to Shay's insight. Instead she folded the child into her arms and just gave her a quiet loving hug.

"Hello?"

"Did I wake you?"

Gena snuggled down further into the bed. Her stomach tightened at the unexpected sound of CJ's deep voice. She wondered if he, too, was in bed. "No. I was just languishing."

"Languishing," he drawled. "Sounds nice. What happens when you languish?" CJ asked.

Gena knew he wasn't trying to be funny. She turned on her side and cradled the phone between her ear and the pillow. Her body sank into the warm bedding as Gena imagined another possibility. She sighed.

"You lie awake thinking too much. You plan and make lists and pretend."

"Anything I should know about?"

"I . . . I don't think so."

"Are you sure?" CJ asked softly.

His question and tone of voice stroked Gena's imagination. But she squeezed her eyes tightly shut and kept her voice steady. "Why are you calling? It's late."

"I wanted to make sure Shay was okay. I got a call from Renee this afternoon . . ."

Gena sucked her teeth. "Did she tell you what happened?"

"I think Renee thought it was worse than it was. She thought maybe Sharon Lee had somehow hurt herself. It threw her off. Renee's not good in a crisis."

"Shay is not a crisis. Shay is her daughter. Renee shouldn't be forgetting that."

"Gena," CJ said patiently. "I'm on your side. I know what the deal is. I told Renee that instead of going off she should try and remember that Shay needs her help right now. This is a big moment in her life."

Gena let out a deep breath. "I'm sorry, CJ. It's funny that you understand better than Renee does. I didn't mean to tear into you like that."

CJ chuckled. "I'm used to it."

"Is that what I've been doing? I don't want that to happen, either."

"Good," he said complacently. "Now we're getting somewhere."

Chapter Four

Gena kept her attention focused on the stage. She pretended an interest in the proceedings so that no one around her would think she wasn't enjoying the evening. She had to admit, however, that she was impressed. Most of what was happening tonight was for Renee. Gena glanced around the room, where a thick hum of conversation filled the air in between presentations, accolades, and jokes from the Master and Mistress of Ceremonies. Nevertheless she felt oddly disconnected from everything that was happening.

The banquet room of the Plaza Hotel provided a grand environment for celebration, and the hundreds of people in attendance for the dinner and awards ceremony were dressed and turned out as if they were in the presence of royalty. They were. Hollywood royalty. New Jersey royalty. The commoner who'd captured the golden ring, and was made a queen. Gena looked at her sister across the span of their dinner table. Tonight, Renee Saxon was at her best.

She was dressed in a startling red gown that was cut straight, from the square neckline to the hem. The small puff sleeves of the dress were studded with rhinestones to match the sparkle of the shoes she wore. The dress was simple but elegant, and stood out from the overdesigned garments of the other women at the affair. It was an outfit that was carefully planned to showcase her physical attributes, while giving the appearance of modesty.

Gena looked at her niece sitting demurely next to her mother. For the past day and a half, Shay had behaved as if the changes she had undergone had somehow cut her off from the little girl she had been, as if she was now required to act a certain way. She was careful and quiet, not wanting to draw attention to herself, yet accepting her new situation.

The night before Renee had called her daughter from her new home base at the Plaza Hotel. She and Shay had been on the phone for an hour. From the living room Gena had listened to giggles and laughter, fussing and exclamations, pleading questions and surprises between mother and daughter. Somehow Renee had managed to find a way to reach out to Shay as sometimes only a mother can. Or maybe Shay had made it easy by being forgiving, as only a child can.

Shay was dressed in a pale yellow dress that seemed to add two years of maturity to her still flat girlish figure. Her hair had been twisted into a knot and adorned with feathery hair combs from her mother's arsenal of accessories. Renee had also presented her daughter with a pair of small diamond ear studs to wear with her outfit. Gena had thought the earrings much too sophisticated for her niece, but had remained silent, given Shay's obvious delight with the grown-up gift.

Finally Gena let her gaze shift to CJ, who was seated on the other side of Renee, whispering instructions and information. Gena felt a catch in her throat as she covertly watched him. He was formally dressed for the evening. From the moment she and Shay had arrived by limo from New Jersey, Gena had been captivated by how handsome and in command he appeared in a tuxedo. He had navigated them through a maze of security and press that reminded Gena of the arrival at the airport earlier in the week, and her visit to California the year before. CJ had been at the limo door when it pulled up in front of the hotel to help her and Shay out. And he had held her hand and gazed into her eyes with a kind of intensity that was not hard to interpret. He had whispered in her ear. "I've been waiting a long time for this moment to happen again."

Again . . .

Remember . . .

CJ turned his head and caught her gaze on him. Gena was mesmerized, vulnerable, and afraid. Yet she couldn't look away. Because for the first time in a very long time, she was allowing herself to daydream again.

The dinner plates had been cleared away, although Shay had been the only one to eat with the hearty appetite of the young. The lights slowly dimmed in the great room, and conversation automatically faded away into an expectant silence. Spotlights went on, and there was polite applause as the emcees again took their places at the podium for the final round of award presentations.

In the dark Renee held her daughter's hand tightly on one side, and CJ's on the other. Gena watched her sister's moment of glory, felt familial honor and sisterly pride. She saw Shay's barely contained joy and excitement. From across the table Gena watched . . . and her entire world began to change.

A long and glowing lead-in was given as to the purpose of the award. The recipient's professional credentials and background were highlighted. Then, with appropriate awe and deference, Renee Saxon's name was announced. Enthusiastic applause and a standing ovation followed.

Renee stood up slowly as the light searched her out and focused on her. She smiled with grace and charm into the sea of admirers beyond the bright light. She nodded and stood for just a moment before turning to CJ to kiss him briefly, and to receive an affectionate hug from Shay. And then Renee carefully made her way to the stage, escorted by an attendant who helped her up the short flight of steps. Alone, Renee regally approached the presenters to receive a Steuben crystal bowl and a gilded-framed certificate of proclamation, signed by the Mayor of the City of New York.

"You folks sure know how to party," Renee joked in home-girl fashion. She got appreciative laughter in response. And then her voice changed. "Thank you." Renee smiled now with sincere gratitude and pleasure. "I can't begin to tell you how deeply honored I am to receive this award. But honestly, you give me much more credit than I deserve."

CJ and Shay exchanged quick looks.

"That's not in her speech," Shay said in a stage whisper.

Gena caught the anxious surprise in her niece's voice, and turned to CJ to see his reaction. He, too, appeared taken aback.

"All of your past recipients have really done important things for the black community. They have saved lives, made improvements, given money, and developed programs. The difference can be seen and quantified." She chuckled with a demure shake of her head. "I just learned that word this week . . ."

There was more delighted laughter.

"All I do is pretend to be other people. What I do is fantasy and make-believe and is too easy to be seen as being important. But I am *really* happy that what I do might, in some way, give you pleasure or a few hours of entertainment."

The room was dead silent, and Gena felt her heart pounding in her chest. She had never heard her sister speak so seriously before and wondered why she'd chosen this moment in front of a large audience to become introspective. She stole a glance at CJ, and even in the dark Gena could make out the flexing of his jaw muscles as he waited through the rest of Renee's acceptance speech.

"What I have learned is that our families are truly important. And the way we love and treat each other . . ."

There was scattered applause.

"I would not be where I am this moment without the support of my family. It would not have been possible for me to be here tonight to accept this award, if my family had not been understanding and patient and believed in me . . . and made sacrifices for me."

Renee's eyes unerringly searched out her table, past the bright light shining on her. She smiled as if she really could see Gena and Shay, and held out her hand.

"It's only fair now that *my* family share in this award. Gena . . . Sharon Lee . . ."

A murmur of surprise rippled through the crowd, and then the applause started again. The spotlight shifted to the table just in front of the stage and podium. Shay turned a bewildered and apprehensive face to Gena. But Gena quickly stood up and reached for her niece's hand. There was absolutely no time to think about anything else except moving onto the stage to stand with her sister.

CJ grabbed her other hand, and Gena held on

tightly as if her life depended on him. He carefully led her and Shay toward the stage in the dark as the applause continued. Just before she began the climb to the stage, CJ detained her for the briefest second, placing a hand briefly on her back and leaning to whisper to her.

"It's okay. I'll be waiting right here for you."

Gena had no idea what he meant. In any case the remark was quickly wiped from her mind as she and Shay found themselves in the overpowering light of attention, standing next to Renee. The applause died down. Renee looked at Gena.

"This is my big sister, Gena, who encouraged me when I was just seventeen years old and made it possible for me to go to LA to make my first film." She turned to Shay, who stood shyly behind her. Renee urged the little girl forward. "And this is Sharon Lee Saxon. My greatest accomplishment . . . my daughter. We call her Shay . . ."

Gena's stomach roiled as a collective gasp whispered across the room, and the applause began yet again. It went on and on. Gena stood with a fixed smile on her lips. Shay and Renee awkwardly tried to hug one another while Renee held her awards. Flashbulbs suddenly started to go off. Several people appeared near the front of the stage with video cameras.

For just a second Gena thought of discreetly backing away and leaving the moment to Renee and Shay. But the light followed her, and she stopped moving. Instead she too began to applaud her sister and niece. For despite everything, it was a triumphant moment for them both. They had discovered one another. They had finally become mother and daughter. Renee had managed in one dramatic moment to reunite the family, and bring them all . . . in a sense . . . home.

With Shay and her sister following behind, Gena headed offstage left. CJ was waiting for her, just as he'd promised. And for that instant Gena didn't care who CJ was supposed to protect, or who he worked for, or what his own motives might be. He had eyes only for her, eyes filled with compassion. And CJ's gaze had all of the signs of something else Gena had noticed the summer before, but had denied herself . . . the possibility of love.

"We're going to be interviewed together," Shay said with a childlike dignity that disguised her real happiness at the turn of events.

They were lounging in the large living room of Renee's hotel suite. The two awards were on the glass-topped coffee table along with other evidence of the evening's ceremonies that Shay had collected as souvenirs. Renee was sitting on the end of the sofa with her shoes kicked off, and Shay sat on the sofa arm next to her.

Gena, walking aimlessly about the room, then stopped to kiss her niece's cheek and gave her a quick hug. "That's going to be so exciting. Are you nervous?"

Shay glanced at her mother as she answered. "Just a little bit, but Mommy said she'd show me what I should do."

"And CJ will make sure the studio people don't get crazy, right CJ?"

"Right," CJ nodded agreeably as he stood next to Gena and glanced down at her. His gaze took in the slightly pinched wide-eyed expression on her face. "They asked to have you on, too."

Gena shook her head. "Forget it. No one's going to be interested in me. And I have to go to work," Gena said in a light tone.

Renee chuckled dryly. "Honey, don't believe for a moment this won't be work. There's going to be a lot of questions about you and Shay and how come I never talked about my daughter before."

"So what are you going to tell the press?" Gena asked curiously.

"The truth," Renee said without hesitation. "Straightforward and simple. This is my baby . . ." she crooned as she pressed her cheek against her daughter's. "I was very young when she was born, but I want people to know that I'm not ashamed of that."

"And now everybody will know I have a real mother, too," Shay said ingeniously.

The smile never wavered from Gena's face, even as a sudden flow of heat seemed to pour over her. She felt CJ's hand on her back as a prickling of tears gathered behind her eyes. He stood close enough to her that no one else noticed his gesture of empathy, but Gena knew he was aware of the erect stiffness with which she held her body.

"You sure know how to grab people's attention . . ."

"Gen, I'm sorry I didn't tell you beforehand what I was going to do, but I knew you wouldn't agree to come onstage if I had. And don't blame CJ, 'cause he had no idea, either."

"I was a little scared to go up there, but it wasn't so bad," Shay giggled, unaware of the adult dynamics around her.

"Does that mean you've changed your mind and you want to be an actress?"

Shay grimaced and shook her head. She played with her mother's earring. "No, I don't think so. I'd rather go in space than in front of a crowd of people."

Gena held out her hand. "Come on, hon. Let's go to our room. I think everyone's tired . . ."

"I thought Shay could stay here with me tonight," Renee announced smoothly.

Gena looked back and forth between her sister and niece. "But . . . we have to get up early. The limo is going to drop me off at work in the morning and drive her on to school."

"Shay has the interview with me in the morning on some of the network locals. Three, as a matter of fact. CJ set it up after a couple of journalists in the audience started asking so many questions."

Gena turned an accusing look on CJ, but he met her glare with steadfast and clear purpose.

"It's time, Gena. There are going to be a lot of questions to answer after tonight. I didn't know beforehand that Renee was going to make that announcement. But now I have to do something about it."

"I can miss school for one more day. I got my book report done, and I passed the math quiz the other day."

Shay made a pleading face at her aunt, with the kind of guile and sweetness that had gotten her her own way for much of the week. The move reminded Gena so much of Renee that she felt not so much defeated as just outnumbered and maneuvered. Silently Gena reached into her evening purse for the flat electronic key to the hotel room assigned to her and Shay. She held it out to the young girl.

"Why don't you go down the hall to the room and get your things. Be careful, and hurry back."

"I will," Shay exclaimed. She grabbed the key and hurried out the door.

As soon as the door closed behind her, Gena turned to her sister.

"I don't think I would have used tonight to make such a grand announcement to the world, but it had to be done. I just hope, Renee, that this wasn't all a publicity stunt. I hope this wasn't about damage control."

"I meant what I said up there tonight," Renee said, wounded by Gena's suggestion.

"I agree with Gena," CJ said, standing with his hands in the pockets of his dress slacks, his deep voice thoughtful. "You might have warned us. There was probably a better way to handle this."

"Gena would *never* have agreed, and she knows it," Renee shrugged. "It was easier to get it out to a whole lot of people instead of a few at a time. Then, it's just like gossip. This way, *I* said so, and it's done with."

There was a certain skewed logic that Gena knew she couldn't argue with, and she wasn't going to. She could feel CJ's attention focused on her and knew he felt the same way. She took a deep breath and stood with her arms folded over her chest. It was the only way to steady the tension coiling within her and to control the tremors.

"So you've acknowledged Sharon Lee as your child. You've accepted the responsibility and apparently made peace with her. What about her?"

"What do you mean, what about her? I'm her mother!"

CJ shook his head. "We know that. But on Friday night you fly back to LA. What about Shay?"

Renee made an impatient gesture and got up from the sofa. The grace and thoughtfulness she'd displayed earlier in the evening was now replaced with willfulness. "I know this is what Shay wanted. Don't you see how happy she is?"

"She's happy right now. Tonight. But what about when you have to leave, Renee? Have you thought at all about what happens to her then?" Gena asked reasonably.

Renee looked from her sister to CJ. They weren't going to let her get away with not answering. She squared back her shoulders and nodded as she took a deep breath.

"I've already talked to her. I told her if she wanted to she could come home with me to LA . . ."

"The child's home is here, Renee," CJ objected quietly.

"What did she say?" Gena asked, her voice so soft and strained that the words seemed forced out of her.

Renee turned to her sister with that same posture, that same look of determination she'd used her whole life to charm and persuade . . . and then get her way.

"She said yes."

Gena let herself be led, and then stopped obediently in front of the door for which CJ produced a key. She blinked out of her lethargy and frowned at him.

"This isn't my room."

"I know that," CJ murmured, opening the door and swinging it wide before Gena.

She stood her ground and stared stubbornly straight ahead. "I'm not going in." Gena pivoted sharply, but before she could take a single step, CJ took hold of her arms and forced her to face him.

"Just kick that thought to the curb, Gena," he said uncompromisingly. He pulled on her arms, and she stared wide-eyed at him. "This isn't about trying to play you. I just don't think you should be alone right now."

She continued to stare at him while a curious ironic smile curved her mouth. "Don't worry about it. I have to get used to it. Why should you care, anyway? All you do is protect Renee. You're one of the people who never says no to her . . ."

"Feeling sorry for yourself?" His grip on her arms wasn't as firm now, but still held her attention.

"Yes," Gena admitted through clenched teeth. And then the rush of anger drained out of her as her body went slightly limp under CJ's strong hands. She closed her eyes, and a veil of pain changed the contours and features of her face. "Yes . . ." she murmured, biting her lip.

CJ made some sort of harsh sound from deep in his chest. It was filled with sympathy. He looked into her face and saw her soul laid bare, and it pulled at his heart. CJ shook his head, and his voice dropped even lower.

"I know what you're feeling."

"How could you?"

"I have a son that I see by appointment. When it's convenient for his mother, or when his school schedule allows. I do the best I can, too. And I try to make sure that he knows I love him. Renee and I aren't that different, Gena. If I had a chance to be with my son, believe me, I'd grab it with both hands."

She stood silently listening to him, and her control frustrated CJ. He'd know exactly what to do if she started to bawl and sob, if she'd thrown a tantrum. He'd dealt with Renee often enough. And his ex-wife, Joyce. But the way Gena held herself together made him feel helpless, because he knew she could take care of herself. He wasn't sure she needed anyone. It also suddenly explained more about her than he'd ever imagined before.

CJ sighed and began to slide his hands up and down her bare arms as she hugged herself. "Come on inside. I'm going to order something from room service."

"I don't want anything."

"Coffee. We could both use the caffeine," he joked dryly. "It's safer than alcohol." He leaned toward Gena to whisper in her ear. "And I don't want to have this conversation in the hallway."

CJ led her into the darkened suite and turned on one lamp on a credenza against a wall. He went directly to the phone to make his call to room service. And then there were several other calls quickly in succession as he saw to Renee's schedule for the next day.

All the while CJ kept his attention on Gena. She didn't bother to sit, but stood staring into space, looking tired and deeply pensive. When he finished the last call, CJ replaced the receiver and turned to her. The night's events and Renee's stubbornness had taken him by surprise, too. But he wasn't sorry. He'd learned a long time ago to work with the cards that were dealt him, whether it was losing his son . . . or learning about love the hard way.

CJ sighed as he slipped off his formal jacket and tossed it carelessly over the arm of a chair. He loosened his tie and deftly unfastened the top buttons of his dress shirt with one hand. He slowly circled the arrangement of chairs and coffee table until he was standing close behind Gena and could smell the subtle sweetness of her perfume and hair . . . an essence of *her*. And he could feel the stiff control in her body again. Her dress was a basic black slip dress, the straps just a string of rhinestones, leaving her long neck bare. It was cocktail length, showing her long legs to best advantage. Her heels made Gena a comfortable height next to him. "Gena . . ." He reached out to touch her.

"Don't, CJ," she turned her head away.

He ignored her. "Look, I know Renee just put it out there, but you knew this was coming. You've probably been afraid a long time this would happen. Why haven't you prepared yourself? Renee certainly had. Even Shay was ready."

Before she could respond, there was a knock on the door.

With a muttered oath at the poor timing, CJ went to answer and accept the tray with the coffee. After he'd closed the door again he quietly returned to Gena, putting the tray down on the table. Her back was to him.

Carefully he put his hand on her shoulder. She jumped at his touch. Before she could move or pull away from him, CJ moved his hand to curve around the side of her neck with his thumb stroking the prominent line of her spine. He squeezed gently in a kind of massaging motion.

"Look, maybe it's not as bad as you think," he said. "Renee talks before she thinks sometimes. She says she wants to move back to the New York area. There might be some TV work next year, or a play . . ." He felt her trembling under his hands. "Gen . . ."

She gasped quietly at the way CJ used her name. He was the first person to call her that. Renee must have gotten it from him. How had her sister known? Gena tried to pull away, not only from CJ's touch but from the magnetic draw of his comforting attempts to make everything better. But CJ easily maneuvered her to turn around. When she finally did, he enclosed her in an embrace that went beyond the understanding and comfort into something much more significant.

Gena began to cry almost silently, her pain locked inside. She didn't want CJ to witness her disappointment. But suddenly . . . *finally* . . . she didn't necessarily want CJ to let her go, either. There was something warm and protective about being in his arms.

"Everything's . . . changing," her voice cracked poignantly.

"About time," he responded.

"I'm going to lose Shay."

"Gena, if you don't let her go, you're going to lose her anyway."

"I know, but . . . I raised her," she sniffed, covering her nose and mouth with a temple made of her hands. Tears flowed over her fingers. Her bent elbows pressed into CJ's chest. "Sharon Lee is all I have."

The sound of Gena's crying tore at CJ because he had never seen her so vulnerable before. And, he realized, no one had ever been there for her before. His hands tightened, drawing her in closer. His fingers kneaded her back and shoulders, stroked the back of her neck. "No, she's not," he answered, kissing her face.

She shook her head. "I know there's Renee. We're family . . ."

"I'm not talking about Renee. I'm talking about *me,*" he whispered urgently. "Look at me . . ." He cupped under her chin with his hand and lifted her face. Slowly Gena's eyes fluttered open, her lashes and cheeks damp. CJ stared into her dark eyes. "Gena, I'm talking about us . . ."

Gena focused on the one man who'd captured her imagination, and whom she'd tried to deny for almost a year. She felt a coursing of warmth flow through her body as memories were stoked to life again. She instantly relived the images of her and CJ on the terrace of the house in California. Of late-night wine and laughter, and feeling herself succumb to the charm of his thoughtfulness, his humor . . . and the way he had treated her, as if he'd discovered something surprising. Well, she had, too.

They had connected. It had been magic and exhilarating. And when the early-evening kisses had led to full-fledged desire, and to her bedroom, Gena had believed then that they had found something important and strong together. The start of something. Until that next morning when Gena had been led to believe that her sister's demands for his attention and CJ's sense of obligation to Renee would burn out any light of hope.

And now here was CJ telling her it wasn't too late.

And she wanted to believe him.

Gena continued to just stare at him, absorbing his caresses, feeling her senses stirred and stimulated. And feeling a sudden need that went beyond the memory of the last time they were together; it outweighed even the painful realization of her sister's careless announcement. She reached up and rubbed her hand over CJ's cheek, searching beyond the intense look in his eyes. Feeling the reflexive muscles of his jaw under her hand. He grabbed her hand and kissed her fingers.

"What are you going to do?" she asked in a curious tone.

"That depends on you." He hugged her and laid

his face against hers. "Everything you've always done has been with Shay's welfare in mind. She's always come first; isn't that right? I didn't figure out until this week that part of your backing off from me and what we had last summer was about taking care of her." He slid his hands up her back, looking seriously into her sad eyes. "But who takes care of you?"

She closed her eyes, enjoying the feel of his cheek next to hers.

"I've been trying to let you know how I feel about you. I'm for real. I was hoping you'd figure out for yourself that you could love Shay and your sister, that I could take care of my responsibility to Renee and my son and there'd still be something left over for you and me. That's why I kept writing those letters. That's why I came with Renee this time to New York. It wasn't about being there for her. It was about getting close to you while we still had a chance."

Gena listened as CJ's voice crooned to her. It was caressing and persuasive. It was sincere. He rocked their bodies gently to and fro, and pressed kisses to her cheek. She'd stopped crying, realizing there was more reason to feel joyful than there was to feel any loss.

"I read your letters," she murmured.

He was surprised. "I thought maybe you threw them out."

She shook her head. "I kept them in a box." Her fingers teased just inside the opening of his shirt against the hollow of his throat. "I was afraid to read them until this week."

He began to trail his kisses up the side of her neck to her ears. Her weight shifted and leaned into his. He chuckled. "Why? What did you think I was going to say?"

"I thought you were going to hand me some line. I thought you were going to be slick."

He frowned at her. "Is that how I seemed last June?" he asked curiously.

Gena pursed her lips and shook her head again. "No," she said softly.

"So what did you think of my letters?" His voice was gravelly and low. He waited patiently for her answer.

Gena looked into his face, her eyes filled with surprise and composure and a shy recognition of the truth. "No one's ever sent me . . . love letters before."

It took a moment for CJ to realize what Gena was really confessing. And then he arched a brow, and growled in a sexy suggestive tone. "No one else better even try."

"Tough guy . . ." Gena grinned at his subtle threat as CJ laughed. Her attention shifted to his mouth. Slowly she reached out to touch her fingertips to his lips, and his smile faded as he studied her intently. "CJ . . ." she murmured thoughtfully. "What does CJ stand for?" Gena asked.

For a moment he didn't answer. He shook his head slightly. "I've been in Hollywood more than ten years. You're only the second person who's ever asked me that."

"Who was the other?"

"My accountant. He needed my full name for my tax returns . . ." He chuckled dryly. He kissed her forehead reverently, and then her nose. "Curtis . . . James . . . Brock," CJ whispered, just before he finally kissed her lips.

It occurred to her, as she felt his mouth expertly cover hers and coax a response, that she didn't have a clue as to why she wouldn't have remembered what this was like, or how CJ made her feel, or even how much she wanted him. But *he* really had remembered.

And CJ was right. Of course she loved her niece and sister. But this was different. This was just for herself . . . and him.

He wasn't rushed or urgent. He didn't demand because he didn't have to. They came together to pick up right where they'd left off. There was something tantalizing for Gena about feeling the desire build up slowly, instead of overwhelming them with heat and passion. In CJ's third letter he'd written to her that perhaps he'd already lost his chance with her, and he was afraid he'd never again know a woman as loving or as sweet. Gena had cried, because those had been her sentiments about him.

They didn't have to second-guess each other anymore. And there was no reason to wait. Tonight, next week, or next year, they were still going to feel the same about one another.

When CJ reached for the zipper on the back of her dress, Gena hid her face, her anticipation, against the front of his shirt. The cool air brushed over her bare skin as the dress opened and CJ eased the straps from her shoulders. Gena lowered her arms so the dress could be removed, and he tossed it, with a flick of his wrist, on top of his jacket. And then he held her against his body. He was more interested in touching Gena, in letting his hands explore the smoothness and warmth of her slender body. He already knew what she looked like completely naked. Everything about her was indelibly stamped on his mind.

Gena began to undo the rest of the buttons on his shirt, and CJ stood still, watching the expression of desire flush her features to a sienna glow. When she was done, however, she stared at his chest. CJ began to remove the rest of his clothing, his gaze forcing her to look at him, to recognize what was going to happen . . . and what it was going to mean.

They forgot about the coffee . . .

The decision had been made. Holding hands, they walked into the second room of the suite, where the bedding had been obligingly turned back by hotel staff. In the dark, with just their instincts and a mutual need, CJ and Gena began to make love. Memory guided their hands and lips and tongues. Anticipation syncopated their movements to slow motion.

On the king-size bed foreplay took forever. They had a lot of catching up to do. Their breathing and other sounds of pleasure were like a love song. Low and sensual. CJ stroked away her fears.

Gena wasn't surprised when CJ took the time to provide protection for them. And then he consumed her. Filling Gena's body and bringing it to life. She responded with trust, her skin heated and sensitive and aching for the cupping of his hand around her breast, the feel of his lips on her neck, his marauding tongue claiming her mouth. She arched upward to meet his rhythmic thrusting. Déjà vu blended nicely with reality and left them both breathless. The door to their feelings, hesitantly opened in the past, swung wide into the future.

Gena accepted what CJ had to give. It transported her. He made her realize that she was no longer just a sister, an aunt, a surrogate, or a caretaker. CJ reminded her that she was a woman . . . and a woman he wanted to love.

At four o'clock in the morning Gena tried to ease out of CJ's arms, out of his bed to search for her clothing. His hand snaked out to capture her wrist and easily pulled her back to the pillows. CJ rolled toward her and planted a sleepy kiss on her mouth.

"I have to get up. I have to go back to my room."

"Why?" he mumbled sleepily.

She rubbed his chest and gave in momentarily to his cajoling as he swung a leg over hers to anchor her in place. "Because . . . Renee might call you," she whispered. "Or she might call me. Shay might return and not find me there."

"So what?" he asked reasonably, stifling a yawn.

"They might worry if they can't find me and . . ."

"You don't want them to know you stayed with me last night, right?"

"Well . . . I don't think we should give people . . ."

"The wrong idea?" CJ was almost fully awake now. He shifted in the bed so that he and Gena faced one another on their sides. "So what's the wrong idea? That you and I have a thing going on for each other and decided to hook up? That we made love behind their backs? That we're falling seriously in love? What's wrong with that?"

Gena didn't have a reasonable answer, because there wasn't one; and she felt relief that CJ could put it into words so well. That meant that last night together had *not* been an apparition. She'd enjoyed the intimacy with CJ exactly as she'd enjoyed that night with him last June. She flashed a secret smile, which couldn't be seen in the dark.

What *was* wrong with that?

"You know what I think?" CJ finally sighed as he shifted yet again and lay on top of her, rolling Gena onto her back. He slipped his hands under her buttocks and rotated his hips against her, reminding her of her own needs. And his. "Renee has already figured it out. And Shay is going to think it's cool that you and I are getting it on . . ." he said with humor, nuzzling his mouth and nose into her neck.

She tried to pinch him. "CJ! The child is only twelve years old."

"The child is more in tune than you are. Sharon Lee has already told me she wants you and I to get married. I think there was some talk about you having babies." He laughed at her expression and kissed her open mouth. And then he kissed her again, his tongue teasing her lips as his mood changed and his body grew hard and urgent. "Cat got your tongue?" He eased her legs apart.

"CJ . . . We haven't talked. We've spent very little time together. We are a *long* way from marriage and children . . ." Gena gasped as he slid effortlessly into her, causing her to moan and close her eyes. She clasped her arms around his neck and reached blindly for his mouth, wanting him to kiss her again. "Curtis . . ."

"We're a lot closer than you think," he drawled.

Chapter Five

Gena closed the door to her room and felt immediately disoriented. Having spent the night in CJ's suite, in his bed, she felt now as if she'd walked into a stranger's room where she didn't belong. Her overnight bag was open on the luggage stand. Some of her personal things were laid out. But all Gena was experiencing was a sense of loneliness. This was what it was going to be like going home. This is what it would feel like once Renee returned to California, taking Shay and CJ with her.

For the moment, Gena didn't know what to do with herself. She'd walked the short distance from CJ's room in her evening dress and stockinged feet, carrying her evening pumps. She dropped them now on the carpeted floor, and they landed with a muted thud. She was about to head for the bedroom and a shower when there was a knock on the door. For a moment she believed it was CJ, coming after her. But when Gena eagerly opened the door, Renee stood in the hall.

They stared at one another. Renee looked her sister up and down, and a sly smile formed on her full mouth. She silently stepped around Gena into the room. She was dressed in a lavender silk jogging suit. Her face was cleaned of makeup, and her hair was combed back, sleek and unstyled.

"Well . . . I guess I don't need to ask how you slept last night. Or where."

Gena closed the door, a flush creeping up her neck into her face. "Where's Shay? Is she still in bed?" she asked, circumventing her sister's impertinence.

Renee faced Gena and sat on the edge of a chair. "She ordered breakfast from room service, and she's watching TV."

Gena nodded and then tilted her head at her sister. "What's wrong?"

"Are you sure you want to get involved with CJ?"

Gena thought about Renee's comment while she took her time walking to another chair to sit opposite her. "I think that's between me and CJ. He works for you, but you don't own all of his life, although I bet you'd like to."

"You only slept with him one night. It probably doesn't mean anything. You don't want to get yourself hurt, girl."

"It wasn't just one night."

"Oh, yeah . . . there was last summer when you came to visit. What happened to you? You used to be so straight and so responsible."

Gena smiled slightly. "That Gena's on a leave of absence."

Renee looked as if Gena had also taken leave of her senses. "Is this because of me or Shay? Did CJ promise you something?"

"No. No . . . and no. I stayed with CJ last night. I wished I'd stayed with him last year when I first realized that I . . . I could fall in love with him. He's a good man. You ought to know. He takes good care of you, too."

"That's his job. He's not going to give that up."

Gena shrugged indifferently, but smiled. "That's his decision, not yours. I'm glad we had last night. It's funny . . . last night at the awards you made a big issue of how important family is. Above everything else, you said, we should remember that family comes first. Well, I did that, and I'm still about to lose everything. You'll go back to the West Coast. You have a life there. Shay will go with you this time. You're her mother. CJ will go, too. But I have to stay here and continue with what's left of *our* family."

Renee looked wounded. "You never said you were unhappy."

"That's because I wasn't. I didn't have to give birth to Sharon Lee to love her as my own child. But she's not." Gena leaned forward, earnestly. "I resisted CJ and what we felt for each other for a whole year, Renee, because I was scared and I was trying to do what was best for you and Shay. Now I think it's my turn," she finished softly.

Renee stood up and slowly approached her sister. "I bet I got on your nerves this week."

Gena looked sharply at her sister, and she started to laugh quietly. "You *always* get on my nerves. But I love you, and I think you're great, and I wouldn't change anything about you, Renee."

Renee sighed, "Well, that's a good thing, since you can't and I wouldn't let you." She headed back toward the door. She stopped with her hand on the knob and looked over her shoulder at Gena. "I came to see if you could pick Shay up after you finish work today and take her home with you. I'm having dinner with a couple of producers who are trying to get me interested in their project."

Gena blinked at her sister, wondering if she'd heard a single thing she'd been trying to say. She nodded. "All right."

"Look, I just want you to know that I really did mean what I said last night. Sometimes I forget that I don't have to act, I don't have to fool people. You were always there. I could always count on you. I really am grateful."

Gena felt emotion welling up inside. She was too tired and too stressed to fight the urge to cry again. Too conscious of things changing, as they surely had to. She didn't want to be left without something just for herself. "I know . . ." she murmured.

Renee opened the door. "What are you going to do when we all leave on Saturday?"

Gena sighed and lifted her shoulders. The expression on her brown face was sad but brave. "Miss you . . ."

It wasn't until Gena heard her name called out softly that she realized she wasn't reading the book she held but rather was staring into space.

"Can I come in for a minute?"

"Come on, hon. I'm still awake," Gena said in a strong voice, putting the book aside.

Shay opened her bedroom door, and then she stood in the entrance. "Can I talk to you for a moment?" she asked shyly.

"Of course." Gena shifted over and patted the space next to her. "Are you going to try and talk me into letting you stay home from school again? I'll have to do a lot of explaining to your teachers . . ."

Shay climbed onto the bed next to Gena. "No, it's not that. I'll go in tomorrow."

Gena watched the young girl. She was wearing a T-shirt with the singer Babyface enlarged across the front. Her slippers were shaped like rabbits, complete with floppy ears. But ever since that fateful afternoon earlier in the week, Shay had shown a kind of reticence around everyone. She hadn't gotten comfortable with her body yet, and so many other things had happened as well. "What's the matter?"

"Well . . . I was just wondering . . . do you think my mother is going to be an actress for a long time?"

Gena stared at her niece, trying to read into the question some other hidden meaning. "I guess so. As long as there are good roles for her to play, and people want to watch her movies. She's very popular right now."

Shay nodded thoughtfully. "That means she'll have to stay in California, right?"

"Probably." She took hold of Shay's hands, which were nervously twisting the bed linens. "Hon, talk to me. What's on your mind?"

Shay bumped about on the bed to get comfortable, finally leaning against her aunt. She intertwined her fingers with Gena's. "I don't want to go to LA. I want to stay here with you."

Gena was stunned. She opened her mouth to speak, and then closed it again. She needed a few seconds to digest Shay's announcement. "But . . . Renee said she asked you . . ."

"Yeah, she did. And I thought I did, but then I changed my mind."

"Why?"

Shay shrugged. "Mommy's always too busy. What if she can't come to Parent Night at school? What if I don't like the other kids out there? I'm going to miss my friends. And . . . I don't want to leave you."

Gena felt her throat close up. She had programmed herself to get through the rest of her sister's visit, say her good-byes to Shay, and deal with the disappointment of not enough time with CJ. She'd imagined that only her own heart was about to break. She hugged her niece against her. "You're not leaving me. This isn't forever. I can still write and call and visit and so can you."

"It's not the same thing. I won't be able to talk to you when I need to. You can't help me with my homework. Mommy doesn't know anything about how to become an astronaut. She won't be able to help me." She turned to look poignantly into her aunt's face. "Aunt Gena . . . can't I stay here?"

"Of course you can, but what about your mother? How do you think she's going to feel about that?"

"I don't know. But it doesn't mean I don't love her," Shay was quick to emphasize. "Her life is different from mine."

"Don't you want to think about this a little more? Maybe you're just a little nervous."

"I did. I know she's going to be my mother forever . . . but my real home is here. You're more like a mommy anyway. Besides, you'll be here all by yourself till CJ asks you to marry him," Shay added coyly.

Gena shook her head, bemused. Where did all of this come from? Why was everyone assuming so much more than she was? She stroked Shay's cheek. "Sweetie, are you very sure this is what you want?"

"I'm sure."

"When are you going to tell your mother?"

Shay sighed, as if a burden had been lifted from her shoulders. "I did already. She didn't even get mad at me or anything. You think maybe she was glad?"

"What *did* she say?"

Shay suddenly giggled. "She said she wanted to be just like me when she grows up."

"She's late again," Shay sighed. "If she doesn't get here soon, she's going to miss the plane."

"No she won't. CJ won't let her," Gena said confidently, even though she was beginning to worry, too.

"But there isn't going to be enough time to say good-bye," Shay predicted.

Gena tried to laugh lightly at her niece's anxiety, although that was the very thing she was concerned about as well. Not about saying good-bye to Renee. She was used to the habits of her sister, who made grand entrances and exits, leaving others to clean up the debris in her wake. What mattered most to Gena right now was what she and CJ were going to say to each other. Gena glanced at her watch. Fifteen minutes before departure.

Her stomach was already in revolt, somersaulting with tension and anxiety. Gena wondered what was worse; the anticipation of CJ's arrival last week . . . or his imminent departure now. That they'd had so little time together . . . or there would be no other time at all.

"Thank you for waiting, ladies and gentlemen. Flight 399 to LA is now ready for boarding. We ask that those passengers with small children, or those needing special assistance please proceed to the gate . . ."

Gena and Shay exchanged glances.

"She's not going to make it," Shay sang with acceptance and calm.

"Yes she will," Gena countered. *He had to . . .*

On Thursday night, after Shay had made her confession about not wanting to live with her mother on the West Coast, CJ had called her. Gena remembered how the very sound of his voice had filled her with hope, and calmed the doubts that had snuck up on her in his absence. He'd whispered his feelings and reminded her now that they'd come this far, there would be no turning back. But they hadn't spoken of where they were headed or how they would get there.

"Are they boarding yet?"

Gena turned swiftly, her heart lurching with anticipation. But it was only Laura . . . carrying, once again, the fur coat and a new stack of reading materials for her employer's long flight. "They've just started."

"Will the first-class passengers please board at this time . . ."

"Where's my mother?" Shay asked.

"Right behind me. I just ran ahead to make sure they knew we are making this flight. Excuse me . . ." Laura said as she hurried to the counter with a set of tickets.

Shay suddenly jumped to her feet and pointed

down the corridor. "Here she comes now," she said with relief.

Gena stood up, hugging herself.

Ten minutes . . .

"Is CJ with her?"

"I don't see him," Shay answered as her mother swept into the lounge. "Hurry . . . they're boarding the plane . . ."

"Don't worry, sweetie. The airlines may operate on EST, but I'm on CPT." Renee's makeup was impeccable, her outfit stylish, comfortable for traveling but meant to catch everyone's attention.

"What's CPT?" Shay frowned as her mother gave her an absentminded kiss and hug.

"Ask your aunt," Renee answered dryly. "Well, I'm off. You be good and do what Gena tells you."

"I will," Shay mumbled, her face buried against her mother's chest as they embraced. She twisted her face to glance into her mother's face. "Mommy? Are you sorry I'm not coming with you?"

Renee stared at her daughter. Her face changed from speculation to wistfulness. "Yes. I am, Shay. Look, I made a decision when I was seventeen years old about what I wanted. I guess you're old enough to do the same. You know your life will be normal here with your aunt. Besides, it might not be that much fun living with me. I have this big wonderful house in LA with a pool and everything . . . and I don't even know how to swim! But it's not a real home. It's where I work. Every time I come back to good old Wayne, New Jersey, and the neighborhood, that's when I realize what home is.

"You stay in school here with Gena. But you can come and be with me whenever you want, you hear? Maybe when school gets out for the summer. I want to show people what a smart little girl I gave birth to."

Renee then turned to her sister. She just stared at Gena with a smile of irony on her brightly glossed mouth. "You make me work hard when I came back home. I have to make my own bed, and pour my own coffee, and fold my bath towels . . ."

Gena smiled. "You must be glad to be leaving."

Renee pursed her lips and shook her head. "You're wrong, girl. CJ told me we can't afford to forget where we came from. You and Sharon Lee keep me in check. I don't get special treatment here. I'm just part of the family. It feels good." She took a step closer to her sister and looked carefully at her. "You know, if it wasn't for me you never would have met CJ."

Gena flushed at her sister's observation, but shook her head slowly. "No. If it wasn't for me neither would *you*."

Renee chuckled in appreciation. "So we're even?"

"I wasn't keeping a score or anything, Renee, but . . . I'd say things somehow worked out well."

"This is the final call for Flight 399 to LA. Will all passengers please board. Thank you . . ."

"Bye, Mommy . . ." Shay said in a tearful voice. "I'm going to miss you."

"I'm going to miss you, too," Renee murmured, holding her child.

Gena felt her stomach roil. She looked off down the long corridor in the direction of the terminal building, but still did not see CJ. Shay was right. There would be no time to say good-bye. Not the kind she wanted.

Five minutes . . .

Renee kissed Shay once more. She gave her sister an awkward hug. "Bye, Gena. Thanks a lot, for everything." Blowing air kisses, Renee passed through the exit.

There was an instant silence after her breezy farewell.

"Well, that's everyone except CJ," Gena tried to say lightly. "Maybe he doesn't like good-byes."

"Maybe he decided to stay here with you," Shay offered guilelessly. "CJ said he was going to get out of Hollywood. He said he was going to manage his own business for a change. He said he wanted to be closer to Nicholas. They could be part of *our* family, right?"

"One thing at a time . . ." CJ said dryly from behind as he approached, accompanied by another airline representative.

"I'll let them know you're here," the uniformed woman said, using the phone at the ticket desk.

When Gena turned around to see CJ, she felt like

her heart had climbed into her throat. She was nervous, excited, and resentful all at the same time that he could have this kind of effect on her. She just stared at him, however, suddenly too shy to move.

CJ handed Renee's red leather Coach tote to Shay. "Run and give this to your mother. She left it in the limo. Tell her if she's forgotten anything else, it's tough."

Shay laughed, grabbed the tote, and hurried back to the departure gate.

Then CJ turned to face Gena and started slowly walking toward her. The collar of his jacket was turned up around his neck. His beard was neat and had recently been trimmed back to keep it flat against the contours of his masculine face. His gaze was dark and direct. When he stood in front of Gena, he calmly bent to press his lips to hers. No hello. No good-bye, either. Just all the possibilities in between.

His mouth was cold from the winter air. Even his body radiated it. But warmth spiraled through Gena as he moved his mouth against hers and took hold of her arms. CJ released her mouth slowly, savoring the last touch and taste of her.

"The plane isn't going anywhere without me," he said easily. He touched her chin and mouth, studying her features carefully. "I had to make sure you remembered Wednesday night the same way I did."

"I do," she whispered, nodding briefly.

"Good," he said in relief. "And you'll remember

what I said to you, about us getting together and doing this right?"

"I will."

A slow smile curved to his lips as CJ gathered her into his arms and just held her. His sturdiness made Gena feel less vulnerable and doubtful. And he made her feel peaceful. She looped her arms around his neck. If anyone was watching she didn't care. Shay came back through the gate, a slightly frantic airline attendant right behind her.

"CJ! Come *on,*" Shay beckoned.

"Sir, we really have to . . ."

CJ calmly put his hand up to cut off the commands and urgency. He continued to stare into Gena's eyes, missing her already. When he kissed her this time, it was thorough and real, and deep and lingering. It was filled with promise and desire.

"When are we going to see each other again?"

He chuckled at the seductive play in her voice. "As soon as possible. We have a lot of time to make up for."

Gena realized that the way she and CJ had said good-bye filled the moment with love. It had not been spoken between them, and now she knew there was no need. CJ had proved it to her during the visit this past week with Renee. He released her and pushed her gently away.

"Good-bye, Curtis James," Gena said softly.

He grinned at her. "I'll write."

Then he abruptly turned and walked through the

departure gate to the waiting plane. The door immediately closed and locked behind him.

Shay stood next to her bemused aunt and held her hand. She spoke in a sage voice with surprising insight. "CJ said he already felt like one of the family. Do you think Nicholas will like me?"

Gena nodded. "I'm sure . . ."

She already knew . . . had learned . . . Curtis James Brock was as good as his word.

And his letters.

GUESS WHAT'S COOKING

by Eva Rutland

Chapter One

"Remember. Nobody in the house till I get home."

"I know." Tonya shifted her book bag to the other shoulder and glanced up at her sister. Darlene didn't look like a person who'd just got engaged.

"And don't stop anywhere. Come straight home from school."

"I know." According to the books Tonya read, when a person got engaged, she emerged with lips bruised from all that kiss kiss kiss stuff, and she was all aquiver inside and glowed all over the place. Darlene's lips hadn't been bruised one little bit when they called her in last night to toast their engagement with ginger ale in her champagne glass. And she wasn't . . . well, you couldn't tell about that. Darlene glowed all the time. But she sure didn't look quivery. Maybe when you got engaged to somebody as brisk and businesslike as Leon, you didn't—

"And phone me as soon as you get in."

"Okay." She looked to see if Darlene's bus was in sight. It wasn't.

"You didn't phone me yesterday."

"Forgot."

"And when I called, you weren't there and I—"

"I told you. I just ran down to the Leskovitzes' for cooking oil."

"Okay, but don't forget today." Darlene reached out a hand and expertly fluffed Tonya's too curly hair. "You might stop in at Miss Selina's if you like."

Her that's-entirely-up-to-you look didn't fool Tonya one little bit. If Darlene had her way, Miss Selina would still be baby-sitting her. The law says a person can stay alone when she's eleven, but Darlene had made her wait until she was twelve, almost thirteen. *And she's still treating me like a baby now when I'm almost fourteen and in high school, for Pete's sake!*

"Oh, there's my bus. Bye, honey." Darlene dropped a kiss on Tonya's forehead and joined the line of people waiting to board the bus that would whisk them to the subway station. Trim and smart in her gray business suit, she paused for a moment and called over her shoulder, "Maybe Miss Selina will help you with your algebra."

Tonya grimaced. Why did you have to take algebra and all that math stuff when there were calculators that could figure out anything! Anyway, Miss Selina might be a retired schoolteacher, but she didn't know squat about algebra. And Darlene didn't know much more. She giggled, remembering Darlene's mystified expression as she tried to make sense of all those equations.

"So what's funny?" Sophie, who had crossed the street behind the departing bus, looked curiously at her.

"Oh, nothing much," Tonya answered, falling into step beside her. Sophie Leskovitz might be her best friend, but nobody was going to laugh at Darlene. Darlene might be a half sister, but she was the very best sister a person could have. Even now, Tonya could remember how scared she had been when Dad died. Only a few months after Mom. Maybe he missed her, or maybe he was just tired. A sudden pain in the chest and he had slumped over and died . . . just like that. She had never felt so alone in her life . . . until Darlene got there.

Darlene was as grief-stricken as she, but in her arms Tonya had felt safe and secure. "I know how you feel," she had said. "But Dad's out of his pain, and we've still got each other. I'm going to take care of you. Everything's going to be all right."

And it was. Well, as all right as things could be without Mom and Dad. Darlene was pretty efficient . . . in most things. Before Tonya hardly realized it, Darlene had settled things in Cleveland and whisked her off with her to this flat in Brooklyn, and ever since had been fussing over her like she was a baby. *So busy taking care of me she can't take care of herself. She doesn't know she's not in love with Leon. And if I didn't do the cooking—*

"Ready for the algebra quiz?" Sophie asked.

"I guess," Tonya said. Right now there was more on her mind than algebra. Darlene. How to get her unengaged. "We'd better hurry," she said as she heard a bell sound, and the two girls ran to join the throng entering Camden High School.

You'd think Miss Selina lived outside on the landing instead of the second-floor flat, Tonya thought. That afternoon when she got home from school, the wiry gray-haired woman was sweeping the landing. And when they had left that morning, she had been taking out her garbage and had walked downstairs with them. Darlene said she was a lonely old lady who wanted to talk. So Darlene had talked, telling about her engagement and showing her that big diamond.

"So!" Miss Selina said as Tonya came up the steps, "You're about to have a handsome stepbrother! I know you're happy about that."

"Er . . . umh . . ." Tonya guessed a smile wasn't exactly a lie.

"Such a fine young man." Miss Selina wielded the broom briskly, though there wasn't much to sweep. "Yes, indeed. A very successful stockbroker. None of us could get into that field when I was young. Yes indeed, Darlene has done very well for herself. As my old mother would put it, she won't have to hit a lick at a snake."

That meant Darlene wouldn't have to work. But

Darlene loved her work. She placed abused and neglected children in foster homes, and she said it made her feel good every time she saw an unhappy child happily settled.

"Things will be better for you, too, child. A good home, probably in an area where there's a better school. Camden is getting so crowded."

"Yes'm. But I like Camden," Tonya couldn't help saying. "I'm a cheerleader this year, you know."

"That's nice," Miss Selina said, but didn't seem impressed. She was still talking about Leon. "I knew Leon's mother. She taught with me at PS 10. A good family. And he's lucky to get Darlene, too. She's such a sweet girl."

"Yes'm. I better go on up and phone Darlene," Tonya said, and raced up the stairs.

She liked living on the top floor. It was nice, with a roomy dining/living area and a neat little kitchen. Two bedrooms, so they each had one, and there was even a small patio. Cozy. She didn't want to leave it for some fancy house Leon was planning to buy.

Tonya phoned Darlene. "I'm home, and I'm going to start dinner and then go down and sit on the steps. Okay?"

Dinner was a cinch. She had washed the mustard greens yesterday, and placed them in a plastic bag in the fridge. She took out just enough for dinner, added salt and pepper, and arranged them in the steamer with one cut-up strip of bacon, ready to be cooked at the last minute. Dad said fresh vegetables should be eaten raw or immediately after cooking, and not much cooking or you'd lose the vitamins. He said his mom always cooked her greens a long time with fatback or a ham bone, but he guessed that was all right because they always ate the pot likker, which they sopped with corn bread, and he guessed that's where the vitamins were. Anyway, he had taught her to steam fresh vegetables with only a wee bit of bacon or butter for flavor. Then Tonya took out a leftover baked sweet potato and peeled it. She was always careful about leftovers because Dad said a woman could throw more out the back door with a teaspoon than a man could bring in the front with a shovel. Tonya giggled. Dad was so funny.

She sliced the potato, sprinkled it with nutmeg and cinnamon and a little butter, ready to place in the oven when the muffins were almost done. The muffins she prepared from a ready-mix package. Sometimes she made corn bread or crackling bread from scratch, but Dad said some of the ready-made packages were good and downright convenient. And today she wanted to get downstairs before Greg came home. Sometimes he would stop on the steps to talk, and he always had good advice.

Her room was a mess. Darlene would fuss, but not much, and would probably straighten it up herself. She felt so guilty because Tonya did all the cooking. But Darlene could hardly boil water. Not her fault. Mom had done all the cooking when she was home. And when Dad had retired and Mom got sick, Darlene was already working in New York. It was Tonya who had helped and learned from Dad. So it was a good thing she got home three hours before Darlene, sometimes four, depending on which subway train Darlene caught.

Tonya liked doing her homework on the front steps. That is, when it was real sunny like it was today. She would lift her head every now and then, turning this way and that, trying to get her skin dark all over like Darlene's. She had light tan skin like both Mom and Dad, and if she wasn't careful, some parts, like her forehead, would tan more than the rest of her face. Her hair was a problem, too. A funny color brown and very crinkly. It wasn't so bad now that Darlene had had it cut and used a curling iron to smooth out the crinkles, but it would never be as black and silky as Darlene's. Mom had said Darlene looked like her real Dad, who must have been real good-looking. But not very nice. Darlene said she was glad when they left him.

Tonya glanced up from her history book to see if Greg was coming. He worked at Franchise Tax and usually got home a couple of hours before Darlene. Greg was nice. He had moved into the downstairs flat three months ago when his uncle and aunt, Mr. and Mrs. Weston, had left for Arizona on account of Mr. Weston's asthma. They had left Greg in charge. He lived in their downstairs flat and collected the rents and took care of everything.

Tonya liked to talk to Greg. The thing was he

didn't tell you to do this or don't do that. He just asked you a lot of questions until you figured it out for yourself and knew exactly what to do. Like when she was figuring whether or not she should go out for cheerleading.

"You like to watch the game? Get excited?" he had asked.

"Oh, sure. Every time our guys get a touchdown, especially when the score is tied." She got excited just thinking about it.

"Want to jump up and cheer them on and tell everybody to yell with you?"

She had nodded and grinned, seeing herself in action.

"So. There you have it."

She wasn't so sure. "Luanne . . . some of the girls trying out are real good."

"Competition, huh?"

She had nodded.

"Like a game, wouldn't you say?"

Again she had nodded.

He had shrugged. "You win some. You lose some. Either way, games are fun."

So she had treated it like a game, and she had won. She was on the junior varsity cheering squad. They had been practicing every day, and Tonya could hardly wait for the first game this coming Saturday.

And then there was the time she had asked about her helping Tom with his English papers.

"A test?" Greg had asked.

"No. Just essays and things he has to hand in. Tom is terrible. He doesn't know when to capitalize, and he leaves out commas and can't spell beans. But he's the best player on the junior varsity squad, and if he doesn't get good grades . . . well, you know. Sometimes in study period I just look over his papers and kinda point out some things."

"You're pretty smart?" Greg had asked.

"Straight As. Never so much as a B. All the way through school. I was accelerated, and that's why I'm in high school already." She knew she sounded smug, so she hastened to explain. "Darlene says it's because I read a lot. Even when I was little, Dad read to me, and I . . . well, I just kept it up."

Then Greg had asked a whole lot of other questions that made her figure out that she had had many more advantages than Tom, and that people with talents ought to help other people who were lacking in those talents.

Then Greg had started another series of questions. "Do you look upon school as a learning experience?" By the time she had answered the rest of his questions, she knew that correcting Tom's English papers was not only helping the football team, but also the teacher and Tom's life in the future, which was a benefit to the whole community. Wow!

Yep, Greg was pretty deep. She hoped he had time to talk today. Sometimes he didn't. He was a writer in his spare time, and sometimes he would rush right by her with a "Sorry, kid. Got a hot idea. Got to get it down."

She was almost beside herself when she saw his lean form a block away. He always walked from the subway station for the exercise. He walked rapidly, his coat flung over one shoulder and a paper bag in one hand. Hamburger, french fries, and milk shake. A dumb dinner. But he always said he was too busy to cook. Anyway, maybe he would stop on the steps to eat. She was relieved when he reached them, and sat down beside her.

"Hi, kid," he said, opening the bag. "Want some french fries?"

She shook her head. "No thanks. You don't eat enough fresh vegetables."

He grinned and bit into his hamburger. "You sound like my mother."

"Where is your mother?" Suddenly she was curious about him. They had never talked about his family.

"Kansas City. Want a first draw?" He held out the milk shake.

"No thanks." She didn't have time to talk about his family. She'd better get on about Darlene before he finished eating and went in. "I wanted to ask you something."

"So shoot."

"How can you stop another person from doing something you know they shouldn't do?"

"Sometimes you can't."

"Well, I mean if they haven't done it yet and you want to try to stop it."

"Depends."

"On what?"

"On who the person is and what your relationship is to them. Stop beating around the bush, kid. Who would you like to stop from doing what?"

"It's Darlene. She just got engaged to Leon, and I know she shouldn't— Oh, Oh!" She looked anxiously up at Greg, who had choked on his milk shake and was standing up, coughing like crazy. "Are you okay?"

He nodded and sat back down.

"You shouldn't bolt your food like that."

"Yes, ma'am." He wiped his lips with a napkin.

"Well, what should I do about Darlene?"

"Butt out."

"What?"

"Butt out."

She stared at him in amazement. He always talked things over with a person, made you figure it out. "Just 'butt out'? That's not the way you usually talk to a person who has a problem."

"Oh?"

"No. You always ask questions and—"

"All right. I'll ask you one question. Who's planning to marry Leon, you or Darlene?"

"Darlene. But—"

"Bingo!

"Bingo?"

"Right. It's Darlene's problem. Not yours."

"It certainly is my problem. I'd have to live with them in that fancy house he's planning to buy, and I don't want to live with Leon."

"Oho! So it's yourself you're thinking about. Not Darlene."

"No. Honestly I'm not just thinking about me." That was true. This was absolutely the first time she had thought of herself in connection with the marriage. "Darlene doesn't love Leon."

"How do you know that? Wait . . . let me rephrase that. What makes you think you know whether Darlene loves the man?"

"Well . . ." No need to talk about the glowing and quivering. Greg might be a writer, but he probably didn't read enough romance books to know the symptoms. "The thing is, Darlene and Leon don't suit."

"Why not? Isn't Leon a nice guy?"

"Oh, he's nice, and very generous. He's always bringing Darlene presents and me, too. I think he's rich. He's a broker, you know. He's always taking Darlene out to dinner, sometimes with his big clients."

"That's good, isn't it?"

"I guess. Only . . . well, Darlene is more of a jeans-and-pullover type of person. I think she'd rather hang around home and eat mustard greens and corn bread than go out for champagne and steaks."

"You think. She goes, doesn't she?"

"Yes, because she likes to please people . . . not just Leon, but anybody. She's a listener, you know. And Leon and his clients just love that. Because they're talkers. But serious talk . . . mostly about stocks and bonds and making money. Serious stuff like that. I know because Darlene always makes me go with them if Miss Selina isn't at home. They talk, and Darlene listens just like she cares about stocks and bonds when she'd rather be at home reading a book or playing a game. I don't think Leon knows how to play. Do you know the one time he went to the park with us, he wore a three-piece suit? And he never laughs. It would be pretty terrible to live all your life with somebody who never laughed, wouldn't it?"

Greg stirred uneasily. "Maybe Darlene will teach him to laugh and play. People compensate for each other, you know, and if Darlene and Leon love each other . . ." He spread his hands.

"Oh, Leon loves her all right. But that's nothing. Everybody loves Darlene. And not just because she's drop-dead beautiful with those deep dimples and that black wavy hair and smooth chocolate skin, and not just because she's a listener. She listens to everybody, even Miss Selina if she's just talking about the way the garbage people pick up the trash. The thing is, Darlene is a caring kind of listener. And there's the way she looks at you with those big wide-open eyes of hers, like she's telling you you're wonderful, even if she's just telling you to wear your raincoat or saying thank you to the man who just brought the mail. You know what I mean? Like you get a lift just . . . What's the matter?"

"Nothing."

But something was the matter. She was trying to figure it out when he stood up.

He gathered up his trash and picked up his coat. "Look, kid. Some things are your business and some things are not. Other people's love lives are not. If your sister has decided to marry this Leon guy, best you learn to live with it. See you later, alligator."

"After while, crocodile." She watched, still wondering what had upset him as he went in and shut his door. Well, she decided, he might be deep, but he doesn't know everything.

Chapter Two

Darlene held tight to the strap in the subway car and swayed to one side, trying to avoid the man who was standing too close to her. The subways were running slow, as usual. She hated to be late getting home. She didn't like to leave Tonya alone so long. Tonya was a good kid, but there was so much going on nowadays. She couldn't help but worry. Once she and Leon were married, she meant to put Tonya in private school, plus they would be living in a better neighborhood. Actually their present neighborhood wasn't too bad, but the rent for their flat sure was straining the budget.

Today was payday, and her check would have been deposited in the bank. She shut her eyes, mentally trying to add up the bills that were due. She wanted to lay aside enough to get Tonya a good jacket before the heavy weather set in. And there was the thirty dollars due for the cheerleader outfit. That was a first. Tonya was so excited about making the cheerleading squad and Darlene was glad for her.

She wanted Tonya to be as happy as Tonya's father had made her. When her mother married Sam Davis, it had been like coming out of a cold stormy night into a cozy warm room.

She hadn't thought so at first. Not that first day when he knelt before her and asked, "How would you like me to be your daddy?"

Too scared to speak, she had just stared at him out of knowing eight-year-old eyes and shrank back against her mother. She didn't want anyone to be her daddy. Daddies got drunk and talked loud and ugly and hurt people. She had been glad when they left her daddy and moved to Ohio. Life had been hard, but better without him. She hadn't even been sorry when her mother told her he had died. So when Sam Davis asked again if she would like him to be her daddy, she shook her head.

Thank goodness her mother had married him anyway. He had moved them from their little one-bedroom apartment to the house on Simpson Street, where she had her own bedroom and a swing in the backyard. A happy house where a dad read stories, played games, and filled their lives with love and laughter. And then there was Tonya, a sweet baby sister to love and cuddle. Now Tonya complained that she was being cuddled too much. She must remember that the child was growing up. A cheerleader, no less. Saturday was the big day, the first game, and she could hardly wait to see her baby sister in action.

* * *

"I don't think you'd better count on me for tonight, Leon," Darlene spoke into the phone. "I've got to take Tonya to a football game, and I doubt we'll get back before six."

"Does she have to go? Isn't it raining out there?"

"Only a slight drizzle. I hope it'll hold up. And yes, she does have to go. She's a cheerleader, you know." She glanced at Tonya, who was staring disconsolately out of the window. She did look cute in that outfit. But the weather . . . That white wool sweater with the big red C in front was warm enough, but the skirt was pretty short and her legs bare. She wondered—

"Where is this game?" Leon asked.

"At her school."

"Then, why do you have to go? For Christ sake, Darlene, she walks there every day, and it's hardly dark before six."

As if she would miss it! "The days are getting shorter, Leon. Anyway, I don't like her going alone." She knew Leon liked her to dine with him, especially when he had an important client with him, but today was important for Tonya. "No," she said firmly. "It's too late to ask anyone else, and besides I want to be there. This is her first game as a cheerleader."

"Do you think we'll be rained out?" Tonya asked when Darlene got off the phone.

"Oh, I doubt it. It's only a light rain." Baseball got

rained out. But football? Hadn't she seen a game played in the snow? But maybe in high school—

"But do you think we'll have a crowd? It is raining—" Tonya looked anxious.

"Now, don't you worry about that. You'll have plenty of rooters. Now, put on your raincoat and let's get out of here." If it was raining hard, she would hail a jitney or a cab.

When they reached the ground floor, Greg Weston was coming out of his flat. "Well, what have we here?" he asked, grinning at Tonya, who was pulling on her raincoat.

"This is our outfit." Tonya pulled back her raincoat to display it. "You like it?"

"All right!" His eyes twinkled in appreciation. "That's pretty nifty. Who are you playing?"

"Norwood."

Darlene had descended the steps and called to Tonya, "Come on. It's stopped raining. We can walk."

"Wait. I'll run you over."

Darlene started to protest, but Greg said it was no trouble. He was just on his way to the mall for office supplies and that could wait. So they piled into the battered Ford he used only on weekends and were on their way, with Tonya talking a mile a minute about how they were going to beat the socks off Norwood.

"Sounds exciting," Greg said. "Think I'll stick around to see it."

So when Tonya tossed her raincoat to Darlene and went down to join the other cheerleaders, Greg climbed with Darlene to one of the choice seats in the stadium.

The rain had had no effect on attendance. The grandstands on both sides were full. The visiting team received and went steadily down the field. Seventy-four yards in eleven plays for the touchdown. A two-point try failed. At least that's what Greg said. Darlene really didn't know much about football. But she did know that Norwood scored six, Camden zip.

During the second quarter, she was still trying to make sense of the wild scrambles when she heard Greg give a gleeful shout and stand up.

She pulled on his sleeve. "What happened?"

"He fumbled and we recovered," he answered, but was too excited to sit down. With the rest of the crowd, he was shouting, "Go, man, go!" Then she heard a low "damn" and he sat down.

"What?" she asked.

He explained that Camden had failed again, after recovering a fumble on Norwood's ten-yard line.

"Oh," she said, really sure of but one thing. They were losing.

But Tonya and her peers never let down. Darlene watched their enthusiastic cavorting with pride. She might be a little prejudiced, but she thought Tonya was the best. So graceful, especially when they did that thing they called the Cougar Crawl.

"Aren't they great?" she asked Greg.

"Yeh." He grinned. "You'd think we were twenty points ahead. If cheering could do it, we would be!"

She laughed. "You should talk. You're as bad as they are." And he was. As wildly enthusiastic as any Camden student, football player, or cheerleader. She was glad he was along. Not only was he explaining the plays to her, he made it fun, even if they were losing.

At the half, it was twelve and zip. Camden had fumbled and Norwood recovered on their twenty-yard line, running it in for the touchdown. But they failed again to convert the extra point.

The Camden cheering squad lost neither faith nor fervor, and gave a winning halftime performance. Tonya, during a brief respite, found them and anxiously whispered to Darlene, "Am I doing okay?"

"Indeed you are," was Darlene's equally quiet answer. Then she gave her a hug and exclaimed out loud, "Outstanding!"

"You guys are great, kid," Greg said. "Keep it up."

"We're going to win, too," Tonya said, her face bright with enthusiasm.

"We'll get them in the second half. Just wait and see!"

And so they did. Fourteen unanswered points by the end of the third quarter. They traded touchdowns in the fourth quarter with Camden, pulling out a two-point win. Nineteen to twenty-one.

"May as well wait here for Tonya," Greg said. "Give the crowd a chance to thin out."

The crowd, wild about the win, wasn't quick thinning out, and it was some time before Tonya joined them, her eyes bright with excitement.

"Wasn't it great?" she asked.

"Great," Greg answered. "And the cheering squad wasn't bad, either. I like that Cougar Crawl you did."

"Yeh. And did you see Tom make that touchdown?"

"We did. We saw it all, Tonya, and it was spectacular." Darlene stood up. "Come on. Let's get out of here."

"Wait, Darlene. I'm going . . . that is, can I go with them?"

"Who's them? And where are you going?"

"Anne and Sue and Jeff and Tom, when he gets dressed. We're just going to the Burger Basket."

Darlene's heart gave a thud. Tonya was growing up. "I don't know about that. I'd rather—"

"Please. Tom's brother is going to drive us."

"Tom's brother?"

"Sidney. Down there." Tonya pointed to a boy standing with a group at the foot of the stadium. "He's sixteen."

Sixteen! And he didn't look much older than Tonya. Darlene's heart pumped faster. "Look, I don't think this is such a good idea."

"Please. We're just going to get burgers and talk about the game and all."

Darlene felt the pressure of Greg's hand on hers. "Tell you what," he said. "Darlene could go with me to the office supply store, and you can go with them. Then we'll swing by the Burger Basket and pick you up. Say . . ." He looked at his watch. "About eight. Okay?" He turned to Darlene. "Okay with you?"

"Well . . ." She didn't want to wipe the joy from Tonya's face. This was a pretty good compromise. "Okay," she said.

Tonya said all right, but not to come in looking for her. She would watch for them and come out at . . . couldn't they make it eight-thirty?

They settled on eight-thirty, and after Darlene had been introduced to Sidney, who, as far as she could tell, seemed a sober straightforward young guy, and had cautioned him to drive carefully the three or so blocks to the Burger Basket, and had pressed a five-dollar bill into Tonya's hand, she left the stadium with Greg.

"I don't know if I should have let her go," she said when she was settled in his car. "She talks a lot about this Tom. And now with him and the others and just his brother driving . . . Isn't that kinda like a date?"

"Kinda." Greg shifted gears and backed out of the parking slot.

"And isn't she a little young for this sort of thing?"

"Kinda."

"So you think so, too!" She frowned at him. "But

you were the very one who set it up. I was about to say no and you said—"

"Hold on!" He had stopped for the light and he turned to smile at her. "Look. When you're kind of young, this is the kind of dating you ought to do. Kind of readies you for the real thing, doesn't it?"

"I guess that does make sense." She returned his smile, remembering that Tonya said he always made sense, and wondering if it was what he said or the way he looked. Strong and sure, with a confident smile that banished any doubts you might have. Well, almost any. "Guess I worry too much," she said.

He glanced at her. "About Tonya?"

She nodded.

"She's not very smart, huh?"

That made her indignant. "Tonya! She's smart as a whip. Above average in everything."

"But not very levelheaded?"

"Of course she's levelheaded. Much more so than any other kid her age. I'd trust her anywhere and . . ." She broke off, seeing his mouth quirk. "Oh, you're putting me on!"

"No, just trying to figure out why you worry." He gave a bark of laughter. "From my short acquaintance with your little sister, I'd say if she found herself facing a tiger in the jungle, the tiger'd better watch out!"

She chuckled. "Maybe. But there are things more

dangerous than tigers in our city streets, and I want Tonya—"

"Safe and secure, cozy and warm. Wrapped tightly forever in your arms."

"Oh, no, I know that's ridiculous." She sighed, because that was exactly what she did want. As safe and secure as Tonya's father had kept her. "I just wish I could do more for her."

"Like what?"

"Put her in private school for one thing."

"Why?"

"She's so smart. I think she deserves the best."

"Isn't she doing all right where she is? She told me she's a straight-A student."

"Yes, but . . . Oh, Camden is so crowded. I don't know how many languages are spoken at that school. And so much goes on."

"So you'd prefer a private school?"

"Yes." If only she could afford it. "I know I can't always shield her, but I'd like to protect her as long as I can."

"I see." He glanced at her. "The best protection is preparation, you know."

"What are you saying?"

"I'm saying that the experience she is getting at Camden, dealing with all kinds of people and situations, will be a better preparation for life than any cozy little private school you choose. So, as long as she's doing all right and is happy . . . Ah, here we are," he said as he pulled to a stop in front of the office supply store. "Want to come in with me?"

He did make sense, she thought as she followed him into the store. She watched as he made his purchases and chatted with the clerk, who evidently knew him. He had such an air of confidence and self-assurance. Like Leon. But more relaxed. Leon was always more . . . well, not exactly anxious . . . alert, watchful. Greg had an almost lazy come-what-may air, and she liked the way his lips curved, as if he was always about to smile. He was taller than Leon and darker, with a rich red cast to his brown complexion. Striking against the tan suede jacket he was wearing. Leon's eyes were not as dark and . . . Now, why was she comparing him to Leon?

Because, she thought resignedly, she compared every man she met with Leon. Once you had decided to marry someone—

"Need anything?" Greg asked. "Pens, paper, paper clips, or something?"

"Nothing, thanks. Here, let me help you," she said, taking a bag from him as they made their way out of the store. "And what on earth are you going to do with all that paper?"

"It's for my printer." He stored the supplies in the trunk of his car, and looked at his watch. "Seven. We've got an hour and a half to kill. Coffee?" he suggested, pointing to the sign over one of the shops.

She nodded, still wondering about all that paper.

The Coffee Mill was clean and quaint with neat

little booths upholstered in blue and white. The air was warm and welcoming, with the rich aroma of coffee of various blends, as proclaimed by the sign over the counter . . .

"All this is very confusing," she said. "Do you suppose I could get just plain coffee?"

"What! When one has a choice of such exotic blends?"

"Well . . ." She looked at the sign, and pondered. "Maybe I'll try the Brazilian Mocha."

"Good." He chuckled. "Live dangerously. I'll try the Kenya Java."

When they were settled in a booth, she took a sip of the hot brew. "Different," she said, wrinkling her nose. "And . . . well, not bad. I think I like it."

He tasted his, sputtered, and pushed it aside. "I don't intend to live that dangerously," he said and, when the waitress brought their sandwiches, ordered a milder blend.

Darlene bit into her turkey sandwich, and looked at the man across from her. Not as handsome as Leon, but she liked his clean-cut appearance, his strong chiseled features. She found herself wondering about this stranger who had popped up out of nowhere a few short months ago. "The Westons were lucky," she said. "To have you take over for them when they had to move."

"Lucky for me, too."

"Oh? Why?" She had wondered why a grown man

had been so readily available. He hadn't even had a job at first.

"It was a good excuse and a chance to leave Kansas City."

"That sounds as if you were running away from something." She was ashamed of the digging, but couldn't stem her curiosity.

"Not exactly running, but . . ." He hesitated, shifted his position, took a swallow of coffee. "Well, maybe so. I was working with my dad, you see, and I knew he didn't want me to leave. But he thought Uncle George needed me so . . . here I am."

"Yes." She knew that Mr. Weston's doctor had ordered him to leave immediately. There was no chance to see after their personal things or care of the property, and she suspected that the income from the property was essential right now. "It was good of you to take over for them, and according to Miss Selina, they couldn't have a better person. She says you stopped that leak under her sink and even replaced her old oven."

He grinned. "Well trained. I've been plumbing, wiring, and swinging a hammer since I was about twelve."

"Oh?" She was surprised.

"Yep. Dad was a handyman and made us work with him. That is whenever we weren't in school learning business and whatever it took to get a contractor's license, which he was determined we should get."

"And did you?"

"Yep. We both got it two years ago."

"We?"

"My brother and I. Which is one reason I don't feel so bad about leaving." He stirred uneasily, and she could tell he did feel guilty. "J.C., my brother, is still there, and he's really into the business."

"And you're not?"

"Not really. And I think my leaving might have been good. Starting a business isn't easy. We were taking on bigger jobs, but we'd had to maintain a bigger working crew, and buy tools and supplies and . . . well, splitting profits two ways instead of three will make a difference. J.C. is married with two kids and needs a solid income."

"And that's why you wanted to leave? For J.C.?"

"Oh, Lord, no. For me. I was dying to get to New York."

"Why?"

Greg hesitated. He didn't like to talk about his writing, but there was something about the way she looked at him . . . not just idle curiosity, but as if she cared. So he told her. "New York. It's where everything is happening. The best place for a writer to be."

"Oh! You're a writer!"

"Well . . ." She sounded so impressed he hated to disillusion her. "I'm not so sure I qualify as *a writer*. Oh, I've sold a few articles, but my real interest is in the theater. I've written a couple of plays, and—"

"Oh!" She leaned forward, cupping her chin in her

hands, eyes bright with excitement. "Tell me about your plays. I had no idea you were a playwright."

"Wait a minute!" he said, laughing. "I'm afraid I don't qualify as a playwright, either. Not until I'm produced. I thought I might have a better shot at it here in New York."

"And have you? Had a shot at it, I mean."

"Oh, yes," he said eagerly. "I've been working with this off-Broadway theater. A workshop, really. But they do readings for new plays. It's been a real learning experience."

"I can see that. No wonder you like being here."

"Yes." He shifted in his seat. "I am sorry about Uncle George's illness, but don't you see? Not only did it give me a place to live until I got a job, but it also provided me with access to the center of the theater world."

"I do see," she said, smiling. "So tell me, Greg Weston, why do you sound so apologetic?"

"Apologetic? No, I'm not . . . I . . ." He threw up his hands. "Okay, Tonya said you were a good listener. She didn't tell me you're also very perceptive." He sighed. "The truth is, I keep wondering about leaving Dad and J.C. in the lurch. They're both better carpenters than I, but . . . well, not too sharp at figures. Cost analysis, business trends, stuff like that."

"So they left the business end to you?"

"Yeh. Still, we're a small business. I keep telling myself they're better off . . . splitting the profits only two ways. And, as I said, J.C. is married with two kids, and needs more money. So . . ." He shrugged.

He looked so torn that Darlene's heart went out to him. She reached out and touched his arm. "It's hard, isn't it?" she said. "When you're the kind of person who thinks of others as well as yourself?"

"Oh, it's not that," he protested.

"No?" She smiled at him. "Maybe not. But would you like to know what I think, Mr. Weston?"

He nodded, looking as if he was eager to know what she thought.

"I think your dad and J.C. will do just fine. Remember, your dad managed alone before either of you boys came of age. Besides, you're only a phone or a plane ride away. And, if you have this opportunity to make your dreams come true . . . What do they say? When opportunity knocks . . ."

"Oh, I know it's a long shot," he said, "but it was like a gift, and I grabbed it." Darlene thought he still looked doubtful, as if he was trying to thrash things out in his own mind.

"What does your father say?" she asked.

"That I'm a damn fool. That construction is a lucrative business, and the writing profession is iffy."

Greg is different from Leon, she thought. Leon would never desert a lucrative profession for one that was iffy. If it doesn't pay, don't play was Leon's motto.

"What do you think?" Greg asked.

"I think that money isn't everything. At least three

fourths of a person's life is spent at his job, and a man who loves his work is very lucky. Keep up the writing."

"I like what you say, but I am forced to remind you that a great portion of my work time is now at Franchise Tax."

"You won't be there long," she said. "Not with your determination, your insight, and all that paper waiting in the trunk of your car!"

He laughed and Darlene laughed with him, watching how his full lips curved around very white teeth, wondering how it would feel to have those lips on hers. She felt the heat rush to her cheeks and was glad she was too dark for it to show. Never before in her life had she looked at a man and wondered how it would feel to kiss him. They hardly knew each other, and here she had been running on, asking questions and prying into his business! What must he think of her!

Greg was thinking that yes, she was drop-dead beautiful, and he got a lift just talking to her. She really listened to what he said, taking it all in as if she really cared. Her lips parted, her eyes, those gorgeous dark lustrous eyes, focused on him as if they were telling him that he had made a good decision, that he was capable of tremendous undertakings and . . .

He suddenly remembered something else Tonya had said: "The way she looks at you with those big wide-open eyes like she's saying you're wonderful, even if she's just telling you to wear your raincoat or saying thank you to the man who just brought the mail."

Her eyes might be on you, but her heart's with that guy she's gonna marry!

And what's with this heart business, buster! You can't afford to fall in love. Not until your writing catches on and you can quit that job at Franchise Tax.

Abruptly he stood up. "We'd better go. Time to pick up Tonya."

Chapter Three

Darlene gave Tonya the idea. Actually all she said was that Greg was nice. That didn't mean much. Darlene thought everybody was nice. So maybe it was the way she said it.

That night after the game they were both in their crowded little bathroom. Tonya was getting out of the shower, and Darlene was at the sink, creaming her face when she said, ever so softly, "That Greg Weston is really very nice." She was staring into that little mirror over the sink, but it was like she wasn't seeing her face, but something else. Or someone else. She didn't seem to be quivering or anything like that. But her expression . . . Well, it gave Tonya goose bumps.

"Yeh" was all she said, not wanting to break the spell.

"I'm glad he went with us," Darlene said as she tissued her face. "He explained all the plays to me, and I really enjoyed the game. Not just your cheerleading, which of course was fantastic." She turned a beaming face toward Tonya. "And then we went for coffee, and . . . I learned a lot about him. He's really very nice."

"Yes," Tonya said again.

"He writes. Did you know that?"

"Yes."

"Plays. I wonder what kind of plays," Darlene mused. Then she threw her tissue into the wastebasket as if dismissing the subject. "Don't forget to brush your teeth," she said as she went out.

Tonya finished toweling herself and brushed her teeth, her mind going a mile a minute. Darlene talked to or about Leon all the time . . . "Now wasn't it thoughtful of Leon to bring you that gift," or "Leon is so smart. He told me about a clever deal he pulled today and . . ." On and on.

Tonight . . . well, it was like she put more in those two sentences about Greg than ever got squeezed into all the thousands of words she had ever used on Leon. It was like . . . Tonya stopped, toothbrush suspended, her mouth full of toothpaste. Yep, the way she talked and looked was like when the heroine first saw the guy she was going to fall in love with. Not that this was the first time Darlene had seen Greg. Except the previous times had consisted mainly of her handing him the rent check and nodding in passing now and again. Yep, she bet this was the first time Darlene had ever really looked at him.

Yeh, the first time. She finished brushing her teeth, rinsed out her mouth.

Now, in those books, even though the heroine got all shook up, at first she didn't know she was going to fall in love with the guy. Sometimes she didn't even like him, maybe hated him for some reason. But circumstances or something kept throwing them together and . . .

Circumstances. That was hard. Darlene never got home until after Greg had shut himself up with his computer. Anyway, the weather was too bad for anybody to linger on the steps. And Leon took up the weekends and as many evenings as he could get. Leon sure complicated things. In those books, the heroine was hardly ever already engaged to somebody else.

Maybe if they had to call Greg up for a leaking faucet or a burned-out wire . . . Not much chance. There was never anything in their flat that needed fixing, the way it always was at Miss Selina's.

Circumstances were not likely to throw Darlene and Greg together. Not enough, anyway. But Tonya kept thinking about it. She thought about it all day Sunday when Darlene went with Leon to his mother's and she spent the day with the Thompsons next door. The Thompsons' brownstone had never been converted into flats, and the third floor was used as a studio by Mrs. Thompson, who was an artist. Carol Thompson was Tonya's second best friend, but she went to private school and was seldom home on account of piano or ballet lessons or something. Yet Tonya always had a good time when she did see her.

Like on Sunday Mrs. Thompson, who was interested in African art, took them to the city for a matinee performance of the African Ballet. Fantastic! And when they got back, Dr. Thompson had dinner waiting for them.

You would think that Dr. Thompson, who was a dentist, couldn't cook, but whatever he had fixed sure did smell good.

"Shrimp gumbo Louisiana style," he said. He was from New Orleans and was always bragging about the food there. "Everything's ready as soon as the rice is. Why don't you girls set the table. Tonya, Leon told me the good news, the lucky dog." Tonya was reaching into the drawer for silver and must have looked surprised that he knew. Anyway, he went on to explain that Leon was his broker as well as a member of his fraternity, and had told him of the engagement. "Darlene's lucky, too. Leon's one sharp cookie. Like all Alpha men." He sang a funny song about everyone except Alphas being dogs or going to hell. It made them laugh and he bowed as he declared, "We are the smartest, the finest, the cream of the crop."

"Which is what any man will tell you about whatever fraternity he's in," Mrs. Thompson said. "Monroe, take off that silly hat and sit down and ask the blessing."

"But you know who's best. That's why you married me," he said, doffing the chef's hat he had fashioned out of a paper bag and kissing his wife before he sat down.

Tonya wondered if Leon would give Darlene impromptu kisses like that. She knew he'd never sing silly songs or cook dinner in a goofy chef's hat. That made her feel sad. She didn't want Darlene to marry Leon. But her conscience pricked when Dr. Thompson began to talk seriously about what a fine man Leon was and the good investments he had advised. He said he couldn't be more pleased, that it really did him good when he saw two young bright people like Darlene and Leon getting together.

Maybe she was wrong. Only she kept thinking about the way Darlene had looked that night when she talked about Greg, and how she never looked like that when she talked about Leon. Anyway, there wasn't anything she could do about it, so she might as well, like Greg said, butt out.

Maybe she would have if she hadn't run into Greg on her way home from Sophie's Monday afternoon. Sophie was in her class, and they often studied together. They spent the afternoon gathering evidence for a forthcoming debate. Sophie's mother had brought them a snack from their deli downstairs. Pastrami on rye with slaw, kosher dill pickles, and Dr. Brown cream sodas. Scrumptious! Louisiana gumbo yesterday and kosher today.

Tonya was thinking it was fun to experiment with different kinds of food when she saw Greg on his way home from the subway. He was walking fast, his raincoat closely buttoned, the collar pulled up against the icy drizzle that had just sprung up. And . . . yep, carrying a paper bag. He ought to have a better dinner than that. She didn't know what kind of food his folks had in Kansas City, but she bet he would like her dad's kind of cooking. She often took a dish to Miss Selina, and she could take . . . No. Tonya almost stopped dead-still, thinking. If she invited him up—

"Just getting home from school?" Greg asked, glancing at her book bag.

"No. I've been over to Sophie's getting ready for a debate." Circumstances. Anything that threw people together . . .

"What's the subject?"

"Huh?"

"What're you debating?"

"Oh. Military intervention by the United States for human rights in other countries." She hadn't even thought about dinner today, but maybe tomorrow she could ask him.

"Great subject. How's it going?"

"Huh?"

"Hey, where's your mind today? How are you doing with that hot issue?"

"Okay, I guess. Sophie's pretty smart."

"I thought you were."

"Yeh, but I'm not too great on the con side." They had reached the house now. "See you," she called, and raced up the steps to see what she could fix tomorrow.

Not much. They had been so busy this weekend they hadn't shopped. Soup was the only answer, she thought as she surveyed the fridge. But she was good with soup, and there was always so much left over they had to store it in separate containers. Easy reason to ask neighbors to share. She better ask Miss Selina, too.

Dessert. She found a package of dried peaches in the cupboard and dumped the contents into a pot of cold water to soak. She would prepare them tonight . . . sugar, cloves, lemon. Greg would love those mouthwatering peach tarts. She debated about inviting him tonight just to be sure he'd come. But then it would look planned and not a spur-of-the-moment-hope-it's-okay kind of thing. She would just have to take her chances. He usually came straight home with that dumb paper bag, and ought to be hungry for something different.

As soon as she got home the next afternoon, she threw her books aside and began to prepare. She took the contents of the vegetable bin from the fridge . . . stems saved from mustard greens and cauliflower, a quarter of a cabbage, celery, parsley, a few string beans, and dumped them with a whole onion into a big pot of water. These she boiled, blended, and drained, added potatoes, carrots, a container of blackeyed peas from the freezer, a can of stewed tomatoes, then flavored the mixture with bouillon cubes, herbs, salt, pepper, and a wee bit of sugar. Nutritious, filling, and nonfattening . . . an excellent dish for a dieter. At least that's what Dad said.

Now for the tarts. The top of the coffee can served to shape the rolled out dough into neat circles, each of which she filled with juicy peaches. Then she folded over the dough and closed it with the tines of a fork. Dad said his mother fried them, but, conscious of cholesterol, he always baked them. So she would, too. Only at the last minute so they would be a little warm.

As she worked, she watched through the window for Greg. The thing was . . . the more she worked, the more she watched, the more pronounced were the nudges of guilt. She kept hearing voices . . .

"An up-and-coming young man. Darlene will be set for life."

"Couldn't be more pleased . . . two bright young people getting together . . ."

"Butt out!"

But she wasn't butting in! Not one single time had she said one single solitary thing against Leon to Darlene. Not once! Asking a person to dinner wasn't asking anybody to fall in love with that person, for Pete's sake. It was just being nice to a neighbor. Especially one practically choking on junk food, she thought as she spotted Greg a half block away. She wiped her hands on her jeans, slipped on her jacket, and hurried to meet him.

Greg was about to put his key in the lock when

he saw the Davis kid racing down the steps. "Tonya! How's it going?"

"Fine," she said, sounding a bit out of breath. "Where's your dinner?"

"Dinner? Oh." He followed her gaze to his empty hands and grinned. "Thought I'd like a change of menu, maybe pick up a sandwich from the deli."

"Want me to pick it up for you? I'm going that way."

He considered, and was reaching into his pocket when she held up a hand. "No. Wait. I've got a better idea. Why don't you join us? We're just having soup." She gave a casual shrug.

He hesitated, thinking of a pair of luscious dark eyes. Since that one-to-one encounter in the coffee shop, he'd warned himself to steer clear of the Davis sisters. Of one of them, anyway. "Thanks, but I'd better not. I—

"Better'n a sandwich. It's good soup. I made it."

"You?" He stared at her, struck by the idea of this pint-size kid trying her hand at cooking. And she looked so anxious. Like Josie, his little cousin, urging him to try the peanut butter cookies she had made. "Well, in that case, I wouldn't miss it," he said, suppressing his skepticism. Josie's cookies were never as tasty as she promised they would be.

"Good. I'm gonna ask Miss Selina, too."

He wondered why that made him feel better. Less vulnerable . . . or something.

"See you about six, when Darlene gets home. Okay?"

He nodded, watching her speed away. Just a bunch of neighbors getting together. So what the hell! As if she'd give him the time of day. Not when she was already hooked up to, according to Miss Selina, the prizewinning, top-selling muckety muck of the century!

Chapter Four

Tonya was quite proud of herself as she dashed out, pretending she was going on an errand. That really made her invitation casual so he wouldn't think it was planned. Now all she had to do was race up the block and then get back to ask Miss Selina and set the table.

And tell Darlene. She knew Darlene wouldn't care. She kept telling herself she wasn't butting into anything, but she felt a little nervous anyway. So when Darlene came, she spilled it out in a hurry. "I made soup, and there was so much, I asked Miss Selina . . . and Greg, too. Okay?"

"Did you! That was nice of you" was all Darlene said before she got into jeans and a pullover and started picking up and vacuuming like crazy. "Miss Selina's place is always neat as a pin. Tonya, take these things into your room and shut your door."

Tonya dumped her jacket and books on her unmade bed, and sighed. Darlene could have kept on that luscious wool dress or at least changed into that sexy lounging outfit Leon gave her for her birthday. And she could have put on a little lipstick, which was all the makeup she ever used.

As soon as he entered their flat, he was enveloped by the inviting and mouthwatering odors of zesty soup simmering on the stove and something sweet and spicy baking in the oven.

"Sure smells better'n a deli sandwich," he said to Tonya. "I'm mighty glad to be here."

"So am I," Miss Selina said from her chair by the window. "Our Tonya is an excellent cook."

"Yeh," Greg gulped, suddenly arrested by the sight of Darlene. The way those tight-fitting jeans hugged her slender figure, the way her rich coffee-colored skin glowed against the pastel pink of that slightly smudged pullover. Her smile. He wanted to crush his mouth against her full curved lips that parted, invited . . . He wanted to run a hand through her tousled hair, and—

Darlene smiled that sweet you're-so-wonderful smile. "We're so glad to have you. We're dressing up for company. See?"

He forced his gaze to follow her gesture to the centerpiece on the table. A few leaves and . . . a geranium?

"Now, isn't that nice?" Miss Selina got up to examine the centerpiece, then looked back at the plant on the windowsill from where it had been plucked. "Tonya may be the cook, but Darlene's the gardener.

All my indoor plants die, especially the blooming ones. But just look at hers." Greg looked. There were only a few plants, but they were certainly thriving, even the geranium and the small pot of violets on the coffee table. "I don't know how she does it."

"She talks to them," Tonya piped up, mimicking, "My, you're looking perky this morning, or you poor thing, you look a little droopy. Would you like a drink of water?"

"Oh, hush," Darlene said as they laughed. "And go check your muffins. We're ready to eat."

Tonya buttered the muffins, and placed them in a basket. Then she struck a meek pose as she ladled out big bowls of soup, apologizing, "There wasn't much upon my shelves, but I'se done my best to suit you. So set down and hep yourselves!"

Miss Selina clapped her hands. "Dunbar . . . 'The Party'! Right?"

"Right," Darlene said, and assumed a husky masculine voice. "I don't believe in 'pologizing and professing! Let 'em tek it as they catch it! Elder Weston, ask the blessing."

Taking the cue, Greg bowed his head, one eye shut and one eye open, and rapidly quoted the remembered lines. "Lord, look down in tender mercy on such generous hearts as these, give us peace and joy, Amen, pass them muffins, if you please!" Amid general laughter, they began to eat. After a few spoonfuls of the delicious soup, Greg raised thumb and forefinger in an okay sign to Tonya. "This is great!"

A smug smile lit her face. "I know. And just wait till you taste my dessert."

Miss Selina continued to talk about Paul Lawrence Dunbar, the late Negro poet laureate. "I guess his dialect poems which center upon our experiences during slavery are the best known," she said, "and probably the most profound, as they're a record of our natures as well as our roots."

"How do you mean?" Tonya asked.

"Take 'The Party,' Miss Selina said. "Can't you see those slaves having fun, even under the most dire circumstances? And making do. Remember Mandy's laden table . . . that coon in all that gravy, laying by that possum's side?"

"Sure weren't picked up from the corner grocery," Greg said. "I see what you mean."

Miss Selina smiled, but she looked serious. "Oh, he told us so much about ourselves. The love of a black father for his child in his 'Lil Brown Baby With Sparkling Eyes.' Our pride in our own talents in 'When Malindy Sings.' And faith. 'The Ante Bellum Sermon,' for instance. Can't you just see that colored preacher standing out in the field, trying to encourage his flock, and warning them at the same time? . . . 'I'se talking about our freedom in a Biblelistic way! Now, don't run and tell your masters I'se preaching discontent.' " She waited for a series of comments and chuckles to subside before she spoke again. "There's history, too. In 'When They 'Listed Colored Soldiers and my Lias Went to War,' don't you feel the pride and pathos of the woman who watched him go? And even in the turmoil of the Civil War, he expresses the love between the races when she grieves for her masters, too, 'though they both went in gray suits, and Lias wore the Yankee blue. Oh, yes," she concluded, "there's a wealth of knowledge in those dialect poems."

"Guess I never thought about it that way," Tonya said. "Dad recited them all the time, and I just thought they were funny."

"Maybe," Miss Selina said. "But I bet you absorbed a few truths, too. Humor can be a powerful teaching tool."

"You think so?" Greg asked. He used lots of humor in his plays, simply because it came naturally to him. More entertaining, too. But teaching?

"Oh, sure. The more we laugh, the more we learn."

"So take note, Greg. Greg's a writer," Darlene said to Miss Selina.

"Aspiring writer," he corrected.

"Why, I had no idea." Miss Selina looked surprised. "What do you write?"

"Well, I'm working on a play."

"My English teacher says we should have more ethnic literature," Tonya said. "Is yours a black play?"

"Not really. It's just about . . . people. A mixed cast."

"Tell us about it," Miss Selina urged, and all eyes focused on him.

He didn't like to talk about his writing. He tried to make it brief. "A group of ecology-minded college students try to stage a protest against a polluting meat products company. They have trouble rallying support. Everybody too busy doing their own thing. The Russian students won't have anything to do with something that might interfere with their plush new-found capitalism, the women are too busy conducting a seminar on harassment, and the blacks ask, 'Save humanity? What about black folks?' "

Amid a crescendo of clapping hands, Tonya exclaimed, "That's funny!"

"And interesting. Can't you just see it in action!" Darlene said.

Miss Selina looked thoughtful. "It sounds like a spoof on ethnicity. A bit against the current trend, isn't it?"

He nodded. "Probably never sell."

"Now, don't despair, young man." Miss Selina shook her soupspoon at him. "That's not a bad theme. It's good to have ethnic pride, but . . . Pride is the first of the seven deadly sins, you know."

"Oh?" He didn't know.

"That surprises you? It shouldn't. Look at what's going on all over the world today. Cruel conflicts between different tribes, different sects, different religions. Sad." She sighed. "Yes, pride can be divisive. And your play makes that point, doesn't it?"

"Wait a minute," he said. "It's just . . . well, just a

takeoff on some incidents when I was in college. It's not all that deep."

"Dunbar probably never thought of his poems as deep, either," Miss Selina said. She nodded at him gravely. "Yes, yours is an excellent theme. Pride can get pretty close to prejudice."

"Oh, yes. And both can be stumbling blocks to what's really important. Like getting a child placed in the right home," Darlene said. "I know." She had taken on Miss Selina's grave tone, and was looking at him like he was some kind of a messiah. Damn! "It's like you're sending a message to the world, Greg. I'd love to read it."

"Maybe when it's finished," he said. And maybe not, he thought, feeling acutely embarrassed. She'd be expecting something profound, when . . .

"Oh, well, it's not all that great. It's just . . ." His voice trailed off. He was drowning in those dark liquid eyes.

"Okay. Dessert coming up," Tonya said. "Who wants milk and who wants coffee?"

"Coffee for me," he said quickly, glad to be off the hook. He tore his gaze from Darlene, reminding himself not to be a fool. That was how she looked at everyone.

Tonya walked into the kitchen to get the dessert, and when she returned, made a point of serving Greg first.

Darlene watched Greg bite into one of Tonya's

fruit tarts. "Isn't my little sister a great cook?" she asked, unable to keep the pride from her voice.

"I'll say. I hope you'll forgive me for making a pig of myself, but this is my first home-cooked meal since I left Kansas."

"Really?" Who had provided home-cooked meals in Kansas? Darlene realized he had talked about a father and a brother, but there was no mention of a mother. In any case, it wasn't likely that he had lived with his parents. "Do you miss Kansas?" she asked. Miss anybody? And why should that interest her?

Because he really is an interesting man, she told herself. That night in the coffee shop—

"Guess I've been too busy to miss it," he said.

Cheerfully busy, she thought. Whistling absent-mindedly as he cleaned off the sidewalk or changed a lightbulb. Not anxious and tight-lipped like Leon when they were on their way to meet one of his clients.

She sat up, annoyed with herself. She was comparing again! Planning a major money investment was a heck of a lot different from changing a lightbulb.

"Do you know you have very dreamy eyes?" she asked. Darn! It had just popped out and sounded downright flirtatious. "I mean," she said, rushing to cover herself. "As a writer . . . you must always be dreaming up some plot or something even when you're doing something else, huh?"

"Er . . . yeh. I suppose." Greg shifted in his chair.

"We're going to play Monopoly. Okay?" Tonya asked.

Darlene looked up to see that Tonya and Miss Selina had already cleared the table. She hadn't even noticed. But she was glad they were setting out the Monopoly board. She was reluctant to see the evening end.

Greg didn't want to see the evening end, either.

He liked being there, happy in the warm hospitality, stimulated by the lively conversation. If he could just manage not to look at Darlene, those eyes, her bright smile, and the way the dimples danced in her cheeks.

Chapter Five

The trouble was he couldn't manage not to look at her. Especially when they found themselves together so often. Miss Selina had them all for dinner the very next week, and he brought dinner in twice, once Chinese food and once barbecue from the Rib House. Tonya's hard-to-resist offers were the most frequent . . . "Come on up . . . I've got chicken and dumplings . . . collard greens and black-eyed peas . . . fried catfish and hush puppies." The tempting dishes teased his palate, but he found he was more hungry for any glimpse of Darlene. Not just a brief glimpse as she hurried from work in trim business attire, or the times he watched from his window as Leon ushered a more glamorous Darlene into his Mercedes. But Greg wasn't envious. He liked her best in jeans, hair tousled, hands in soapy dishwater as they washed dishes and argued over some remark of Miss Selina's. Or in the midst of a game of gin rummy, when her dimples deepened and her eyes twinkled in a triumphant grin as she yelled "Gin!"

Although her eyes aren't twinkling now, he thought as he leaned against the sink and dried the dessert dish she handed him. This was not one of their middle-of-the-week dining get-togethers, but an impromptu invitation from Tonya to "sample my lemon cream pie." A Sunday evening that, in itself, was unusual. Where was the boyfriend? Miss Selina was not there, and, after dessert, Tonya had withdrawn to her room to "catch up on some reading."

He didn't like to pry, but Darlene had been so quiet that he couldn't help asking, "Something bugging you?"

"Something certainly is," she said, giving the dishrag a vicious twist and shaking it out. "My job."

"Oh?" He was conscious of a feeling of deflation. Had he been hoping it was her love life?

"You would think, wouldn't you," she said, almost slamming the dishes he had dried into the cupboard, "that if a person has a master's degree in social work, with a specialty in psychiatry, plus a year of training in child psychology, plus two years experience in the field of child welfare, that people would have some respect for her opinions in that particular field. At the very least, that person should have some say in any decision concerning the welfare of any child that person has been counseling for a whole year!"

She sounded so much like Tonya when she was in a huff that he had trouble keeping a straight face.

"Well, wouldn't you think so?" she demanded.

"Decision," he repeated, trying to unravel all that

she had said. "But I thought . . . That is, isn't that just what you do? Decide what to—"

"Oh, no. No indeed." Her voice was rich with sarcasm. "We can only recommend. The decision, the final decision that may make or break a child's life, is left to the court. The judge who sits on his high-and-mighty bench and listens to a repentant whining parent or an incompetent and therefore frustrated foster parent and makes a decision about a child when he doesn't really know a darn thing about what is going on with that child."

"Hey, cool it," he cautioned. "You're the one who seems frustrated. And not on account of incompetence if you're in possession of all the qualifications you just rattled off. Are you?"

She gave a rueful nod.

"I'm impressed."

She shrugged. "I guess it doesn't add up to all that much. But I do care. And I hate the rules, regulations, and court procedures that get in my way!"

"Your way?" He did smile then. "What's really bothering you?"

"What I have to do tomorrow."

"Which is?"

"Remove one child from a home where he truly belongs and take another one back to a home where she should not be!"

He watched her lips tighten, the pulse at the base of her neck throb convulsively. So different from her vivacious, happy self, whether playing a game or jauntily leaving for work. As if her job was a breeze. Evidently it wasn't. "Do you want to talk about it?"

"No. That won't do any good."

"It might. Come on, let's get comfortable." He led her to the sofa in the living room. "Tell me. What's the removal case all about?"

"These foster parents made the mistake of applying to adopt a five-year-old boy they've had since birth. Eric. Oh, Greg, he's so cute and so clever. Musical. He can actually play some tunes on the piano. The foster father is a music teacher, and he says Eric is naturally talented."

"And they made a mistake in applying to adopt him?"

"A big one," she said bitterly. "Interracial adoptions are taboo. Cultural differences and all that stuff! Oh, Greg, he's so happy there. And now they can't even be his foster parents."

"Why not?"

"The agency is snatching him away because they've become too attached. I've talked till I'm blue in the face, but I feel like I'm the only person on my staff, maybe in the whole world, who thinks loving and caring takes precedence over race."

He felt her rage and helplessness, and wished there was something he could do. Or say. "You're not. There are others who feel as you do."

"I know. The foster parents are going to sue."

"Good."

"I don't know. They don't have much money."

She looked so despondent that he put an arm around her and drew her back against him. "Hey, don't despair. Our court system is pretty fair. Right often triumphs over money. Maybe this family will be reunited."

"Maybe. But tomorrow I'll have to go over there and take Eric away." Her head dropped back against his shoulder in a gesture of despair.

Silently he rubbed his chin in her hair, wishing he had a solution. Or words to help her through the turmoil.

"And then I have to return Emily to her parents, and I don't want to do that, either!"

"Emily?" Her hair tickled his chin. It had the fresh smell of sweet-scented soap.

"A seven-year-old beauty. Really. Golden hair, big blue eyes, and pale skin, which, when we got her, was very bruised."

"Oh. And now?"

"Oh, now everything is hunky-dory!" She sat up and turned to him, scowling. "Her father has had counseling and joined AA, and it'll never happen again!"

"Maybe it won't," he said.

"Maybe it will. Even if it doesn't, she'll always be living in constant fear that it will. I know," she said, her face reflecting concern for all the Emilys in the world.

He took both her hands in his, and hesitated. You can't win them all was not the thing to say. Not when Darlene couldn't think in terms of statistics, or race, or even a case. Only of a child in need of her guidance, her protection. "Yours is a tough job, Darlene. You do what you can, make hundreds of happy placements, I am sure." He paused, took a deep breath, and spoke more slowly. "But, much as we'd like it to be, this isn't a perfect world. There are bound to be some mistakes, some wrong decisions, some imperfect situations."

"I know, but—"

"But these are the ones you worry about," he finished for her.

She nodded.

He gently rubbed a thumb against the back of her hand. "Don't. Most children survive. They learn to cope."

"You're right," she said, lifting her face. "That's what I wanted . . . what I still want to do. Focus on the child. Help them to cope, whatever the situation."

"Oh?"

"Child psychology. That's what I was taking at Columbia when Dad died. I still have two more years to go."

Slowly he drew it from her. Night classes at Columbia while working at County Welfare, sharing an apartment near the school with two other women.

"But then Dad died, and there was no place for Tonya to live." Her smile flashed now, as if it was a joy, a privilege to take on the responsibility of her sister. No mention of her own interrupted plans, her deferred career. Just . . . wasn't she lucky to find this flat? Wasn't it a good area for Tonya? She had friends and was doing well at school. Didn't he think Tonya was happy here?

He nodded, but he wasn't thinking of Tonya. He was thinking of her sister. "You are drop-dead beautiful," he said.

"Thank you . . . I think." Her gurgle of laughter held surprise and doubt.

Perhaps a bit of embarrassment, too, he thought as she tried to pull away. "Tonya's words," he said, taking a firmer grip of her hands. He could not let go. Nor could he tear his gaze from her eyes that held a beauty far deeper than physical. "She's right. She knows you pretty well."

"Oh? So what else did my little cocky know-it-all sister say?"

"That you are a listener. She was right about that, too. You listen with your heart."

"And just what do you know about my heart?"

"Not as much as I'd like to." His voice was a coarse whisper as his eyes focused on her quivering lips. "I want to know all about you. What you want, what you think, what you feel. I want to touch you." He tilted her chin and bent toward those full, parted, inviting lips.

He was unprepared for the impact . . . the quickening of his pulses, the heat in his veins. The strong surge of desire mixed with a tangle of emotions, tender and compellingly erotic. He wanted to shield and protect her . . . comfort, care for, pamper . . . possess and pleasure her. The first light touch of her lips and he knew that this was the only woman in the world for him. Slowly and possessively, he drew her close, his hands caressing, his tongue teasing, tantalizing, as he deepened his kiss. When his demanding mouth finally captured hers, she was with him all the way. Her arms clung tightly about his neck, her fingers dug into his hair, and he felt the sweet yielding of her soft body as she pressed closer. He was undone by the fervor of her response. Her need was as great as his. He could fulfill that need, make passionate love until they both cried out in the magic of fulfillment. His exhilaration mounted even as a warning bell sounded. He paid it no mind. It rang and rang and . . . was replaced by pounding on the door. A voice . . . "Darlene! Are you there? Is anybody home?"

She pulled away and looked at him in a dazed languor.

The pounding started again.

"The door." She tried to smooth her rumpled pullover and went to answer.

Who the hell was intruding at this time of night!

"Oh, Leon! It's you," he heard her say.

Greg saw a fair-skinned man with sandy hair bend to kiss her. He felt something deep inside himself burst and explode.

Chapter Six

Leon Cranston threw his camel coat on a chair and slipped a proprietary arm around Darlene. "I missed you," he said, "but the trip was worth it. I got the old geezer's whole portfolio and . . ." He stopped in mid-sentence as he spotted Greg. "Oh . . . er . . . how do you do," he said, his brow rising in surprised, but unperturbed query.

"Greg Weston, Leon." Darlene hurriedly supplied, since Greg stood stiff, tight-lipped, silent. "Greg, this is Leon Cranston, My . . ." A lump rose in her throat, muffling the words, "my fiancé." The smoldering ecstasy of the past moment was strangely kindled by the hot wave of embarrassment, and the confused emotions burst, like flames, inside her. She ignored the fire that threatened to consume her, and carried on, surprised to find her voice normal. "Greg is our stand-in landlord." At his sharp glance, she hastened to add, "and our good friend as well." But she was irked. He was their landlord, wasn't he? He had no right to look as if she had slapped him. Still, she didn't want him to think . . .

"Oh, yes, Darlene has spoken of you," Leon said, extending an affable hand.

For a long moment it seemed Greg might not take the hand, and Darlene was relieved when he did.

"Oh, yes. Cranston!" he said, giving Darlene another significant look. "Tonya has often spoken of you."

Darlene's head jerked up, and their glances locked. Tonya? And not she? But she knew Greg was aware of Leon, and it wasn't like she was trying to hide anything. It was just . . . They had always had so much else to talk about.

Leon seemed not to notice the implication. "New to the city, aren't you?" he asked, and launched into an amiable conversation. Darlene resented his cool serenity while she was all on edge. She resented it still more when his pleasantries soon developed into smooth probing concerning Greg's occupation and business interests. More interested in Greg's portfolio than what he's doing alone with me at this time of night!

She was appalled at herself. Did she want Leon to be angry . . . jealous?

And why was she more concerned with what Greg was thinking! As if he was due an explanation rather than Leon. Which reminded her . . . "Greg came up to sample Tonya's lemon cream pie," she explained as soon as there was a lull in Leon's questioning. "It's delicious, isn't it, Greg?"

"The best," he said evenly. He refused her offer of a second helping, and got out as fast as he could.

Darlene watched the door close behind him, feeling a strange sense of loss. And a keen awareness of the heavy pounding of her heart and the vibrations still skittering through her whole body.

"So . . . what mischief did you get into while I was gone?" Leon asked. Then added, "Hey! I'm joking. Come on. Where's that pie?"

"Coming right up," she said, hurrying into the kitchen.

He followed her in and sat at the little breakfast nook. "Did you go over those listings?"

"Listings?" She set a serving of pie in front of him.

"The houses I marked on that brochure. Any one of them appeal to you?"

"Oh." She had forgotten to look. "I haven't had a chance. Saturday I went to a football game with Tonya." And with Greg again, she thought as guilt surfaced. And tonight . . . what on earth had come over her! Her hand shook as she set two mugs of coffee on the table.

Leon took a forkful of pie. "Scrumptious! Tell you what . . . whatever house we settle on, Tonya'll have to check out the kitchen. We have to satisfy the chief cook."

"Yes." How could one kiss so unnerve her? Coffee. Perhaps that would sober her. She took a deep swallow. It burned her tongue, but did not stifle the little shocks of delight still pulsing through her.

"Get the brochures," Leon said. "We'll go over them together. There was one house I particularly liked. I think you will, too. There's a private girl's school only a few blocks away."

She tried to catch his enthusiasm. This was Leon. Dear Leon, who loved her. And he was making such plans to care for her and for her sister. Leon would give Tonya the kind of security Tonya's father had given her. Dear Leon. They were so lucky.

She stood up and went to get the brochures.

"I owe you an apology, Greg," Darlene said, keeping her eyes on the Monopoly board. This was the best time to do it, casually, while Miss Selina and Tonya were haggling over the price of Marvin Gardens.

"Oh?" He met her eyes, something he had avoided all through dinner.

"Sunday night . . ." She hesitated, wondering how to put it. It was her fault that things had gotten out of hand, and she wanted to tell him so. But she didn't want to make a big thing out of it and was glad that Miss Selina had asked them in for chili, giving her an opportunity to set things straight. In this setting she hoped to avoid any awkwardness. Or intimacy. She cast a glance at the other two, who were still haggling, oblivious. "I had no right to dump my troubles on you."

"No problem. What are friends for?" he said, his expression unreadable.

"No way!" Tonya's voice rose in protest. "You can't charge that much. It's not worth it!"

"It's worth it to you, young lady. You want the whole section so you can build. Demand sets the price, doesn't it, Greg?"

"Er . . . demand. Yes," Greg answered, though it was clear he had no idea what he was responding to. He looked directly at Darlene, and she read the question in his eyes . . . *What the hell are you trying to tell me?*

She colored under his gaze, but answered steadily. "One shouldn't impose on a friend," she said. "It wasn't fair of me to cry on your shoulder."

"Any time. It's always available."

"No. Don't joke," she said, not liking his glib response. "I'm serious, I'm so ashamed."

"Ashamed?"

"For falling apart like that. For . . . for . . ." She bit hard on her lower lip. "Losing control and . . . oh, you know what I mean."

He obviously got it. "Sure. I understand."

"And you forgive me?"

"Hey, like I said . . . what are friends for?!"

Tonya screeched in capitulation. "Okay, okay. I'll pay. And, boy, you stop on my property, you've had it. All right, your turn, Greg. Greg!"

"Huh? Oh!" He threw the dice, made his five moves and had to choose a card . . . " 'Go to jail. Go directly to jail. Do not pass go. Do not collect two hundred dollars.' Guess that puts me in my place!" he said, slamming his token onto the space marked JAIL. Tonya threw him a startled look, and Darlene watched him quickly change his grimace to a smile.

"You don't have to go to jail," Tonya said. "You have a choice. You can pay fifty dollars and get out."

"Oh. Sorry. Sometimes I get my signals crossed," he said, and Darlene knew he wasn't talking about the game.

"What are you going to do?" Tonya asked.

"I'm paying the fifty dollars," he said, shelling out the play money and picking up his token. "I'm getting out of this jam and going on with my life. So watch out!"

Greg's life got so busy that it was easy to keep her out of his sight, if not out of his mind. He had finished his play, and it had been accepted for a reading at one of the off-Broadway workshops. He was ecstatic, and his first thought was to tell Darlene, who had listened to parts of it and had been so encouraging. Then he reminded himself that wasn't a good idea if he was to stick to his resolution. He wouldn't tell any of them until a few nights before the performance, when he would surprise them with tickets.

It was easy to keep his secret, for he spent almost all of his evenings in the city interviewing striving actors and arranging for the performance. This was a big deal for the volunteer actors as well as for himself. Agents and producers were always scouting these workshops.

About a week before the scheduled performance, he got a call from his father. He and J.C. were planning to bid on a big project, a federally funded low-cost housing complex.

"We got a good shot at it," his father said. "Or at least a big piece of the action on account of we're a minority business, don't you think?"

"Yes, I think so. That's great, Dad."

"Yeh, but first we got to figure the cost and get in a competitive bid and . . . Well, son, we need you, and we need you now!"

They did need him. His brother and Dad were both excellent craftsmen, but not worth a damn when it came to figures. And calculations had to be precise not only for the federal project but to determine which current projects to retain, how many new employees were needed, and numerous other details. Too high a bid would lose the project, and one too low might send them under. So much at stake. Not only the livelihood of the two families, but all their workers as well.

The call couldn't have come at a worse time. But there was no getting around it. Besides, as far as the play was concerned, his part was finished, and it would go on without him. He just wouldn't see it.

Darlene paused on the bottom step, glancing at Greg's door. It was shut tight as usual, and she wondered if he was inside. She had seen very little of him since that night at Miss Selina's, and that had been . . . goodness, over a month ago. Funny how the get-togethers that had become routine had abruptly ceased. Maybe because Miss Selina had been away for two weeks visiting her sister, and Tonya was so involved in her cheerleading and the debate team. Even so, why hadn't she seen him around? Cleaning the sidewalk or changing a lightbulb or something.

Had he been deliberately avoiding her? That night when he had kissed her, and Leon had come in . . .

Nonsense. Men are different. They don't get all shook up over one little kiss.

Like she had been shaken? That one kiss, she admitted, had made her feel . . . loved, desirable. And on the verge of an intimacy so wonderful, so fulfilling that . . .

She stifled the memory. One kiss. Just an illusion. Or just the cap to a rare moment of sharing. They had shared so many good talks. Had been such good friends.

They were still friends, weren't they!

She considered ringing his doorbell . . . "Hi! Just hadn't seen you around and I wondered . . ."

No. She'd feel as foolish as she had felt when she tried to get back on the just-friends track in the middle of a Monopoly game. When, maybe as far as he was concerned, they were still on that track. Maybe, for him, a kiss was just a kiss, and she was blowing things all out of proportion. Goodness, she had been kissed before, hadn't she?

Yes. But never before, even with Leon, had one kiss . . . okay, she hadn't seen stars or heard bells. It was more an explosion of rioting emotions . . . a dizzy, delicious, exhilarating, take-me-I'm-yours hunger that . . . Goodness, it must have been the mood she was in. Nothing to do with Greg.

She went on upstairs, determined not to think about him. Not to listen for his voice, or his footstep, or his funny absentminded whistle.

"Hello, Darlene. I thought that was you."

"Oh, hi, Miss Selina. How are you?" Darlene asked as she reached the landing.

"Just fine. Come in for a minute. I've something to tell you."

"Good news, I hope." Darlene entered the flat, appreciating, as always, the extreme neatness and the fresh lemony smell of furniture polish.

"Very good news." Miss Selina shut the door and crossed to her little desk. "Guess what this contains," she said, holding up an envelope.

"I can't imagine."

"Tickets." The older woman's face broke into a smile. "You are cordially invited to The Satellite Workshop Theater, Saturday, December 5, for the premier performance of *Pride,* an exciting play by a new young playwright, Gregory Weston."

Darlene stared in astonishment, unable to utter one word. Incredible. Greg's play was to be presented. It had all happened so quickly. Or had it? He must have known. Must have been preparing. And he had not said anything to her. Not one word.

When he had read the whole play to her, discussed it, laughed over it. Talked about changes.

"So he left his car keys," Miss Selina said. "He thought it might be more convenient for you to drive us to the city. Said he didn't like us riding the subway at night."

"But isn't he going?"

"No. I told you. He's going to miss the whole thing," Miss Selina said, obviously repeating what Darlene had been too absorbed in her own thoughts to hear. "It's a shame."

"A shame?" Her heart gave a lurch. Had something happened to Greg? "What's wrong?"

"Oh, nothing is really wrong," Miss Selina said. "Actually it's a very good thing. His dad has a construction company. You knew that?"

Darlene nodded.

"Well, it seems they have a chance to bid on a big federal contract. Greg says they have a good chance at it because they are a minority business, you know. Things have surely changed. In my day . . ." She shook her head. "Well, it is a good thing. A biggie for their company. Only Greg says they need him to draw up the bid. He got an emergency call from his father, and took a plane this afternoon."

"I see," Darlene said, remembering how she had

assured Greg . . . "Only a phone call or a plane ride away." And he had responded.

"He doesn't think he'll make it back for the play. Come on into the kitchen, honey, and let me fix you a cup of tea."

Darlene followed her, needing both the tea and a chance to pull herself together. She didn't know why she felt so sad. Because he had not told her, or because he was going to miss the first performance of his own play?

"Such bad timing." Miss Selina put the kettle on the range and set out a plate of cookies. "But Greg says more is riding on the project than on his play. Anyway, Greg has been at all the rehearsals, getting things perfected and all."

And never said one word to her. The tea tasted hot and bitter on Darlene's tongue.

"I'm just sorry he'll miss his big night," Miss Selina said. "But even so, they're putting it on. Isn't that wonderful?"

"Wonderful," Darlene echoed, trying to get a grip on the emotions rioting through her. It was all so confusing. As explosive as his kiss.

Surprise. Joy. Pride.

And a deep sense of betrayal. He had not told her.

Chapter Seven

Darlene's grasp on the phone tightened. "But I told you I couldn't go with you. That's the night we have tickets for this play."

"Look, this is important." Leon sounded exasperated. "You know I like to have you with me."

"I know, and I'm sorry. But this is . . . rather special."

"What's so special about a play? I'll get tickets for you for another performance."

"But there won't be . . ." She stopped, not knowing if there'd be other performances, irritated that she didn't know. Greg hadn't told her anything at all! "This is the first performance, and it's Greg's first play, and—"

"Who's Greg?"

"This guy in our building. You met him."

"Your landlord, huh? His play is more important to you than I am?"

"Oh, for goodness' sake, Leon, it's not that. He's a . . . well, we're kinda like family, here in the same complex and all, and since he's not going to be able to see it himself, we thought . . . Well, Tonya and Miss Selina are really looking forward to it." She did not tell him that not for anything in the entire world would she miss this play.

They went into the city early, deciding to treat themselves to dinner before the performance. Tonya and Miss Selina were in high spirits, talking a mile a minute and eating heartily at the modest restaurant across from the theater. Darlene's anticipation was as potent as theirs, but she was quiet and could hardly touch her food. She finally ordered a glass of wine, hoping it would relax her. But her nerves were still on edge when they walked across the street to the theater. What was the matter with her? It was only a play.

But it was Greg's play.

"Golly!" Tonya exclaimed as they entered the lobby and found it quite crowded. "I didn't know there'd be so many people here."

"Oh, yes," Miss Selina said. "These little workshop theaters are quite popular. Not only for the public, but agents and producers as well. And don't forget those opinionated critics, who can make or break a production with a few well-chosen words."

What would they think of this production, Darlene wondered. Would they know it was good? Or . . . "against the current trend" as Miss Selina had said? Would they resent this and castigate him? Anxious and tense, she stirred in her seat, trying to spot the powerful persons who held Greg's dreams in their hands.

But once the lights dimmed and the curtains parted, she was completely absorbed in the play, which came alive before her. She breathed with it, smiling and nodding, drinking in the familiar lines, oblivious to the appreciative chuckles and the roars of laughter around her. When it was over, she stood with the audience, clapping wildly as the delighted performers took curtain call after curtain call. Then she turned a glowing face to her companions. They hugged each other, grinning like fools, knowing without a doubt. Greg's play was a success.

Greg returned the following week, just in time to see the second and final performance. He had read the reviews and knew the play was well received. He was glad. At least something had been accomplished by his brief stay in New York.

He wished . . . No, he didn't. When a man had built a lucrative business with his bare hands, as his father truly had, his sons ought to carry it on. They had reached a good compromise. He would be in charge of the business end, and Dad and J.C. would manage construction. Not a bad deal, though right now things were pretty rough. There was so much hanging on this potential federal project. He had managed to get the bid in on time, and it looked like they had a good chance, but . . . well, you could never tell about those things.

Meanwhile, he had given his notice to Franchise Tax. While finishing up there, he would also find a real estate agent to take over his uncle's property.

It was probably good that he was leaving. Avoiding Darlene right here in the same building was getting harder and harder. When he was in Kansas, she would disappear from his life forever. His heart lurched at the thought, and there was a desolate ache deep inside him.

Well, hell! She was going to disappear anyway, wasn't she? Whenever she and . . . What was taking that Leon so long! If he were in his place . . . !

He wasn't. And he'd best get to his own business. If he hurried, he'd have time to see the real estate broker and catch a bite before the play. He snatched up his coat, opened his door . . . and walked straight into Darlene.

"Greg! You're back!" Her eyes lit up, the dimples danced, and her face shone with pure pleasure. At seeing him? "Oh, I'm so glad. You can see your play tonight. Greg, it's wonderful! Absolutely wonderful!" Her words tumbled over each other as she tried to tell him . . . how each actor performed, how the audience laughed, what Miss Selina said about learning from laughter, and how . . . "It was you, Greg. All you. Miss Selina said that a writer puts some of himself into everything he writes. And it must be true because I kept seeing you. Each expression, each line reminded me of you. So sensible, and so funny. Did you read what that critic said . . . about how cleverly you combined common sense and humor?"

He had, but . . . She liked it. She bubbled with enthusiasm and praise, and he reveled in it. He was so enraptured by the sight of her, so pleased by what she had said that he couldn't speak or even nod.

She didn't notice. "I know I had read it. But it comes alive onstage. It really does. I wish . . ." She stared at him. "Could I . . . Is anyone . . ." She hesitated, then put it bluntly. "Do you have a date?"

He shook his head.

"Then, could I go with you? I'd love to see it again."

"Sure. I'd like that," he said, knowing nothing would please him more. "I had planned to leave early to make a short stop, but if that's inconvenient, I could—"

"No problem. Just give me five minutes." She must be a little crazy, Darlene thought, as she ran upstairs and changed into her black sheath. It was as if she didn't want to let him out of her sight. All right, why shouldn't she go! Tonya was at Sophie's, spending the night on account of that debate, so she had the afternoon and evening free. Still, she had been rather brazen, inviting herself to join him. But she didn't care. Instead she sped down the steps, anticipating the fun, liking the appreciative gleam in his eyes as he watched her descent.

"You're going to have a new landlord," he told her as he pulled to a stop before a real estate office.

"At least this broker is going to take charge for Uncle George."

"You . . . you're moving?"

"Back to Kansas."

"Oh." The news settled like a stone in the pit of her stomach. "Right away?"

"Two weeks. Maybe three. As soon as I get things wrapped up here."

"Why are you leaving? Especially now with your play being so well received." Two weeks! Then she probably wouldn't see him again. Not ever!

"They need me at home. Business is really expanding."

"But what about your writing?"

"I'm taking my computer with me," he said, laughing as he picked up a folder and opened the car door. "Back in a minute. Want the radio?"

She shook her head. She felt miserable.

The restaurant where he took her for dinner was also near the theater, but more posh than where they had dined the week before. Linen tablecloth and napkins, candlelight, and low chamber music. She was glad she had worn her smart black sheath.

She looked up at him as he pulled out her chair. He seemed so composed, so relaxed. Didn't he care about leaving? "Greg, are you sure you're doing the right thing," she ventured as he took his seat before her. "Leaving, I mean. Things are going so well for you here."

He shrugged. "Oh, sure . . . right now. But like

Dad says, this writing business is pretty iffy. I still need a steady job. And Dad needs me more than Franchise Tax."

"But you said the reason you came here was to be near the theater world. To make the contacts."

"No. The reason was Uncle George," he said, smiling. She liked his smile, his teeth so white against his dark skin, the way his eyes squinted. "But it gave me the chance to be where the action is."

"Oh."

"Hey, don't look so down! Don't worry about me. I've made the contacts. And I can write in Kansas as well as in New York."

"Of course you can." But he wouldn't read the lines to her. They wouldn't laugh together.

"Tell me," he asked, "What happened with Eric? Did his folks sue?"

He remembered! "They did, but withdrew it."

"Oh? That's too bad." He frowned.

"Not really." She leaned toward him, keeping her voice low. "I had a long talk with the judge, who proved to be very understanding. He ruled that Eric be returned to them as foster parents, and they withdrew the suit."

"That's good?"

"I think so." She looked across at him, doubt surfacing again. "I know such a case could set a precedent, but I had to think of Eric. This way, there'll be no long drawn-out court battle, and Eric will remain with people who love him during his formative years, possibly all his life if he likes."

"Clever girl." The understanding and genuine admiration in his voice banished the doubts. She felt herself grow warm, bolstered by his reassurance. "And, how are things going with Emily?" he asked.

"So far so good. Her father's still in counseling, still in AA, and no bruises reported. I've got my fingers crossed, and I'm keeping close watch."

"I'm sure you are." He lifted his wineglass. "To you. I wonder if the kids in your charge know how lucky they are!"

"I don't know about that, but I know I'm going to miss you. Nobody else tells me how great I am." Her smile masked, but did not stifle, the ache.

This time she enjoyed the play even more, sitting beside Greg, feeling the pressure of his hand at the sound of a well-remembered line or the appreciative laughter from the audience. He took her backstage with him to drink champagne and rejoice with the riotous enthusiastic cast, and to listen to the earth-shattering prophecies.

"This one's gonna go, man!"

"We got it made this time."

"Next stop, Broadway!"

As they turned to leave, they were approached by a man who asked them to join him for a drink. "I'd like to talk with you," he said, handing Greg his card. Amos Cadrill, theatrical agent. He thought Greg's play had real potential.

"I can't make any promises, but I'd like to take it on," he said when they were settled in a relatively quiet corner of a nearby bar. He wanted to take a look at whatever else Greg had, and no, where Greg lived presented no problem. "I make the contacts. You just deliver the goods. If Greg could arrange to meet at his office during the following week . . ."

They settled on a date and time, and Mr. Cadrill took his leave.

"He's from one of the top agencies," Greg said. She could tell he was excited. And who wouldn't be!

"Just think," she said. "You got all those good reviews, and now an agent wants to handle you, and this is your very first play!"

"First produced, you mean," he said, grinning. "Remember, I've been scribbling a long time. A lot of junk filed away—"

"Excuse me!" she interrupted. "You mean a wealth of material destined to soon reach the spotlight, acclaimed by all, and—"

"Stop it. My head's big enough with just a glimmer of potential success," he said. "Let's dance."

She went willingly into his arms. It was prophetic that at that moment, the band struck up with "Let's Have a Celebration," for the sense of celebration was zooming through their veins. They succumbed to it, their feet stamping in rhythmic jubilation to the exhilarating tune, hearts, minds, and muscles reverberating with sheer joy and excitement. Greg bribed the band leader, and he played the tune over and over again. Other dancers joined with them, singing along with the soloist, rejoicing in whatever they were celebrating. It was wonderful!

Soon enough, exhausted, both band and dancers settled for a more mellow tune. Greg held her close. It felt so right, her head upon his shoulder, his muscular body pressed to hers, moving slowly and easily together. She was so happy, so—

Abruptly he moved back, almost pushing her from him. "Time to go," he said. "Busy day tomorrow."

Dazedly she followed him, wondering what could be so busy on a Sunday. She should be sleepy, she thought, as Greg maneuvered the car through the traffic and onto the bridge. She had had two glasses of wine at dinner and two cocktails at the bar. But she wasn't sleepy. It had been such a glorious evening, and she couldn't stop talking about it . . . the play, the after party backstage, what the agent had said, and the miracle of possibilities. Greg answered in monosyllables. He seemed intent on driving.

When they reached home, he walked with her up to her flat, took her key, and opened the door. "Thank you. I enjoyed having you with me," he said, handing over her keys. "Good night."

It was over. But she didn't want it to be over, didn't want the evening to end. "Thank you," she said. "It was a wonderful, wonderful evening, and I wouldn't have missed it for anything in the world. Oh, Greg, I am so happy for you." Impulsively she threw her arms around his neck and lifted her lips to his. She felt herself crushed to him, felt his mouth take complete possession of hers, and she was lost to all but feeling. The pulsating waves that rippled inside her as his tongue teased and tantalized created the whirlwind of passion that had gripped her only once before.

"Oh, Greg," she whispered, pressing closer to him, her arms tightening around his neck. "Greg," she whispered again, throbbing with a need she couldn't explain, a wanting that nudged and clamored to be filled. Her fingers tangled in his hair, pulled at his earlobe, caressed his face, urging, demanding . . .

"Stop it!" He pushed her away. His words were short, clipped, as if he had trouble breathing. "How much of this do you think I can take? Make up your mind, lady." He gave her a level look. "But your mind is made up, isn't it?"

"Greg, I'm sorry. I . . ." She stuttered, feeling abandoned, confused. "It was just that I felt . . . I wanted . . ." She stopped. How could she explain what she didn't understand herself? "I didn't mean to—"

"Oh, I know you didn't!" His words were angry, explosive. Then he seemed to mellow. "Okay, I'm sorry. I don't mean to take advantage of your . . . moods. But I . . . how did you put it? I lose control, too. And, damn it, Darlene," he said, his voice sharp again, "I can't stand this 'take-me-I'm-yours kiss' that tears me apart one evening, followed the next day by 'excuse me I'm sorry, I lost control'! I . . . Oh, forget it! See you." He turned and bounded down the steps.

Chapter Eight

Tonya flung her book bag over her shoulder and followed Darlene down the steps. "It's going to be at Luanne's house. It's her birthday, and she's just inviting the cheerleaders and a few guys."

"We'll see," Darlene said. "You have her telephone number? I'd like to call her parents."

Tonya winced, but said nothing. She knew she wouldn't get to go unless Darlene was sure parents were chaperoning. "I could grab a ride with Jody or—"

"No. I'll call Leon."

"If he can't, maybe . . ." Tonya stopped. Greg's name was not exactly mud, but it hardly got mentioned these days. Since last weekend.

Darlene did not glance at Greg's door. "I could go along with Leon, and we could pick you up later," she said as they stepped outside.

"Okay." More checking, Tonya thought, but she was not about to rock the boat. "Look, could you pick up a present for me today? She likes those woman detective novels or maybe some junk jewelry."

"Sure."

"It's going to be fun. Tom's coming, and Luanne has a CD player, and there'll be dancing."

"That's nice."

Tonya looked at Darlene. It wasn't like her to be so subdued. She might treat her like a baby with all that persnickety checking-everything-out stuff, but she was always excited and enthusiastic about whatever Tonya did. Now she just wore that same lost, sad look she had had all week. Tonya watched her sister board the bus and waited for Sophie, wondering what had gone wrong.

She was pretty sure it had something to do with Greg, and she felt a surge of guilt. If she had never . . .

But she didn't butt in. She didn't. She had just invited him to dinner, had exposed them to each other. They had taken it from there, hadn't they? And right away . . . well, you can't really see sparks fly. But, just like in a novel . . . Well, they both lit up. Really. Like they caught a spark from each other. They radiated all over the place even if they were just eating dinner or arguing over something Miss Selina had said. Sometimes during a game she caught them whispering to each other, and Greg often lingered behind to read what he was writing to Darlene. She could hear them chuckling after she had left them alone.

Then all of a sudden ... boom! Everything stopped. Greg got too busy to ever come to dinner, and then he was gone for a while, and Darlene got that tight-lipped anxious look. And now ... Honestly you'd think that now that he was back and she went with him to see the play again and got the good news from that agent and all that ...

Something had happened.

Tonya's fists clenched, and she had trouble breathing. If Greg had said or done anything to hurt Darlene ...

"Hey, what's with you? Somebody rain on your parade?" Sophie teased as she ran up. Then she looked anxious. "Did Darlene say you couldn't go to Luanne's party?"

"No. At least she said she'd see. It's ... oh, nothing!" Tonya swung into step beside her friend and unclenched her fists. Why was she mad at Greg? He wasn't engaged. At least he had never talked about anyone else, and the way he looked at Darlene ...

Tonya sighed. Greg said a person shouldn't butt in, that people should be left to handle their own affairs. If it was Leon Darlene wanted ...

She sighed again, trying to reconcile herself to the situation. Leon Cranston might not set off any fireworks, but she guessed he was all right. Anyway Darlene had been contented with him and ... well, fairly happy.

Until she had laughed with Greg.

* * *

At the last minute, there was a chance Tonya might have to miss the party. Mr. Taylor, Leon's boss, had invited him, along with several other top brokers and their spouses, to be weekend guests at his home in Bedford Hills.

"But Luanne's party is Saturday night," Tonya cried.

"We'll work it out," Darlene said, and did so. Tonya was to spend the weekend with Sophie, whose parents would escort both girls to and from the party.

Darlene came home early Friday, and that afternoon they were both packing for the two coming events when the call came in.

Darlene, who had picked up the phone from her bedside table, assured the caller that yes, she was Miss Darlene Davis, Tonya's sister and guardian.

"I'm John Whitmore, Tonya's algebra teacher."

"Oh, yes, Mr. Whitmore." Darlene pushed her overnight case aside and sat on the bed, feeling apprehensive.

"Firs', I must say that Tonya is a fine well-behaved young person with perfect attendance, and, I understan', has an excellent scholastic record. But . . ." There was a pause. "She's really having difficulty grasping algebra." There followed a long discussion, the upshot of which was a forthcoming deficiency notice and possible failure in that particular subject.

"I do appreciate your call," Darlene said. "And I

will talk with Tonya and see what can be done to bring her grade up to par."

I'll find a tutor, she thought, as she replaced the phone. She should have done that before. She knew Tonya was having trouble with algebra. But they had gotten busy. Too busy. Maybe she should cut down on her activities. No. She ought to have fun, and the cheerleading and debating were both healthy and constructive. Anyway Tonya was bright. With a tutor, she would soon catch up. We'll work it out, she thought, as she went in to talk with Tonya about what she had decided was only a small problem.

She was totally unprepared for Tonya's reaction. The look of shock on her face, the almost hysterical cry, "A deficiency notice! No! Oh, no! I've never had a deficiency notice in my whole life!"

"I know, dear, but—"

"I hate him!" Tonya screamed, flinging herself facedown and beating her fists on the bed, unmindful of the pile of clothes.

"Tonya, don't!" Darlene reached out to rescue a sweater. "Aren't you planning to wear this to the party? You'll ruin—"

"I'm not going to any dumb party."

"Of course you are. Just because—"

Tonya sat up, tears streaming down her face. "You think I'm going to walk in there and have everybody laugh at me!"

"Don't be silly. Nobody is going to laugh at you about a deficiency notice, which, I remind you, you have not yet received, and if you did, who'd know about it but you and me!"

"Everybody! Because everybody knows everything that goes on at that dumb school! And Tom . . ." Tonya gave a groan. "Tom will know I'm flunking. "I've been helping him with his lessons, and he thinks . . . he thinks I'm the smartest girl in the whole school. He said so. And now . . ." She fell back on the bed, sobbing uncontrollably. "I hate Mr. Whitmore. I hate him!"

This was a Tonya Darlene had seen only once before. When her father died. But this was not a life-or-death matter, and she tried to tell her so.

"Tonya, listen. You're taking this all the wrong way. Mr. Whitmore just wanted to warn you—

"That he's going to flunk me! I'm so embarrassed!"

"Don't be silly. It doesn't mean you're going to flunk. You have time. And, anyway, there's certainly no reason to be embarrassed. Tonya, we'll get a tutor Monday. You can catch up. Now, get up and take your shower so you can be on your way before I leave."

"I told you I'm not going. I'm not going to Sophie's, and I'm not going to any dumb party!"

Darlene was still trying to reason with her when the phone rang. She went back into her bedroom to answer.

"Are you ready?" Leon asked. "I'll be leaving here in about an hour."

"Yes, I'm almost . . ." She glanced toward Tonya's

room. "That is . . . something has come up. I may not be able to go." She tried to explain.

"I don't believe this" was Leon's exasperated reply. "For Christ sake, Darlene, you and Tonya both are making a mountain out of a molehill."

"It's not a molehill to her."

"You mean you're going to let one little deficiency notice break up a whole weekend! Yours as well as hers. You've got that kid spoiled rotten."

"That's not true. It's just—"

"That you can't make a move until you've got her wrapped all right and tight and happy!"

Darlene gripped the phone, wanting to deny it. But it was true. She did want Tonya happy. "Look, Leon, for her this is important. I—"

"What about me? You're breaking up my weekend, too, and it's a pretty damn important one. Do you know how few, if any, of us ever get near Bedford Hills? It's a big deal for Taylor to have us, and I don't want to miss it."

"I know. Look Leon, you can go even if I—"

"No. I'm not going without you. Taylor asked particularly that I bring you." Now Leon began to plead. He liked her by his side. Liked the impression she made. Didn't she know that was one of the reasons he loved her? "Besides," he finished. "I have a surprise. Something I want to show you Sunday on the way back. Please, Darlene, don't let me down again."

His last words pricked, rebuking her. She had been

neglecting him. "Give me a few minutes. Let me talk to her. I'll call you right back."

But there was no talking, at least no reasoning with Tonya. She wasn't going anywhere. Darlene could go. She would be all right. Just leave her alone.

Darlene was distraught and more than a little angry. And torn. She didn't want to let Leon down again. But she couldn't leave Tonya. Not alone and not in this state. Even though she was being ridiculous. This didn't make sense.

Sense. Tonya said Greg always made sense.

Darlene didn't hesitate. She forgot his curt words on that last night. Forgot that he had been avoiding her. Forgot the feeling of everything between them being cold and finished.

She needed him.

Greg was on the phone with his uncle, trying to decide what to store and what to leave behind when the doorbell rang. It was followed by rapid knocking and Darlene calling his name. She sounded frantic.

"Let me call you back. There's someone here." He put down the phone and rushed to the door.

Darlene looked up at him, her eyes wide and frightened. "Oh, Greg, I'm so glad you're here. You've got to talk to Tonya and tell her it's all right. Please, Greg."

"Sure," he said hesitantly. "What . . . what's all right?" So all right that it's got you all fired up, he wondered. "Come in and tell me what this is all about," he said, pulling her in and shutting the door.

"One of Tonya's teachers called to say he was sending her a deficiency notice, and it's got her so freaked out she says she's not going to a party she has been talking about for a week. I don't know what to do. I thought maybe if you talked to her and told her . . ." She stopped suddenly, staring at him. "What . . . what's so funny?"

"You," he choked, unable to stifle the laughter. "You come tearing down here like the place is on fire about a simple thing like a deficiency notice."

"And you stand there laughing like a hyena while Tonya is up there crying her eyes out. It's not a simple thing for her. You know how proud she is."

"Cocky, you mean. All right, don't look at me like that. She's a bright competitive kid, and I'm proud for her, glad she's tops. But look, Darlene, it's okay for her to stumble a bit. Kinda puts her on the level with the rest of us. Understand?"

"Oh, yes, I understand that you're going all philosophical when all I wanted you to do was talk to her. Make her see that it's not the end of the world so she can go and enjoy her party and . . . Oh, never mind." She reached for the door.

"Wait a minute. I didn't say I wouldn't talk to her. I was just trying to make you see that it's not the end of the world."

"Thank you. But I don't have time for a lecture. I've got a hysterical sister on my hands, and I've got Leon waiting—"

"Oh!" he broke in, suddenly gripped by a blinding

rage. "Why didn't you say so? I'll get up there right now and try to coax Tonya out of whatever stupid mood she's in that's keeping you from your precious—"

"Never mind. Forget it!" She flung the words over her shoulder as she spun out of the door.

He was right behind, racing up the steps with her. "Oh, I couldn't forget it. We mustn't keep Leon waiting."

Darlene was mad enough to spit, but she kept her mouth shut. She was worried about Tonya, and . . . she didn't want to keep Leon waiting. If this smug know-it-all could help . . . well, let him! She stood, anxiously waiting, as he knocked on Tonya's closed door.

He jerked his head at her. "Go on. Get ready for your date. I'll handle this." As she turned toward her room, she heard him speak in a firm voice, "Open up, Tonya. We need to talk."

Her anger vanished as quickly as it had come. She finished her packing and got into the shower, confident that Greg would handle it.

Greg sat beside Tonya's bed, his own rage subsiding. He could see that the kid was pretty torn up. And he had known about Leon all along, hadn't he!

"Okay, Tonya. Let's talk."

"I don't want to talk."

"Plan to stay buried in that pillow forever?"

No answer.

"Miss out on a lot of things that way. Football. Cheerleading. Parties."

No answer.

"Guarantees that others miss out on things, too, doesn't it?"

He saw her shoulders stiffen, but she was still silent.

"One thing for sure. Darlene won't be going out with Leon tonight, will she?"

Tonya sat up and faced him, her eyes blazing. "I'm not stopping her. I told her to go ahead."

"And you knew she would, didn't you? She'd walk right out and leave you kicking up a storm, freaking out on account of some nonsense about a deficiency notice."

"It isn't nonsense. It isn't! I've never received a deficiency notice! Not in my whole life!"

He smiled. "I've got news for you kid. Fourteen years is not a very long life. If you live as long as I hope you will, you'd better be prepared to meet many more challenges."

"Challenges?"

"Well, that's all a deficiency notice is, isn't it? A notice that you'd better get on your p's and q's, and, being the bright kid you are, you can do it. Look, I'll help you."

"You're leaving."

"Not for a few weeks. It shouldn't take long for you to catch up. Unless you're a complete blockhead, of course." That brought up her fighting spirit, and in a few minutes they were planning study sessions and agreeing that Mr. Whitmore wasn't really hateful. Also Tom's confidence might increase to find she wasn't quite so perfect, but was human like everyone else.

"Now, go on out there and let Darlene know you're okay," he said when he saw that she was truly calm. "You know she won't make a move unless you're happy."

"All right." She started to get up, then hesitated. "I didn't . . . wasn't trying to stop her from going," she said, looking earnestly up at him.

"Are you sure?"

She gave an emphatic nod. "Really. I had decided that since things didn't work out with you—"

"With me! What are you talking about?" Damn! Did he carry his feelings on his face? Or had Darlene said something that made her think . . . Hope welled within him.

"Nothing," she said hastily. "I have made up my mind that Darlene is going to marry Leon and I can live with it. He's a nice guy."

"Right." He could live with it, too.

But it was going to be hard, he thought when he followed Tonya into the living room and saw Darlene. She looked delicious in a pair of smooth-fitting lavender slacks and a long matching sweater that molded over her slender hips. She looked at him with those wide-open expectant adorable eyes that silently asked, "Is she okay?"

His almost imperceptible nod was not needed. "Everything is all right, so you needn't worry," Tonya said, as if Darlene had been the one in a tizzy. "Greg is going to help me catch up. I'm going to take my shower, and I'll be ready when you are," she said, disappearing into the bathroom.

Those adorable eyes were still focused on him, and he could hardly stand it. And when she rushed to him, threw her arms around him, and thanked him effusively, he became completely unglued. Maybe it was the familiar soapy scent of freshly washed hair, mingled with the aroma of a tantalizing exotic perfume, or the sweetness of those caressing arms, or the pressure of her soft body against his, or the thought that the caressing arms, the soft body, belonged to someone else. Whatever drove him, he unclasped her arms and almost roughly pushed her away. "Stop it! Can't you see what you do to me? Don't you know I love you?"

Her eyes stretched even wider, her mouth forming an incredulous inviting oh. "Greg! You never said . . . I didn't know . . ."

"Now you do! And the only way you can thank me is to get the hell out of my sight and stay there!" He turned and bolted before he gave in to the impulse to take her back into his arms and kiss her senseless.

Chapter Nine

Darlene, slightly numb, stared at the door that had closed behind him, trying to unravel exactly what he had said.

Then her heart began to reverberate in spasmodic jerks. Joy. He loved her. He loved her. He, too, felt it . . . that powerful surge of compelling erotic passion, the sizzling vibrations of delight, the exultation of being intimately attuned and wonderfully breathtakingly alive! She wanted to run after him, tell him—

The sharp peal of the phone interrupted her reverie. She shook her head to steady herself and went to answer.

"You said you'd call me back."

Leon. She forgot! "I meant to. But so much was happening that—"

"Darlene, don't tell me you're not going."

"Oh, no. I mean yes. Whenever you get here. I'm ready."

"Good. This weekend means a lot to both of us.

I'm sure Taylor is going to give out the end-of-the-year bonuses, and if it's the usual percentage, we're in clover, Darlene. We won't have to wait any longer. I told you I had a surprise." His words spilled over, no longer able to hold it. "A house I've had my eye on. I think you'll like it. If you do, we won't have to wait any longer. See you in a few minutes."

Slowly she replaced the phone. Leon. Good stable Leon. He had been making plans . . . for her. While she . . .

Good Lord, was she losing it! She was committed to Leon. Had been for a whole year.

She couldn't be unfair to Leon. She couldn't. Just because another man had walked into her life and had her spinning like a top, her emotions in a whirl.

Leon. Safe. Stable. Dependable. Wasn't that what she wanted?

She went into her bedroom to check. Luggage. Coat. Gloves.

She called to Tonya. "Are you ready to leave? I don't want to keep Leon waiting."

Bedford Hills was a luxuriously gated community of towering hills and well-tended shrubbery on two-acre estates. The Taylor home was one of the most luxurious, and they had opened all of it for the enjoyment of their guests, the indoor swimming pool, the exercise and game rooms, the spacious living room with its several comfortable conversational areas. Like a top-rated hotel with all the comforts of home,

Darlene thought, surveying the large and well-appointed bedroom she shared with Irene Morris, a beautiful vivacious blond. Darlene had thought Irene was the guest of a tall freckled man with red hair, but it turned out he had come with her. Irene, Leon told her, was one of the firm's top brokers.

"This is going to be a fun party," Irene declared as they unpacked. "Let's go for a swim before dinner."

It was fun, Darlene decided, as they cavorted with a merry group in the pool. Indeed, she enjoyed every moment of the weekend, participating in her usual charming listening-with-interest way to the talk that flowed about her, the money market, the vacillating price of gold, and who had made a pile in commodities. She was proud of Leon, who held his own and was evidently well respected by his peers in the field.

And all the while, deep inside her, bubbled an undercurrent of joy that had nothing to do with what was going on around her. Greg loved her. The knowledge was a radiating beam throughout her whole being, bringing a sparkle to her eyes, laughter to her lips, and a throb of happiness to every beat of her heart.

"You are the greatest," Leon told her on Sunday afternoon as he put the Mercedes into gear to drive out of the complex. "You charmed everyone."

"Easy." She blushed, realizing Leon was just as proud of her as she was of him. "Everyone was charming to me, I think because of you."

"No. It was you. Your usual gracious self." He

glanced at her. "Only more so. A special glow. As if . . . you liked the group? The party?"

"Oh, yes." But the glow had not been for the group or the party. Or for Leon. But how could she tell him?

"Just wait till you see this house. We'll be giving some parties of our own, Darlene."

She had to tell him.

No. It wouldn't be fair. She couldn't hurt him.

The house was some distance from Bedford Hills and certainly not as opulent. But it, too, was in a gated community, on a half-acre lot, and quite spacious. More house than she had ever dreamed of. She followed Leon's enthusiastic progress through every room, watching him watch her. Did she like it? Wasn't this a good room for Tonya? Would she like wallpaper here? The house was so far out she would need a car of her own. What kind did she think she'd like?

She looked at Leon, a lump forming in her throat. He was offering her so much.

"Leon, it's absolutely beautiful. Wonderful," she said. "But not for me. It wouldn't be fair." When a man offers all this to a woman, she ought to be overflowing with gratitude, love, and loyalty. All she could think was that she'd rather be in a two-room shack with Greg.

Leon looked astonished. "What do you mean, not fair? You deserve—"

"No." She put a finger to his lips. "You deserve

much more than I can ever give you. I don't love you, Leon. I thought I did." Maybe what she really loved was the security he offered. For herself, and for Tonya. The kind of security Tonya's father had provided for her. Sam Davis's face flashed through her mind, and with it came a flash of understanding. He had not had many material possessions. His security had been time, patience, love and laughter. Like Greg's . . . even in the short time they had known him. It was Greg she had called when—

"Darlene! Talk to me. What are you saying?"

She became aware that she had forgotten all about Leon. When she looked up at him, the tears were streaming down her face, but her voice was steady. "I'm saying I can't marry you, Leon. You are a fine man. I truly like and admire you, but I don't love you. You deserve more than I can give you."

He protested, but she was adamant, declaring he would someday thank her.

She gave back his ring, feeling the weight of it lift from her finger. She was free.

The only thing Darlene could cook was oatmeal. And it was the only way she could ensure that the late-rising Tonya got a hot breakfast before rushing off to school. Monday morning when she was handed the hot bowl of cereal, Tonya noticed the ringless finger. Her heart lifted. Maybe . . .

But Darlene didn't say anything, so she didn't, either.

Neither did she say anything to Greg when he came up that afternoon for the tutoring session. For all she knew, Darlene and Leon could have just had a little spat that would soon be patched up. Anyway she was not about to butt in. Let people mess up their own lives.

Darlene got home as soon as she could Monday afternoon, but Tonya was alone, books and papers scattered on the table before her.

"Did Greg come up to go over algebra with you?"

"Yeh. And he made everything so clear. You know something, Darlene! I'm not the dumb one. It's Mr. Whitmore . . . talking so fast and chalking up numbers on the blackboard like they're gonna disappear if he doesn't hurry! He's the dumb one. How does he expect a person to know what he's talking about when—"

"Did you ask him for dinner?"

"Who? Mr. Whitmore?"

"No, silly. Greg."

"Oh. Yeh, but he couldn't come. You know something Darlene . . . maybe Mr. Whitmore isn't dumb. Maybe he's got one of those brilliant minds that goes zip-zip-zip-got-it, and he thinks other people should—"

"What did he say?"

"Mr. Whitmore?"

"No! Why do you keep talking about him? Greg. Did he say why he couldn't stay?"

"Busy. Getting things stored and all that stuff. But

he says he's not going to miss our study sessions. Says that by the time he leaves, I should be a whiz."

"Getting things stored." The only thing she knew for sure was that Greg was leaving. "I love you" doesn't necessarily mean I want you by my side forever.

The radiance his declaration had engendered dimmed, and the happy beat of her heart subsided to a doubtful thud.

Tuesday and Wednesday were a repetition of the same. By Thursday she was downright angry. No man had a right to tell you that he loved you, than stalk out of your life forever! She had a great mind to tell him so. To go downstairs right now and ask him. Did he mean one thing or the other! If he did mean the other, if he really meant to go away and stay out of her life forever, could she bear it?

She swallowed convulsively, feeling like . . . what was the saying? A cat on a hot tin roof. Anxiously perched between hope and doubt. She ought to confront him, force him to speak his mind. Like . . . Something between a sob and a chuckle caught in her throat as she thought about the slave girl in Dunbar's poem, who urged her swain to "speak up and 'spress himself."

Well, darn it, if that was her heritage . . . so be it! What did she have to lose?

She looked around for an excuse and spotted the remains of Tonya's devil's food cake. "Did you offer Greg a piece of cake?"

"Forgot." Tonya crossed her fingers. "You know, Darlene, this algebra is pretty simple. When you change sides, you just change signs and—"

"You should have. It's very good. Think I'll run down and take him a piece."

"Okay." No need to tell her Greg had already wolfed down two hefty slices. Let people fiddle with their own lives. Out of the corner of her eye, Tonya watched Darlene depart with the cake. She crossed her fingers again. Maybe . . .

Darlene stood in front of Greg's door. Hesitated. Turned to go back upstairs. Turned again to the door, determined. She would just ask him right out what he meant when he said—

The door was opened by a disheveled Greg. He had changed to jeans and discarded his coat and tie, but he was still in the white shirt he had worn to work. It was now rumpled, open at the throat and the sleeves rolled up. His feet were bare.

Darlene was disconcerted. He never looked this untogether even when he was cleaning the sidewalk.

"I brought you a piece of cake, and I wanted to . . . to . . ." Her voice faded as she surveyed the clutter. Books and papers piled everywhere. Shoes and socks on the floor. Coat and tie on a chair, and more clothes on the sofa. Cartons, some filled, some empty. Potted plants dry and dying. He might be good at installing ovens and changing lightbulbs, but . . .

"This place is a mess," she said. Mrs. Weston would be appalled. She was almost as neat as Miss Selina.

"I know." He looked a little sheepish. "Damn it, I guess there's so much to do and so little time to do it. I've still got two more weeks at Franchise Tax, Cadrill wants revisions on the play, and I've got to get this place ready to lease before I leave."

"Trying to do everything at once, huh?" And never missing one single tutoring session with Tonya, she thought. How thoughtless they had been, imposing on him!

He shrugged. "Well, it's gotta get done. Dad needs me back as soon as I can get there, Cadrill wants the revisions yesterday, and Aunt Meg requests that all her precious china be packed just so. Hey, do you think I'm doing this right?" he asked, moving to the kitchen.

"Looks like it," she said, checking the dinnerware he was carefully wrapping in newspaper. "But you better get a professional to pack the stemware. Leave the cups. I'll do those. But I can't work in this mess." She moved to the sink to rinse out the cold coffeepot, then dumped a half-eaten hamburger and other disposables in the garbage. "This gives us more working space," she said as she wiped off the counter.

Greg's a giving person, and everybody pulls on him, she thought, feeling somewhat irate as she wrapped the cups, packed linens, and gathered up old newspapers and dried-out plants to be discarded.

A bit of order was beginning to emerge from among the chaos by the time Greg went out with a load for the dumpster.

Better hang this up, she thought, picking up his coat.

Maybe it was the familiar scent of his aftershave that wafted from the coat, or just the look of the room, rather bare except for a few cartons and the papers stacked by his computer. Whatever it was, she was suddenly acutely and painfully aware that Greg would soon be out of her life forever. She couldn't seem to move. She was still standing in the center of the room, holding his coat, looking lost and frightened, when Greg returned.

"What is it?" he asked, his face startled and anxious. "Oh, my darling, what's the matter?"

It was the "my darling" that finally got to her. "Don't call me that!" she sputtered, feeling hot rage boil through her. "You ought to be careful what you say. Words can hurt."

"But, I only . . . I didn't . . . what did I say?"

His puzzled look enraged her more. "You know darn well what you said. You said you loved me, and you didn't mean a word of it."

"Oh, I meant it all right." Now he sounded cold and hard.

"No, you didn't. If you did, you couldn't just stalk out and leave me wondering if you meant it or not. And you wouldn't go away and walk out of my life like you are!"

"Darlene, what the hell do you expect me to do? You're all set to marry another man."

"I expect you to stick around long enough to find out how I feel about you loving me and find out if I love you. Maybe find out that engagements can be broken. When you love someone, you stick around to talk things over with them and—"

"Hold it!" He took her by the shoulders and shook her. "It's true? You've broken with that guy?"

"I have, but not on account of you! It's because—"

He didn't let her finish. He took her in his arms and swung her around. "I don't care why. Oh, Darlene, my sweet, my love, my angel, I love you, I love you!"

"Then, if you do love me," she said when, quite breathless, he set her down. "If you love me and I love you, why are you going to Kansas and I'm staying here? You could stay here and commute, you know, when your dad needs you, or I could move to Kansas and—"

His eyes twinkled. "Darlene Davis, are you proposing to me?"

"No, I'm not!" she said, indignant. Then . . . "All right." She grinned. "Maybe I am."

"I accept," he said quickly, the grin widening. "And if you think I'm going to have you anywhere within reach of that Cranston guy, you've got another thought coming. It'll be Kansas for both of us."

She smiled. "That does make sense, I suppose. I could probably get a job. Social workers are—"

"Wait a minute. You proposed. That's enough women's lib. I don't care whether you work or not. Maybe you'd like to go to Kansas State University and finish that psychology course. Whatever. Just as long as you're with me. That's all I ask."

All I ask, too, Darlene thought, feeling the earth tremble beneath her, the delightful vibrations spinning through her, as he again took her in his arms and pressed his mouth to hers.

It was quite late when Tonya heard Darlene come into her bedroom and turn on the bedside lamp. "Wake up, Tonya. I've something to tell you."

Tonya sat up in bed, blinking. "What?" But, sleepy as she was, she knew. There were all the symptoms. Bruised lips. Sparkling eyes. Golly, Darlene was even quivering.

"Tonya, wake up and look at me. How do you feel about moving to Kansas?"

"Kansas?"

"Yes. You see, I'm not going to marry Leon. I'm going to marry Greg. What do you think about that?"

"I think it's about time." Tonya yawned. "Darlene, please turn off the light so I can go back to sleep."